Newport Community Learning & Libraries
Cymuned ddysgu a Llyfrgelloedd Casnewydd

THIS ITEM SHOULD BE RETURNED OR
RENEWED BY THE LAST DATE
STAMPED BELOW.

Newport
CITY COUNCIL
CYNGOR DINAS
Casnewydd

To renew telephone: 656656 or 656657 (minicom)
or www.newport.gov.uk/libraries

D1346628

THE TANGLED WEB

THE TANGLED WEB

Grace Thompson

This first world edition published in Great Britain 2000 by
SEVERN HOUSE PUBLISHERS LTD of
9–15 High Street, Sutton, Surrey SM1 1DF.
This first world edition published in the U.S.A. 2000 by
SEVERN HOUSE PUBLISHERS INC of
595 Madison Avenue, New York, N.Y. 10022.

British Library Cataloguing in Publication Data

Thompson,   Grace
The tangled web
1.Brothers and sisters - Fiction
I. Title
823.9'14 [F]

ISBN 0-7278-5508-5

Typeset by Palimpsest Book Production Ltd.,
Polmont, Stirlingshire, Scotland.
Printed and bound in Great Britain by
MPG Books Ltd, Bodmin, Cornwall.

THE TANGLED WEB

One

"Having a thief for a brother is a life sentence!" Amanda Clifford told her friend Gillian angrily as they prepared her brother's room for his imminent return from yet another prison sentence. "Being brought up in a Children's Home is his excuse, his sob-story perfected over the years for the Probation Officers and anyone else prepared to listen. But it was the same for me, and I survived it and qualified as a teacher. So why was it so much harder for him?"

Amanda was enjoying her third year at Haversley Street Infants, where her friend Gillian Harris also worked, as a secretary. This Saturday morning, Gillian had come to empty the room of clutter and sort out the books into the abysmally inadequate shelves in the tiny flat. Beside a willingness to help her friend, Gillian was curious to meet Roy Clifford about whom she had heard so much.

"Roy went to a different Children's Home, perhaps it wasn't so easy for him," Gillian suggested. "They might not have been so encouraging."

"It wasn't easy for me. But you're right, the regime might have been different for the boys – but it wasn't harsh. This is 1953 not 1853! I visited him and found it only slightly different from where I lived. Besides, those days are well and truly gone, thank goodness. No, Roy just likes being a thief and taking from others what he's too lazy to work for."

Pulling the blue and white bed-cover straight, Amanda admitted she felt more like throwing it out of the window. "Why am I responsible for Roy Neville Clifford, recidivist, with eleven prison sentences behind him?" she fumed. "He isn't even clever enough to get away with it! Although that's

1

probably a misleading statement. How many other burglaries and housebreakings has he succeeded in compared to the eighty-three housebreakings and shoplifting offences he's so far owned up to?"

"At twenty-five he should be settling down and looking ahead," Gillian agreed.

"Exactly! But what does he do? He plans 'just one more' session of break-ins just to set him up, as he so urgently explains when I answer yet another knock at the door to the police. D'you know he's done more than five in one night, while people sit goggle-eyed with their new televisions? He says he can't resist it, it's too easy."

She set out Roy's favourite soap and shaving cream and the new toothbrush and paste, all chosen with care to help disperse the stubborn miasma of prison. In spite of her angry words she loved him and wanted him to lead a normal life more than anything in the world. Her anger with her brother had been exacerbated by her quarrel with Edmond. They had been seeing each other for more than a year and he had been adamant she must not take her brother back when he was released.

Defying Edmond had been casually done. He couldn't really expect her to ignore Roy when he needed somewhere safe to stay. She had been so certain Edmond would understand, she had hardly mentioned her brother's imminent arrival until last night. After a frighteningly fierce row, Edmond had glared at her and left without their resolving their differences or making an arrangement to see each other today. She rang, but his mother had explained stiffly that he was unwilling to come to the phone. Not unable, she had noted angrily, but unwilling. She still hadn't worried overmuch. He'd come round.

"What are you going to do, Amanda?" Gillian asked when they had finished the room and were staring out over the back gardens of the closely packed houses. "You can't have him here indefinitely. This flat is too small for you and all these books—" she smiled, "—without a brother and his belongings!"

Amanda smiled back and shrugged.

The two young women were not unalike. Both were fair-haired, with Gillian's helped by bleach, and although Amanda was smaller, slimmer, and Gillian bordered on the plump, the similarity was there in their colouring and the willingness to smile. They both had eyes the colour of a summer sky and cheeks that glowed rosy with health. Amanda's hair was luxuriant and long, worn tucked back in a sort of loose bun. Gillian's slightly wavy hair was kept short. The most noticeable difference between the friends was Gillian's love of jewellery. Nothing of value, just strings of brightly coloured beads and sparkling brooches and hair ornaments. Amanda's taste was restricted to a gold chain around her neck.

Amanda's flat was situated on the outskirts of Cardiff. The school where she and Gillian worked was only fifteen minutes' drive away and, as Gillian lived around the corner with her parents, they travelled together in Amanda's car. The Austin had been Amanda's first luxury. Having been taught to drive by a colleague, she bought his car from him when he changed it for something newer and had never regretted doing so. With local shops providing most of her needs she had been comfortable and contented in the flat, but with big brother Roy appearing every few months before being re-arrested and sent once more to prison, it was slowly losing its appeal.

"This time I'll make sure Roy knows it's the last time I'll help," she told her friend. "My own job might be lost if someone realises I'm supporting a criminal. And Edmond won't put up with the situation much longer. He's very annoyed at me for taking him in again, when he begged me to refuse." She shook her long fair hair loose from its bun, which had become untidy, and glared at the freshly-made bed. "From now on he makes his own bed. If necessary I'll move out and rent a place even smaller than this, where there isn't room for him."

"Is that what Edmond wants you to do?"

"It was his suggestion, yes. But he's right and this will definitely be the last time. Edmond will cool off, but he really won't stand much more of my brother interrupting our lives."

Gillian sat down and started to cut out some shapes which

Amanda wanted for the children to use as part of a maths lesson. It was an excuse not to leave as she wanted to stay until Roy arrived. What would he be like, this criminal brother? Huge and menacing? Small and weasel-like? A greasy, sweaty, swarthy type? She was not prepared to meet someone like the man, who arrived at lunchtime.

He called out and walked in, tall, confident, surprisingly well-dressed and startlingly handsome. His blonde hair was very short and his skin had a light tan: the prison's attempt to disguise the pallor of several months inside, Gillian guessed. She accepted the cropped hair almost immediately. Roy's devilish grin, with his greeny-grey eyes and the confident air, made the unusually short hair an addition to his attractiveness. That he was a criminal who used charm as one of the tools of his trade simply added to his appeal.

"Hi yer, Mand. How's tricks? And who's this lovely young lady then?" he asked, his Welsh accent more pronounced than Amanda's. The different Childrens' Homes had produced other differences besides moral ones.

Amanda introduced them and saw at once that Gillian was impressed with her handsome brother irrespective, or perhaps because, of him being a criminal. She saw the way they were looking at each other and sighed inwardly, resigning herself to losing yet another friend.

As it was a mild April day, and she knew she would have a busy morning preparing for Roy, Amanda had prepared a simple meal of egg salad. There was no welcome home cake. Her small butter and margarine ration made that impossible. 1953, eight years after the war ended and they still had to endure food shortages. "Where's your ration book, Roy?" she asked as she remembered it.

Gillian was easily persuaded to stay and after spending an hour being amused by Roy's exaggerated account of life in one of His Majesty's Prisons, she stood reluctantly to leave. As if he were already in charge of the household, it was Roy who saw her to the door, and from the whispering and giggling, Amanda guessed they were arranging to meet. Gathering up the dishes, she began tidying her impossibly small kitchen,

4

and found room for some of Roy's possessions in the even tinier bathroom.

How long would he stay this time? Would it be a girlfriend or the police who would be the cause of his leaving? As she stacked the dishes in the cupboards she thought seriously of giving up the flat and finding a room instead. Perhaps he *would* be better able to cope if he didn't have her to help him out during the first weeks? If he made the effort and found himself a place to live, and a job – with the assistance of the Probation Officer – he might stay on the straight and narrow and begin to build a life. She knew that if he didn't, he could easily demolish her life as well as his own. But could she pretend to turn her back on him?

While he talked to the departing Gillian, she looked around her at the three rooms, carefully designed to look comfortable and friendly yet not too crowded. After the shortages of the war and in the years immediately following, the fifties had burst out with a wonderful choice of furniture, fabrics and accessories. Putting aside the heavy dark furniture, she had chosen to buy the new contemporary style.

Moulded and bent plywood produced comfortable chairs and tables, which, with their pin legs and bright colours, gave a completely new look to a room. China with abstract designs and angular shapes looked neat, and so different from what had been used before. With abstract designs on wallpaper and carpets, it all blended to give a lightness and a spacious look.

Amanda had chosen to paint her walls in bold slabs of colour and her one armchair was moulded in the shape of an egg. Together with its matching stool, it was her only concession to comfort. Edmond, a traditionalist, hated it.

It had taken her three years, ever since she had started at Haversley Street Infants, to get the flat as she wanted it. Now, with her dining table pushed in a corner, with two cupboards balanced precariously on top, her dining room was Roy's bedroom. Chairs were placed wherever there was space and ornaments had been relegated to boxes at the side of her wardrobe.

She listened again to the voices by the half-closed door. Roy and Gillian were probably making plans to meet later. Anger swept over her. It wasn't fair, she moaned silently. She had no other family and having a brother should be fun, not misery.

At school the next day, Gillian was excited. "Roy has offered to do some tidying up in the garden for Mam and Dad," she announced. "Just until he gets a job; he doesn't like being idle. I hope you don't mind?"

"Of course I don't mind." Amanda smiled and hoped he wouldn't be foolish enough to 'lift' anything left lying about. She couldn't warn Gillian to be careful. Even after all his convictions she couldn't tell people he wasn't to be trusted. Even though that, and his attraction to young women, was why she lost so many of her friends.

She did warn Roy though. "You have to get a job, and fast," she told him sternly. "I don't want you living here indefinitely. As soon as you can afford it you have to find yourself a room. Right?"

"Right," he echoed and saluted formally. "Yes, boss. At once." And he winked to show he hadn't taken offence. "No grumpin' mind if I don't get one first off. It isn't easy, Mand."

He came in the following evening and told her he had a job.

"Not much of a job, Mand. Only labouring for a gardener, but plenty of back-aching work, and that's what I need, eh? Make me too tired to go clambering about on roofs!"

She couldn't hold back from laughter. There was something about Roy that immediately won you over.

Although she resented the intrusion into her life she soon relaxed and began to enjoy his company. He started work early and was often there when she returned from school, with a kettle boiling for a cup of tea. When his work allowed, he cooked for them both. He listened and comforted her when she told him that Edmond wouldn't see her or even talk to her, and laughed her out of her regrets for a man without humour or compassion. She didn't tell him he was the cause of their parting.

6

Roy didn't discuss Gillian but Amanda knew they were meeting. She was anxious about where he was getting the money for entertainment, as his wages were extremely low, and she eventually voiced her concerns to Gillian.

"He doesn't have much money," Gillian assured her. "That's a good sign, isn't it?"

"So how does he manage to go out several times a week? He pays me for food and I don't think there's that much left."

"He hates this, but I treat us to a meal out and a matinée at the pictures on Saturdays. Mam and Dad like him and they cook him a good meal on Sundays, or as good as they can with the rationing. I mean, he needs encouragement if he's to give up his previous ways."

"The love of a good woman?" Amanda couldn't hide the sarcasm, and quickly apologised. "Sorry. I hope you don't get hurt, that's all."

"Roy wouldn't do anything to hurt me. I think he really cares." Gillian spoke confidently. Amanda agreed, but silently wondered if Gillian were about to become another of Roy's victims.

Roy was very nimble and very experienced at moving with practically no sound. Twice each week he slipped out of the bedroom window, moved like a shadow across the gardens then worked his way around to Amanda's car. He made sure he was well away from the area where they lived before parking and making a reconnaissance of a small village. Working in a different village each night, he would choose three houses and, after gaining entry, pick up small items he could readily sell plus any money he found. Then he would hide the proceeds of one before going on to the next house.

One night towards the end of April, he entered a pretty thatched cottage, one of a pair, intending to steal from both. He had no idea of the name of the place, which was about eight miles from Amanda's flat. It was one he had noticed on his nightly wanderings and noted for future attention. He climbed in through a low window which had been left open, after making sure that the bed was unoccupied.

Three bedrooms provided three pounds ten shillings and sixpence, and some jewellery. The place was apparently unoccupied – all three bedrooms were empty. In that case it was worth trying downstairs. Testing every step just in case he was wrong, he went down the curving staircase and found himself in a narrow hallway. Opening the door of what he presumed was the kitchen a light came on and he saw two old women standing in front of a Welsh settle. One held a shotgun steadily and with unnerving accuracy towards his chest.

Gesturing him to raise his hands, she stretched out a hand towards the telephone, the mouthpiece of which was already resting on her shoulder.

"Who are you?" she surprised him by asking. "Before I dial nine nine nine, I want to know who you are and why a strong healthy young man like you should chose to rob rather than work."

His heart was racing but he smiled and said, "Get on with you, I don't want to tell you a thing. Call the police if you want to or let me go, whichever," he said casually. The gun moved infinitesimally and his heart rate increased even more. "All right, I do work, but because I've been in prison, the work is poorly paid and I want to be wealthy."

"What about your family?" the old woman demanded, still holding the gun steadily pointed towards him, her gnarled finger on the trigger. "Don't they help? Families should help each other."

"There's only my sister, and we were brought up in Children's Homes, see."

He took a breath to begin his sob-story but the old woman demanded, "What's your name?"

"Clifford. Roy Neville Clifford." He saw the old woman frown as if the name meant something.

"You have a sister, you say?"

"Now look here, call the police if you have to but don't involve my sister." The finger tightened almost imperceptibly and he answered quickly. "Amanda Clifford. Teacher she is and she knows nothin' about this, right?"

She seemed startled by his words, her dark brown eyes

8

staring at him disconcertingly. "Amanda Clifford? Amanda Clifford? How old is she?"

Roy relaxed slightly but stayed perfectly still out of respect for the gun. The poor old woman was lonely, she just wanted to talk. What unbelievable luck! He was going to get away with it! She'll be offering tea next!

He told her everything she wanted to know, including Amanda's occupation and the names of the Homes where she, and he, were brought up. The woman stared at him for a long time, then the gun was lowered and he was told to leave.

"But first you can return what you stole from me."

"I never took nothin'. Too quick for me you were, you an' that gun!" He was barely holding back laughter as he opened the front door to make his formal leave, but was disconcerted when the old woman, still holding the gun, said:

"Twenty-five you say you are? Amanda isn't your sister, you stupid boy! Amanda Clifford hasn't got a brother and certainly not one that's older than her."

It wasn't until he was in the car that he relaxed enough to think about the old woman's words. Could it be true? He and Amanda had been adopted, he knew that, but they were left in care at the same time and, since they had come from the same address, were both given the name of Clifford. Was it possible that although they were brought up together for those few months, they had been separately adopted and were no blood relation at all? With a strong respect for self preservation he decided not to mention the conversation to Amanda. Even by inventing the situation in which he had met the old woman, to make it acceptable. She'd have no reason to help him if she found out they weren't brother and sister.

Before he drove home at a careful speed to avoid being stopped by an over-zealous policeman, he checked on the name of the village. Tri-nant. Three streams. He was curious, but decided it best forgotten. Cheerful and with confidence restored and even enlarged by his narrow escape, he drove back and slid in through the window.

He wrote off to the Register Office for details of both his birth and Amanda's, explaining that he wanted replacements

9

for lost birth certificates. His own certificate duly arrived but not that of Amanda's. So far as was known, the letter said, there was no registration of his sister's birth. They suggested he had the date or the name wrong and said he should make further enquiries. If he wrote again with more information they might be able to help.

So the old woman had been right. But how had she known? Was it possible that by sheer coincidence he had tried to rob a house in the actual village where he and Amanda belonged? For sure he wouldn't go there again. The old woman was probably ga-ga and was talking nothing but a load of rubbish! But she didn't look ga-ga in the way she held that gun, she seemed to know exactly what she was doing. He shuddered every time he remembered that gun.

Weeks passed and Amanda began to accept that he was there for the forseeable future.

"I know the wages he earns makes it impossible to survive on his own," she said to Gillian. "But Edmond and I have started seeing each other again and, well, it is difficult. Edmond makes it clear that Roy's charm fails to work on him."

"Give him a little longer. I'm sure he'll get a better job once he's proved his honesty."

"Oh, I'm not complaining. I rather like having him around. He's my brother, after all, my only relative, and as long as he behaves himself I'll go on helping him." As with all the other times, she hoped this would be the last and that all the criminal behaviour was behind him.

"Have you met his friend, Dave?" Gillian asked one evening when they were in the library after school. "He seems very nice. Mam and I really think Roy's avoiding the riff-raff and making an effort, don't you?"

A few days later Amanda met Dave and, seeing his short hair and light tan, guessed where he and her brother had met. Gillian must have guessed too, she thought, so she is drifting into an acceptance of Roy's life like other girls before her, believing she can change him into a perfect husband.

Dave was quite a lot older than Roy, probably middle

thirties, Amanda guessed. She wondered if any of his family still supported him. He was looking for lodgings, so apparently not. He was easily persuaded to stay to supper, which was salad, potatoes and sliced spam. After they had eaten and Dave had helped with the dishes, Roy asked, "Would it be all right if Dave stays tonight?" Although she wasn't keen, she agreed.

Dave stayed several nights during the weeks that followed and each time he and Roy went out at about nine and didn't return until long after midnight. Even then she couldn't sleep. She didn't really trust her brother, and with Dave there her doubts increased. She stayed awake long after retiring, listening for signs that Roy and Dave were leaving the flat. She dreaded having to be his alibi and hoped he would avoid returning to his thieving ways at least until he found somewhere else to live. If he ever did!

Then they both stayed out all night and the following day she found a pair of binoculars that were obviously expensive. When she faced him, he denied stealing them and stormed out.

"He's stealing again, I know he is," she said to Gillian.

"The binoculars are mine, Amanda. Roy said he wanted to watch birds in the wood at the back of the hill. Seen a nightingale, he says."

"Oh, I thought—"

"There's nothing to worry about. But he isn't helped by knowing you don't trust him." Gillian sounded piqued. "His own sister, his only relation. Your suspicions will drive him straight back to prison."

"That's ridiculous. He was out all night!"

"They were both with Mam, Dad and me, for heaven's sake! Playing cards we were. It got to be after midnight so the pair of them slept on our floor instead of walking back. Afraid of being stopped by the police they were."

Sighing with relief, Amanda nevertheless warned her brother about not staying where the Probation Officer expected him to be.

"Don't get your 'air off, Mand, I couldn't resist it," he

11

grinned. "Dave left about nine but Gillian persuaded me to stay on, till after her Mam and Dad went to bed. Very persuasive she is, mind, that Gillian." He winked and Amanda was angered by his lies and her friend's dishonesty.

Edmond rarely visited the flat. When they met she was asked to meet him either at the cinema or at the restaurant. He never brought her home, just left her where they had parked the cars and drove away with a haste that suggested relief. When they were together his arm was rarely there and his kisses became less loving and more a formal salute to an aged aunt, she told an amused Gillian. Sometimes she blamed Roy but mostly she was honest enough to admit that if it hadn't been Roy it would have been something else.

It was June before she knew for certain she was being tricked by Roy. She woke very early one morning desperate for a drink and went into the kitchen to make a cup of tea. The dining room door was open slightly and, peeping in, prepared to apologise for disturbing him, saw at once that his room was empty.

He returned at four-thirty to find her sitting in the pre-dawn waiting for him. As he closed the door behind him she switched on the light.

Apparently unperturbed, he asked, "Hello, Mand. What you doing up? Couldn't sleep? Me neither. I've been for a walk."

"What's that you're carrying?" she asked quietly.

"What, this?" He patted the bag, hidden under his coat but causing a bulge her sharp, suspicious eyes couldn't miss. "Oh, just something I picked up at the park gates. Someone must have dapped it down and forgot it. The street light's broken just there so I thought I'd bring it home to see if it's valuable."

He went to walk away but she held his arm, a fierce glare in her eyes. "Then we'll look together, shall we?"

"Sis!" he said reproachfully. "You don't trust me. And here's me thinking you understood my determination to go straight." She held out a hand for the bag and he gave it to her, sad-eyed with reproach, and watched while she unpacked a thermos flask – one of her own – and a half-eaten sandwich. She looked at him coldly as she also removed a short crowbar with curved ends, some metal objects she recognised as skeleton keys and a small claw hammer.

"I didn't do nothin'," he insisted. "I just carry the stuff sometimes to remind me of what ruined my life. Like an alcoholic having an unopened bottle of scotch. I can easily chuck it if a policeman appears, and there's nothing suspicious about an insomniac out for a stroll, is there?"

"Roy, you're on probation."

"Well, who's going to see me? Careful I am. I know how to avoid the police, Mand."

"Sorry, Roy, but I can't cope with this any more. You're my brother and I love you, but it's time you left, found a place of your own."

"Love you too sis, and I understand. Don't think I'm not grateful. Lucky I am to have you. I'll try to get somewhere, I'll really try, but we won't lose touch will we? Proper choked I'd be if that happened, Mand. You're all I've got in the 'ole wide world."

She sat up for what was left of the night feeling wretchedly guilty. She wanted to help him but didn't know how. He was her brother and, as he had reminded her, the only person in the world belonging to her. Giving him a roof over his head wasn't enough. The next day she said nothing more about him leaving and things continued as they were for another week.

Then she was again disturbed at night, and this time it was the now familiar loud banging on the door and the call, "This is the police." More banging and, "Open the door, this is the police."

As she watched the police search her flat it became less and less her home. Every room was ransacked and as it was pulled apart, all feeling of security and comfort faded. She had to find a new place, a single room, a bedsit. She would hate it after this once pleasant flat, but knew that if she stayed and tried to rebuild the ambience she had once enjoyed, she would be too soft-hearted to refuse Roy a bed when he was once again free.

The worst part of his recent string of robberies was Gillian's involvement. She had been flattered and instilled with the sense of adventure, and, taking advantage of her adoration, Roy had left her to explain the presence of a few pieces of jewellery, some cheap watches and cigarette cases in a rarely used shed. Stuff he had intended to dispose of.

The police eventually believed she knew nothing, but she left her job and avoided Amanda completely. She must hate me, Amanda reasoned, for introducing her to my charming and untrustworthy brother. As she had forseen, Roy had cost her another friend.

She believed that she and Roy were alone in the world. Her mother had left them at a police station. How ironic that was, she mused, when you think of the time Roy had spent in one since!

She had been six months old and Roy had been about two. When she was old enough she had searched the area around the Children's Home for a family called Clifford, but no one wanted to own to being even a distant relation. That was why it was so difficult to refuse to help Roy. There was no one else and if she let him go out of her life she would be completely alone. A thief he undoubtedly was, but he was also her brother.

Amanda began to imagine she was being followed. An unknown man had knocked at a neighbouring house and asked about her, and twice she saw someone at the school apparently staring at her as she took her turn supervising the children at play and practised netball with them. On another occasion, she sensed rather than saw someone darting into a shop doorway when she turned suddenly. Most surprising of all, a man took her photograph before hurrying off down a side-street.

She was irritated rather than frightened. It had to be something to do with Roy. Really, his intrusion into her life with his criminal ways was becoming a serious nuisance. She did have a shiver of apprehension when she thought it might not be the police, but someone whom he had crossed in some way. But surely she wasn't in danger from his activities? It was just as well she was moving. Perhaps she would see an end to it once she found somewhere else to live.

To everyone's surprise, Roy was found not guilty of the robberies. Gillian and her parents, feeling sorry for him and believing he had been tricked by Dave, had given alibis for him. It was Dave who returned to prison and Roy who walked free. That Gillian had lied, Amanda was certain. The reason she had changed her job and stayed away from her was probably not because of any regret for being introduced to Roy, but because of guilt over having perjured herself. Either way, Gillian no longer considered her a friend.

Roy was ecstatic. As well as the money he had acquired, he had Dave's as well, and what with the police finding the few worthless oddments they had left in Gillian's garden shed, they wouldn't expect to find the rest. He knew people often didn't know with any certainty just what had been stolen and their haziness encouraged him to think that the police would accept that the money would never been found.

He chuckled as he remembered the old woman with the gun. She probably didn't report the burglary and she didn't even ask for the money he'd taken. He kept that three pounds ten shillings and sixpence as a sort of lucky charm in the back of his wallet. What fools people were.

Dave would know, of course, and he could be dangerous when he was crossed. But why worry? He would be long gone before Dave came out and started to look for him.

Amanda was looking for a new home. Roy knew this and began his own plans. He had a feeling that Gillian would persuade her parents to take him in. What a comfortable billet that would be. In the meantime, he had the remaining tenancy of Amanda's flat, on which she had paid the rent.

Searching for new accomodation took time and it was during the big summer break from school that Amanda eventually found a room. It was small and would necessitate selling most of her furniture, but with a growing determination to make

15

a fresh start, she offered it to a colleague who was getting married and used the money to buy herself a comfortable bed-settee. With room for one person only, she felt guilty but determined to make Roy find somewhere else to stay.

In the village of Tri-nant a pair of cottages were welcoming new tenants. And from one, a steady stream of letters and photographs went forth to a town several hundred miles to the north east of it, where an old woman lay dying. When her enquiries were completed and she was satisfied she had achieved her aim, the old woman paid off the investigator and the following day, changed her Will. When death finally claimed her she was at peace. She had done what she could to right a wrong.

Amanda spent the first weeks of the summer holiday decorating the room and finding small items to make the place her own. During the rest of the time, she prepared for the new school year, designing and making displays and games to develop early skills. The room looked very overcrowded as she painted and sewed and knitted fresh toys for the new intake of children. She hoped her determination to make Roy stand on his own feet hadn't forced her to make a mistake. The room wasn't exactly comfortable.

When the new term began she was filled with her usual excitement at the prospect of a new group of children who would come to her as babies and leave her proudly carrying reading books and with the beginnings of all the main subjects already sown in their lively minds.

It was October when the letter came and she didn't open it until late in the evening, when, abandoning her work, she was relaxing with a cup of coffee and settling to watch the television. She reached over and sifted casually through the morning's delivery. The envelope looked official and at once she thought it was something to do with Roy. What now? More trouble?

The letter was from a solicitor and told her that her Aunt Flora had died and left her a cottage in a village called Tri-nant.

A map showed her it was about eight miles away. She read the letter twice, then studied the envelope, convinced it had been intended for someone else. The name was right; Amanda Gwendoline Clifford. The address was her previous one and had been forwarded by her former landlord. She frowned, then put it aside. It would be easily cleared up the following day with a phone call to the firm of solicitors.

There was no mistake. An aunt about whom she had known nothing had left her a cottage in her Will. The Will explained that Clifford was not her family surname but that the real name of her father was not known. She waited, hardly daring to breathe as she hoped for more revelations, some information that might lead her to members of a family she didn't know she had. But there was nothing further. The bombshell came at the end, in a codicil. Aunt Flora asked that the man calling himself Roy Clifford, a regular offender, should not be allowed to live at the cottage with her.

"A man *calling* himself Roy Clifford?" She puzzled over the wording, then remembered that their name wasn't Clifford, only the name of the family who had adopted them.

At once she wanted to protest but the words died as she saw the solicitor frown. "Your aunt wanted you to have the house for the rest of your life, Miss Clifford, and I think she was afraid that should your brother share it, he might do something which would cause you to sell it. You can't ignore this reasonable request. I'm sure your brother, whatever his morals and behaviour, wouldn't wish that for you. He is after all a convicted and repeat offender."

Although the words were true, hearing them said put her on the defensive. "He's foolish, but not bad!" she protested at once.

"I'm only passing on her wishes, Miss Clifford. Like your aunt, I wish you well."

"Thank you." She smiled then. "I don't know whether I'm sorry or pleased about him not being allowed to stay, and if I'm pleased, whether I shouldn't be feeling more guilty than I do."

"Don't waste energy on guilt, Miss Clifford. It's such a

useless emotion. Especially when it's undeserved. Enjoy the cottage."

"I will. I'm so excited at owning a place of my own, and knowing I might have family somewhere near is added pleasure."

"Oh, there's one more thing. You have a tenant."

"A tenant? I thought this meant I'd move in to my aunt's home?"

"Your aunt hasn't lived there for a long time, apart from visits between tenants, and she requests – only requests, she doesn't insist, you understand? She requests that you allow Mrs Falconbridge a year from when you accept the place before you ask her to to vacate the property. And to be generous if it takes a little longer."

"I'll willingly agree to that. I'll have a year to savour it all." She smiled at him as she began to rise. "A year in my tiny bedsit will make me appreciate it all the more!"

Amanda was nervous driving down to see the property after writing to arrange it with her tenant. She was prepared to meet an irate woman demanding to be left in peace and, as the miles slid under the wheels of her second-hand Austin, the woman grew in size and fury.

What about the condition of the place? The solicitor didn't say anything about that and she hadn't thought to ask. It was probably a ruin. A tumbledown barn. And she wouldn't be able to afford the repairs. After all the excitement, she might have inherited nothing more than a garden plot heaped up with rubble!

Stopping outside Firethorn Cottage, she forgot her fears and her heart beat loudly in excitement as she looked at the place she would one day call home. It was a beautifully kept, white-painted thatched property. Not the ruined and neglected sight she had half expected.

Pyracantha bushes bordered the front garden, thickly covered in red berries and giving the cottage its name. A blackbird flew up from its branches with flutters and calls of alarm as she closed the car door. Opening the wooden gate, she walked up the path of pressed earth that lurched around forsythia bushes and straggly lavender, and approached the front door.

Her hand hesitated as she touched the knocker, remembering that the forthcoming interview would be difficult. Discussing with someone when they must leave their home was not an easy task. She wished she had rung Edmond and asked him to come with her. But that was weak. She didn't need Edmond or anyone else to hold her hand.

During the journey she had rehearsed a speech but when the door opened and a smiling face surrounded by white curls greeted her, the words faded completely.

"You must be Miss Clifford, the new owner. Do come in, my dear."

"Mrs Falconbridge?" Amanda said hesitatingly.

"Yes, dear. That's me. I presume you're here to examine your new inheritance and warn me you won't renew my lease?"

"I'm sorry, but yes," Amanda said. "It's such a thrill to suddenly be the owner of a house, and such a beautiful one – I just have to live in it. After existing in a small flat and then a tinier bedsit, the thought of a whole cottage to myself is bliss."

Mrs Falconbridge led her through the house. "Come into the kitchen first," she said, "and we'll have a cup of tea."

Amanda glanced at the tempting part-views of the rooms, excitement glowing in her expressive blue eyes. She couldn't resist a gasp of pleasure when the kitchen door opened. Brass shone around an old fashioned fireplace and a copper kettle steamed gently over glowing coals. "It's too good to be true!" she exclaimed.

She looked at the lady in front of her, whose eyes shone in a rosy face surrounded by the luxurious white hair. The hair colour had misled her at first and she now guessed that Mrs Falconbridge was no more than sixty.

"Sit down, my dear. After our tea you can see the rest of your house."

While Amanda soaked in the atmosphere of the cosy room, Mrs Falconbridge studied her. The late autumn sun shone through a window and picked out golden streaks in the wisps of hair, making a frame for the young woman's face. There was a gentleness about the girl's expression and bright intelligence in the blue eyes. She liked what she saw.

Amanda's blue eyes darted around the room, storing the impression of a well loved home. A radio sat on a window sill and a work basket spilled its contents over a leather couch against one wall. There was still room for an armchair and a table with two kitchen chairs in one corner.

"This is your favourite room, isn't it?" she asked.

"Except in the summer. Then I use the lounge with its large windows and the main view of my – your – garden."

"The cottage is still yours, for another year," Amanda promptly reassured her. "I'm not here to try and find a way to evict you. I'm content to wait until it's mine."

"Come and see it any time. I love visitors, especially lovely young ladies."

The cottage consisted of three bedrooms and two living rooms besides the kitchen and a surprisingly modern bathroom. "It's enormous compared to what I've had before." Amanda's face was flushed with excitement. "I'll enjoy living here, I know I will."

"I feel it's a happy house," her companion said.

"Did you know my Aunt Flora?" Amanda asked when they were once more settled in the kitchen. "I'd love to know more about her."

"No, she lived in the north-east. I knew her only through correspondence when I first rented, or when there was some repair needed. But her parents lived here and they were, presumably, your grandparents. There must be someone hereabouts who could tell you about them."

Amanda looked at the bright, intelligent face watching her and on impulse asked, "Will you help me find out?"

"Certainly my dear, if I can."

"Perhaps I could come again soon?"

"I'd like that." Mrs Falconbridge reached out and touched her hand. "Tell me about yourself, dear. A teacher aren't you? Will you look for something near here? Eight miles is too far to travel each day."

"I don't think I'd be lucky enough to find a job here, in the village school, do you?" she laughed.

"What age-group do you teach? There's a vacancy coming up for a reception teacher. Would you qualify?"

She felt as if fate were sweeping her along in a direction she hadn't planned, to a destiny she could only have dreamed of. "Reception is what I do best!"

Two

Visiting her house for the first time and then being told there was a chance of a job in the local school was almost more than Amanda could take in.

"A vacancy at the local school? I don't believe it! But I wouldn't be fortunate enough to get it," Amanda laughed.

"I'm not so sure. This is a village from where the young people want to escape, sad as it is. They look for somewhere more exciting once they qualify and I don't think there's more than one other applicant."

"Really? Then I might have a chance?"

"Let's go at once and get the details," Mrs Falconbridge said. "The head teacher is a friend of mine. In fact, why don't we look at the place, see what you think?" She seemed as excited at the prospect as Amanda.

While Amanda waited for Mrs Falconbridge to get a coat, she looked at the collection of souvenirs that filled the shelves of the room. A photograph above the mantelpiece attracted her attention. It was of a young man, probably in his late twenties. A rather serious face looked out at her and the dark curling hair, reminiscent of Mrs Falconbridge, was untidy, as if the photograph had not been planned.

The eyes appeared to frown slightly as if wanting to know who was staring with such interest. Amanda smiled at her fanciful imaginings, but she continued to stare at the photograph. The man looked interesting and she wondered idly if he were the son of her tenant. There was a definite resemblance.

"I see you're admiring my nephew, Rhys." Mrs Falconbridge answered the unspoken question. "I have others but I confess he's my favourite."

"Sorry." Amanda stepped back from the mantelpiece. "I shouldn't be so inquisitive."

"Nonsense, dear. I don't mind a bit."

Amanda collected a camera from her car and as they set off down the road, she was given a running commentary on the owners of the houses they passed. At a place where the road crossed a stream, her guide returned to the subject of her nephew.

"That's Rhys's house." She pointed to a low stone-built property set beside the fast-running stream and partly hidden by trees. Amanda leaned over the gate for a better view.

"What does he do?" she asked. "It looks the perfect place for a naturalist or an artist."

"What a remarkable guess. Rhys is both. He makes wild-life films."

"I'd love to meet him. I'm interested in wildlife too." She patted her camera. "But only as an amateur."

"He's away at present, making a documentary on birds of the highlands and islands in Scotland. He's due home soon, I don't know when, but he'll send me a shopping list when he's on his way."

"How wonderful to have somewhere like this to return to," Amanda breathed. She looked at the low building, quietly hiding in the trees and dappled by the pale autumn sun. Attracted by its air of peace she wanted to walk around its grounds. Regretfully she left the gate and followed her new friend along the road.

Mill Lane School was a traditional grey stone building set in an area of concrete. It was quiet now, it being a Saturday, and after taking a few photographs, Amanda went to look through the windows at the displays of autumn leaves and flowers filling the classrooms.

Stretching up beside her to peer in, Mrs Falconbridge whispered, "There's always an air of expectation in a school-room. It never looks deserted, only pausing for breath. It gives the impression that the door is about to open and a lively stream of children will burst in to fill the empty seats."

23

"Being a teacher is exciting, there's the promise of new discoveries every day."

"I know, dear. I was a teacher myself." It was another thread in their growing friendship and when it was time to leave Amanda felt real regret.

Her mind was filled with exciting new plans as she drove back to town and the bedsit that was no longer a prison. Very soon she would be living in a place of her own in a village called Tri-nant. The people would all be strangers but, with Mrs Falconbridge already a friend, they wouldn't stay that way for long.

The application for the position at Mill Lane School was duly filled and Amanda waited in an agony of anxiety for a response. She was given a date and time for an interview and dared to hope the job would be hers. There was again that feeling of fate having something planned for her and she looked forward to the interview with impatient eagerness.

A phone call the day before the interview gave her a superstitious twinge of apprehension. Mrs Falconbridge, her talisman, would be away from the village on that day.

Amanda dressed with extra care, choosing a pale green suit which she knew was a perfect setting for her light hair and intensified the blue of her eyes. She bought a bunch of flowers which she intended to leave at Firethorn Cottage for her friend.

Arriving in plenty of time, she parked the Austin beside the firethorn hedge and walked to the school. The day was rather gloomy, more November than September, she thought. Clouds seemed low enough to touch the tall trees that lined the narrow road.

Mrs Falconbridge had been wrong and there were several applicants waiting. Amanda's spirits dropped as each one entered the room and left it smiling in hope. When her turn came she stood tall and looked assured, but she walked into the room to face the interview committee with fading confidence.

She was given the subject of drama in the infant school as a subject and as it was one of her favourites, she thought she had done rather well. Then it was her turn to come out of the room smiling and putting a dash of doubt on the faces of the other applicants.

Unbelievably, she was called back and told the job was hers. Not only that, but because the transfer was within the area, she would be able to start after Christmas.

Her feet danced along the road back to the car and she no longer noticed the dull weather. She had to tell someone and was tempted to write a note to go with Mrs Falconbridge's flowers but she didn't. It wouldn't be as much fun as telling her. She took the flowers from the car and pushed her way past the lavender to the front door. Then, as she was about to place them on the floor, she changed her mind and went around to the back porch.

As she stepped inside she paused. Her gaze had casually swept the kitchen window and had caught a movement. Someone was inside.

Her first impulse was to knock and call her friend, but although the glance had been fleeting she knew it wasn't Mrs Falconbridge. Hair on her scalp began to prickle and she quickly put down the flowers and, ducking under the window sill, crept back to the front of the house and peered in.

The intruder was now in the dining room. It was a man, dressed in well-worn outdoor clothes. His back was towards her as he searched through drawers and cupboards. Searching for money, Amanda thought with disgust. It was something her brother had frequently done; invaded someone's private domain and helped himself to whatever he wanted. She felt physically sick with fury.

She ran to a telephone box, dialled 999 and waited in a fever of anxiety for the police to arrive. What would she do if the man left? She thought of her camera, collected it and set herself up out of sight, in the front garden, determined to at least get a photograph of the thief. Having a thief for a brother had not led her to have sympathy with them.

She risked another look through the window and saw him write something in a notebook which he then put in his pocket.

She took a couple of snaps without a flash. They would be better than nothing.

He headed towards the door and there was no sign of the police. Slithering back into a bush she held the camera aimed at the door. As he stepped out she'd get him! Holding her breath and trying to steady her racing heart she watched through the viewfinder. It would be infuriating if all she managed was a blur!

After he closed the door, he stopped as if posing and she clicked, hoping he wouldn't hear the tell-tale sound. The flash she couldn't hope to hide but he was looking down at something and didn't appear to notice. Then she saw he was looking at the flowers she had left. He picked them up and put them inside. After re-closing the door he walked around and down the front path.

As he reached the gate with Amanda tiptoeing behind him the police car pulled up. Amanda froze in fear, her lively imagination envisaging a fight.

She covered her eyes with a slim hands afraid to witness a bloody battle. Her senses were fully alert but all she heard was a low, calm conversation. No shouts, no thudding blows or shouts of agony.

She slowly uncovered her eyes. So, he was going to talk his way out of it, was he! She stepped out and two policemen and the burglar turned to stare at her.

"What are you doing in there, Miss?"

"I'm the one who reported a burglary," she said firmly. "He was going through drawers and I think he stole some money."

"If this was the man you saw, it's very unlikely." The policeman smiled at the intruder.

"Have you searched him?" she demanded.

"I'm Mrs Falconbridge's nephew," the 'burglar' explained.

For the first time Amanda looked at the face and not at the shabby clothes. It was the face on the photograph on the mantlepiece.

"Rhys—" she stuttered. "I thought – you looked so suspicious I was certain that—" She felt colour rising on her cheeks. "Well, you certainly acted like a housebreaker!" she snapped. "What were you doing snooping around while Mrs Falconbridge is out?"

"Collecting my messages and keys. But who are you?" he asked, his eyes beginning to glint with amusement. He drew himself up to his full six feet three inches and said, "It seems to me that if anyone is snooping, it's you!"

"Perhaps you'd give us your name, Miss," one of the policemen said, taking out a notebook. "Just for the record."

"Amanda Clifford and I own Firethorn Cottage. Mrs Falconbridge is a friend and I just left her some flowers." She explained about seeing someone inside and knew she sounded pompous and angry, but Rhys's eyes watching her with that hint of amusement was making her strangely shy. To hide her discomfort she glared at him, her chin thrust forward, her full lips reduced to a thin, disapproving line. "I thought you looked like a tramp!" she added defiantly.

After a few more questions the police left and Amanda searched her mind in vain for another parting shot. She unlocked her car door and put her camera and bag on the seat.

"I should drive carefully," Rhys chuckled, "now the police have your number."

"I always drive with care." But of course she stalled twice before moving off and at the corner the car again spluttered to a halt. Through the mirror Amanda saw Rhys walking towards her and although she tried to get away before he reached her, the car stubbornly refused to start.

"Would you like me to try?" he asked.

"It's all right, I've probably flooded the carburettor." She wasn't sure what that meant apart from having to wait a while before trying again.

"Why not give it a rest and have dinner with me?" he suggested and before she could reply to the surprising invitation he added, "Of course you'll have to cook it. I need to unpack and get my camping gear sorted out."

"You want me to cook your dinner?"

"For yourself as well," he said reasonably. "My aunt usually

27

has a meal prepared and you did say you were a friend. Won't you help a friend?"

Her anger dispersed and she laughed. "That's the strangest invitation I've ever had. And I suppose dinner will be tinned food?"

"Of course."

The car started when she turned the key and Rhys jumped in beside her. He still wore the heavy oilskin and his presence filled the small vehicle. She drove into his drive and stopped outside his garage.

"Oh, I see you know where I live," he said curiously.

"Your aunt and I walked around the village and she pointed out several houses and told me about the occupants. If I'm going to live here I'd like to know something about the neighbours."

"So, you're going to move into Firethorn Cottage and throw my aunt out into the snow."

"Of course. But I'll wait until it's good and deep!"

The garage doors were open and Amanda saw a muddy Landrover full of assorted boxes and camping equipment, including a small tent.

"I'll show you where the kitchen is then I'll start unpacking." He opened the front door and she stepped into a dark, cold hallway. "I usually get a better welcome than this," he explained, opening curtains and letting in the dusky light. "Aunt Catrin comes in and turns on the heating and cooks a meal."

"Spoilt, aren't you?"

He went around turning on switches and soon the rooms began to benefit from the large radiators. He nodded towards a well-stocked pantry and left her to find a meal from the dry ingredients and tins. He chatted as he passed with armfuls of equipment, telling her about his journey from his last campsite.

After studying the cupboard she chose a pie that only needed heating and several tins of vegetables. For dessert, yet more tins, this time fruit, which she would serve with custard, thrown together in a sort of trifle with bananas and a packet of macaroon biscuits. With tinned cream the scratch meal was complete. Not wonderful, but it would do. "I need milk for custard," she demanded and he called back a promise to 'dig it out'.

Rhys came into the kitchen and put his hands on her shoulders to see how she was getting on with the meal. "There should be milk and bread somewhere among this lot." He gestured towards the last armful he had deposited on the hall floor. "If you've finished messing about with the meal I'd be glad of some help."

"I need the milk for custard, and I was going to set the table," she protested. She was uneasy at the contact. His hands warmed her in a disturbing way.

"No need," he said taking her hand and leading her out to the car. "We'll eat near the fire. You'll find trays in the cupboard." On reaching the car, he took hold of her other hand, pulled both her arms out in front of her and loaded them with clothes. "Just drop them on the back kitchen floor," he instructed, "they're to be washed."

"You wouldn't like me to do that too, would you?" Her voice was heavy with sarcasm, but all he said in reply was, "I don't think there'll be time unless you're staying until Aunt Catrin comes back."

"You've got a cheek!"

"Nonsense. Women like tidying things."

"This one doesn't! D'you like being asked to fix drain-pipes and cut down trees just because you're a man?"

"I don't mind at all. Try me."

"I haven't a tree or a drain-pipe. Yet!" she said as she staggered back to the house with the load of jumbled clothes.

The Landrover was slowly emptied and Amanda said, "Dinner, such as it is, will be ready in five minutes. Come on, I might as well carry in one more load."

"I should think so. You owe me that for setting the police on me," he said ungratefully.

The living room was impressive. Windows filled the whole of one wall and although it was now almost dark, no curtains were drawn. The light from the room made the darkness outside more intense but Amanda guessed that during the daylight hours the scene outside, with the stream running past, was an ever-changing one.

The furniture was large, leather-covered and obviously expensive. Another couch matching the one on which they sat and two armchairs stood against the walls and each had a carved table standing near. The walls were covered with books and objects which were obviously souvenirs of Rhys's travels. The carpet was oatmeal, the curtains the same and the walls a plain cream. With the brown leather it should have been dull but the effect was one of orderliness and peace. Amanda wanted to ask who had helped him plan it. But instead she asked about his work.

He told her they were filming the life of some of the rarer sea birds.

"Will you appear in the finished film?"

"We leave that to the professionals. We are what you might call the back room boys." He smiled, then coaxed her to talk about herself.

She explained about her new appointment. "I'm so looking forward to telling your aunt," she said. "It was she who told me about the vacancy and I know she'll be pleased."

"Why not call and tell her now? She's sure to be home at this time of night."

Amanda glanced at her watch and was startled to see how late it was. "Good heavens! I really ought to get myself home."

"Why? Do you have to be back at a certain time?" The question was double-edged. He wanted to know if there was anyone waiting for her.

"I live alone," she told him, "but I have work to finish ready for my class tomorrow. It will soon be Halloween and we're making masks and—" she stopped, afraid of boring him.

"Masks, eh? Would your tribe like to see these d'you think?" He pointed to a shelf on which were displayed some beautifully carved African masks. The wood was so cleverly polished it shone like metal. "Borrow them if you like. You can return them when you next visit my aunt."

30

"You'd trust me with these?" she gasped. "They're wonderful."

"You're welcome – even if you didn't finish my washing."

She smiled at his teasing. "Tell your aunt I'll see her at the weekend."

"Can I tell her you got the job?"

"Yes, you can tell her."

All the way home Amanda marvelled at the strange way her day had ended. Meeting Rhys for the first time in such embarrassing circumstances and then ending up preparing a meal for him. She pictured the suspicious man glimpsed in the cottage, then compared him to the man with whom she had spent an evening.

The dark hair that had looked so unkempt through the window had turned out to be a strongly curled thick mane that many girls would envy but that in no way looked effeminate. Everything about Rhys, including his attitude to women's work, was strongly masculine if not downright chauvinist!

As she opened the door of her bedsit she suddenly felt dejected. How long before she met Rhys Falconbridge again? Not long, she hoped. He was the most exciting thing to happen since the solicitor's letter had told her she owned Firethorn Cottage.

Roy was given the task of planting out a small area of summer cabbage. It was back-aching, tedious work and, with no one to talk to, never ending. He finished the work and told the farmer he wouldn't be coming in again. If this was going straight he'd think again. He stretched his aching back. Going straight? Anything but!

With no money to come, he was immediately tempted to return to crime. He found a sort of job in the local market helping out with the fruit and veg, which, as it involved people, interested him more. No pay but a few tips. One afternoon, a man dressed expensively in a suit and carrying a silver-topped cane left his wallet on the display of potatoes. Using a cabbage leaf to prevent leaving fingerprints, he opened it and removed two crisp fivers and a couple of ten shilling notes. Another fiver he left sticking out slightly and hoped it would be sufficient for the man not to examine the wallet when he came back to claim it.

He didn't tell Gillian he had given up his job and she was pleased and flattered when he went to where she worked and invited her to the pictures and supper afterwards.

Since leaving her secretarial job at the school, Gillian had settled in a new job, keeping the books for a company which owned several houses, flats and shops. She entered the rents paid when the collectors handed in the money, and made a note of any arrears. The work was not without interest, with a variety of problems to solve and people to placate. Tenants called to request repair work, explain their reasons for not clearing any debts, or just for a chat. She liked dealing with people and would have been content, but a worm of unease was eating into her contentment; she was worried about Roy's increasing interest in the people with whom she dealt. After that first visit to the office he began to call regularly and seemed more than a little interested in her clients.

She was so determined to believe he was going straight she had convinced her parents he was the victim of neglect, that love and care had shown him a better way. She had almost convinced herself. Until now, when his questions about the tenants and their movements were leading her to think he was using her. She began to fear he was sizing up the possibilities before breaking in and robbing the places she told him about. So far there had been no reports of any robberies, but knowing he had been capable of a number of break-ins in one night, she was afraid he would carry them out and disappear.

He was always extremely well dressed and the lighter and cigarette case he carried were obviously expensive. He bought gifts too, and they had taxis whenever they went out to restaurants, which were also the very best. He finally told her that the gardening job had long finished and he tried to convince her he earned enough carrying bets to and from the bookies, and in tips as an errand boy for the local fruit and veg market, to pay for it all.

"One day, love, I'm going to be rich," he told her enthusiastically. "I just know it. I'm taking every opportunity to earn money but not to save it. That doesn't make you rich. That's just a life of misery. Money's to be enjoyed and if you've got confidence in yourself, money brings money. Look rich and you feel rich. Feel rich and you convince everyone you are rich. Gillian, love, with you beside me I can't fail!"

He was so buoyantly confident that when she was with him, she was caught up in his enthusiasm and would have believed anything he told her. It was only during the night when she lay restless and unable to sleep that she knew she was lying to her parents and, worse than that, lying to herself. The only possible outcome was a worse misery than she could imagine. These thoughts were pushed aside when he appeared, cheerful, full of plans and hopes and dreams, with never a moment's doubts.

It was a surprise, therefore, when Roy came to her one evening in obvious dismay.

"Read this," he said, thrusting a letter at her.

Gillian read Amanda's letter with a growing disbelief. At first the news that Roy and Amanda had an aunt who had left a cottage was a wonderful thrill, but as Amanda went on to explain about the stipulation regarding Roy's presence, her excitement cooled and she looked at Roy with dismay.

"So when the tenancy of the flat ends you have nowhere to go? Amanda can't help?"

Roy couldn't trust himself to reply. He had been thinking of nothing else. Who was she, this aunt who had decided he was worthless? How did she know about the prison sentences? If she was that close, why hadn't she made herself known?

He was thankful he hadn't told Amanda he was not her brother. If she owned a cottage, surely somehow he could persuade her to give him a share, whatever this miserable Aunt Flora said. Amanda was fair and honest with him. If he kept that bit of news to himself and boxed clever, he'd make something out of this.

"Can she do this? Can she separate Amanda and me?" he demanded, looking at Gillian for explanation. "You know about such things – can she tell Amanda who she can and

33

can't have staying? No, she can't. This has got to be Amanda's doing. She doesn't want me there!"

"Amanda wouldn't be so devious. She cares too much to do that. But your aunt is probably within her rights to insist you don't share the cottage as a permanent address. There might be a time-limit set. You'd have to find out. Perhaps there's an amendment stating that if you don't re-offend, then after a given period Amanda might change the restriction. I'll try and find out for you, shall I?"

"Amanda's done this to me." He wondered if Amanda had learned the truth about their supposed relationship. She had found out and this was why she was behaving in this way.

"She doesn't have a choice," Gillian insisted. "Not if that was this aunt's condition, and you wouldn't expect her to give up her inheritance because of *your* police record, would you, Roy? That's asking too much, even of a generous sister like Amanda."

He calmed down a little and nodded, accepting what she said. "No, you're right, I wouldn't ask that, but what am I going to do? Where will I go when the tenancy ends in January?"

"We'll find you a room. Perhaps near your sister's house. Then you'd at least be able to see her."

"She might not want that. Now she's broken free she could resent my interfering in the new life she's making. New house, new job, new friends, they wouldn't know about me and perhaps she wouldn't want them to."

"They must know. This Aunt Flora of yours knew about you so I doubt it's a secret."

"Will you write to my sister and ask what she thinks?"

"Better than that. We'll go and see her."

Roy began to demonstrate a deep sense of melancholy. "I'm being abandoned for the second time in my life. First my parents, whoever they were, chucked me out, and now an aunt I've never met thinks I'm so worthless she wants to keep me from my sister."

For a while his tale of woe gave him a sympathetic audience and he began to wallow in self-pity. Then one of his mates at the fruit and veg market told him to stop feeling sorry for himself. "You've only yourself to blame, boy. The reason for your aunt's actions was your criminal record. You can't blame that on your sister or anyone else, no matter how hard you try!" the man said. The bald truth was hotly denied and Roy went over the story of his deprived childhood once again.

But the outspoken remarks rankled. Then Roy had a sense of revelation. With Gillian's support he could start again. He'd had similar revelations but they had always ended when temptation was too strong, or he was short of money. Thieving was exciting and often so easy. But he would try. He really would try. He felt that optimistic freeing of the spirit. He *could* go straight. Because he'd been a thief all his life so far didn't mean he couldn't change. He only had to stay out of trouble and Amanda would make things right. He could do it, if he was really determined.

Trying to forget the plans he had made for robbing the houses on Gillian's books was hard. It really went against his nature to abandon what would have been a very lucrative couple of nights. But he managed to push the information to the back of his mind and concentrate on other things. Persuading Gillian into his bed for one thing.

He began to take a greater interest in the job at the fruit and veg stall, hoping for a permanent position. Though not well paid, it would be a beginning. His cheerfulness expanded with his determination to leave the past behind. He was teased by many and doubted by more but he began to make plans in a way he had never done before. One thing he knew was essential; he had to stay away from Dave. If he had to pay back what he owed him from the previous robberies he'd have to resort to crime once more.

Convincing Gillian that having her love was the one thing he needed to give him the strength to make something of his life was surprisingly easy, and during the rest of October they spent very little on the pictures and restaurants, spending the time instead in the flat that had once belonged to his sister. Gillian was contentedly waiting for him to save the money to buy her an engagement ring. He was discontentedly thinking of those houses simply asking to be robbed.

"We won't say anything to your Mam and Dad yet about us, love," he said. "Let's enjoy it for ourselves for a while, is it?"

If he could persuade Gillian's parents to take him as a lodger, life would be sweet. No chance of that if they thought there were night-time wanderings across the landing to worry about!

On Sunday, Amanda returned to Firethorn Cottage having been invited for lunch. As she parked her car she wondered if Rhys would be there. In fact it was he who opened the door. His greeting was hardly conventional.

"Can you drive me to the Cwm Gwyn Arms?" he asked, closing the door behind him and striding towards her car. "I have to collect some stills from the man who does some of my printing. It won't take more than ten minutes, there's plenty of time before lunch. My car's in for a service," he explained as he hustled her back into her seat. "Hurry up, I'll guide you."

"Very kind of you!" she said, but her sarcasm was wasted.

Their route passed his bungalow and the school. They went along narrow country lanes to a small group of houses, one of which was a pub, called the Cwm Gwyn Arms. The house Rhys wanted was next door.

"Shall I wait in the car?" Amanda asked.

"Yes, I won't be a moment." He didn't go in, but took a large envelope handed to him by a little girl. "Have a look at those," he said, getting back into the car. "They're some enlargements of some photographs I took in North Wales."

She took out the photographs of scenery. Fresh green meadows with a backdrop of mountains. There were several close-ups of mountain flowers and one showing a wide expanse of spring squill. There were snow scenes that were breathtakingly beautiful. Trees and dead foliage, water, frost-encrusted banks gave a magical view of winter. The scenery was delicately silvered, and in some touched with pink by the first rays of a winter sun.

"They're for a holiday brochure," Rhys explained. "A friend is planning a holiday experience with a difference. People are shown wild animals and birds in an area where the wildlife is allowed to live undisturbed by man, but with everything arranged so they can be observed."

The photographs came out again when they returned to Firethorn Cottage to be examined and admired by Catrin, who, to Amanda's surprise, had some reservations. Some of the scenic views were not quite sharp. One close-up was wrongly angled. The discussion was rather technical and Amanda didn't join in, she just watched the two people who were obviously such good friends.

Lunch was a light-hearted affair and discussion ranged widely. As they finished their coffee, Rhys said, "Aunt Catrin tells me you're going to search for some relatives. Is that wise?"

"If you had been brought up without knowing, wouldn't you?"

"Perhaps, but if you are interested, why haven't you done something before?"

"I admit to being a bit fearful of what I might discover," she admitted, thinking there might be more relatives like her brother Roy, about whom she said nothing. "When I was in the Home, Matron warned me that besides the risk of finding someone unpleasant, there's the likelihood of someone particularly clever and I might have felt the need to compete."

"That sounds wise," Mrs Falconbridge said. "But has learning about your Aunt Flora changed that?"

"It's made me curious to learn more," Amanda admitted.

"I'll be home for a week, I'll make a few enquiries if you wish." Rhys was staring at her, his deep velvety-brown eyes revealing an interest in her that was exciting.

She hesitated to reply and, sensing her conflict, he put a comforting hand on her shoulder. "Don't worry, Amanda. If anything unpleasant turns up we'll be here, Aunt Catrin and me. And," he added, smiling, "if we unearth Nobel Prize winners, murderers or burglars, we'll keep it to ourselves."

Amanda started with shock at the word burglars. Did he

know about Roy? Should she have told them? Now it seemed too late.

A week later Amanda's car stopped once again beside the firethorn hedge, now sadly denuded of its bright berries. She looked hopefully into the kitchen, half expecting Rhys to be there, but she was disappointed.

"Just the two of us today, dear," Mrs Falconbridge said. "He wasn't satisfied with some of the photographs and wants to try and get the autumn ones before all the colour goes."

Amanda asked polite questions about his plans, hoping to hide her disappointment, but a glance at the penetrating blue eyes of her companion convinced her she could hide nothing.

As they prepared coffee, there were seven loud bangs on the wall: bom diddy bom bom, bom bom. Mrs Falconbridge added another cup and saucer to their tray. Amanda looked at her companion curiously but nothing was said. A moment later there was a knock at the door and a man's voice called, "Catrin? Can I come in?" He entered and Amanda was introduced to Philip Morgan, who lived in the adjoining cottage. They shook hands formally and she found herself looking into a pair of friendly, dark blue eyes in a sun-wrinkled face.

"We have this code," Philip explained. "The 'lucky seven' knock means I'm coming in and two knocks means I need help, come at once."

"What a sensible idea!" Amanda warmed to the man at once. He was obviously taking care of his neighbour as it seemed unlikely he would be the one in need of help.

He was in his late thirties, she guessed, with a figure that could only be described as burly. There was an air of restlessness about him. He was tanned and his piratical eyes shone with lively intelligence. He was, Amanda decided, a free spirit, a man who chose his own way and enjoyed life to the full.

She was enormously disappointed to be told he drove a bus!

"But how can you not be a sailor?" she said with a look of surprise.

"Because I'd be sick before we left the dockside," he replied, with a loud energetic laugh in which they all joined.

"So you aren't a pirate!"

When the teasing had died down, Philip said, "So, you're the new landlady." He looked her over in an embarrassing way, his eyes clearly liking what they saw.

Throughout the evening Amanda tried several times to bring up the subject of Roy. Mrs Falconbridge had been so kind to her she felt she owed her complete honesty, but each time something stopped her. She admitted that the strongest motive for silence was fear of Rhys being discouraged from becoming a friend. They knew she had a brother, but the impression she gave was that Roy was working a long way away in a job in retail marketing. As soon as she had invented the lie she had regretted it and now it was impossible to put it right. The evening ended with her still holding back the embarrassing detail of his prison sentences.

Roy's recent letter had assured her that with Gillian to help him he was making a determined effort to leave his past behind. He had been so understanding about their Aunt Flora's refusal to allow him to share the cottage, he must have changed. If he succeeded in keeping out of trouble there might not be any need to explain, until the prison sentences were behind him and it could all be put down to juvenile wildness. She drove part of the way home with her fingers superstitiously and childishly crossed.

Three

The letter from Edmond telling her he was engaged to someone they had both considered a friend was a relief tinged with sadness. They had drifted away from their once close relationship and although she knew that much of the blame was upon her brother's head, she also knew that theirs would never have been a really successful marriage. The parting was too easily done.

She wondered idly whether she had a decent photograph of Edmond and, also, whether she would keep it if she did. That reminded her of the photographs she had taken of Rhys on the day she had suspected him of being a burglar. Perhaps she would take them to be developed. She imagined how Catrin would laugh when she related the story once again, with illustrations.

Now Edmond was out of her life she felt free to start planning her future without anything dragging her back to the past. Unfinished business no more. If only Roy's future could be sorted so easily.

Apart from moments of weakness, Roy was able to enjoy the feeling of being free from worry over the police investigating his activities. Running bets for bookies from the market stall-holders and those he began to know in the local pubs was against the law and, as he was still on probation, a risk, but he needed some excitement in his life and running to and fro with the written bets and the cash in his pocket and waving to the local policeman on his beat was better than nothing.

He explained this to Gillian, who understood his need for

some spice to compensate for his lack of night-time activities and she giggled with him as he told her of some narrow escapes.

"Roy, you'll never change," she chuckled when he had explained how he had chatted to the policeman for ten minutes while watching the clock, afraid he would be too late to place the bets.

"Casual beyond, I was, love. You'd think I was an actor the way I leaned on the wall as if I had all day to waste. And there I was, watching the minutes tick away, closer to the time when I'd have to stand the bets myself."

"What would have happened?" she asked.

"Well, if the horses had lost, I'd have kept the money, seven pound I had, mind! But if they'd won I would have had to pay out. I've done it before," he told her with a grin. "Made a few shillings that way I have."

"It's risky though."

"That's part of the fun."

He was whistling cheerfully, brushing away the debris of a day's trading when a shadow crossed the floor in front of him and a voice said, "So, Roy Clifford, I've found you at last. Hiding from your old pal, were you?"

"Dave!" Roy felt his legs shake as he looked into the angry eyes of his one-time partner. "I didn't think you'd be out just yet, boy. How's tricks?"

"Tricks? That's more your line. Why haven't you been in touch? Where's my money?"

"Money? What money?"

"Oh, I see, we're playing that game are we?"

"Never 'ad a penny piece, Dave, I swear!"

"I know different."

"Oh come on, boy, let me buy you a drink, is it?"

"I want more than a drink from you, Roy Clifford." The last of the stalls were closed for the night and Roy looked around as if wondering if he could make a run for it as Gillian appeared and waved. Dave gripped his arm tightly before waving to Gillian and moving away. "Don't think you can get away with it. I served time for both of us, remember? I want my money, here, tomorrow, right?"

"Wasn't that Dave?" Gillian asked. "Why didn't he stop and say hello?"

Roy put on his little boy look and lowered his head. "Come to ask for money he has, love. Says I owe him fifty-seven pounds."

"What?"

"Well, we didn't get clean away on that last job. We had to leave the money behind and he thinks I still have it. Depending on it he said, to pay some debts. I don't know what I'm going to do. I haven't got fifty-seven pounds, just the fifteen I've saved to buy your ring and he won't get that."

"Ask your sister! She owes you something for leaving you like she did and owning a cottage and only paying rent for a tiny room. She must be able to give you enough to pay him off. Forget the ring, love, it's more important we settle this. We don't want anything of your past dragging us down, do we?"

"I'll try," he said. "There's lucky I am, to have you."

Roy had no intention of trying to borrow from his sister. She could be saved for when he needed more generous help. She was bound to be feeling guilty about the cottage. No, Amanda could be put on ice for later.

After stalling Dave for a few days, and being threatened with violence, Roy took out the list of houses taken from the files in Gillian's office and began to plan a new spate of robberies. He was drenched with sweat at the prospect of another session of break-ins and the sweat was from the thrill and not from fear.

He would have to leave of course. Once the police realised the houses were all registered with the firm for which his girlfriend worked they wouldn't take long to get to him. Lucky he hadn't told Dave about Amanda's cottage. That might be a useful bolthole if he couldn't get the money in time. Damn it all, he muttered with insincere anger. Why did I spend it! Just when I was beginning to feel settled. But there was a lilt to his step and his smile was wider than it had been for weeks.

*   *   *

It was Philip Morgan, Mrs Falconbridge's neighbour who accompanied Amanda and Mrs Falconbridge on their first foray into Amanda's past. They had decided to begin at the church but to their disappointment, when they reached it, it was locked.

"Tombstones it is, then," Philip said cheerfully. "Where do we start?" He looked thoughtfully around then said, "Your Aunt Flora was married so we need to know her maiden name. Any ideas?"

"Beynon according to the solicitor."

By kneeling down and scraping away at the lichen and mosses that concealed the writing on the neglected stones, they were able to decipher several Beynons, which Amanda carefully noted in her book together with dates. Most were too long ago but some were possibilities.

"These two could have been the couple who lived in the cottage before Flora," Philip said, pointing. "Would they have been your great-grandparents, d'you think? The dates look about right." They all compared notes and discussed their oddments of information.

Amanda looked at the sad rows of graves with their occasional bunch of wind-blown flowers and thought it all too long ago to hope for success. The trail was cold and tenuous and she might as well forget any idea of discovering a warm and welcoming family. If there were any they would be far from this place, where memory had dimmed every trace of their existence.

Amanda saw that Catrin was chilled and at once abandoned further searching. "Come on, it's time for a cup of tea I think. A café, or the cottage?"

They went back to the cottage where the fire burned cheerfully and after preparing a tray of tea, Amanda said the two possible names aloud hoping foolishly they would mean something to her. "William and Sheila Beynon." Could she be their great-granddaughter? A stirring of hope grew within her.

"Flora couldn't have been your mother," Philip said as the discussion continued. "She was too old."

"I understand she died without children and so did her

43

brother, Tom," Mrs Falconbridge told them. "At least, Tom didn't marry. The only hope seems to be their sister who went to live in America."

"If the American sister married and had a daughter, could that daughter be my mother?" Amanda sighed then. "Oh, it's all hopeless. How can I trace the existence of someone who lived in America – if she existed at all! There are too many gaps and guesses. Her name wouldn't even be Beynon so where would I begin?"

"You aren't giving up after one afternoon, are you?" Philip teased. "I thought you were made of sterner stuff!"

"Of course not," Mrs Falconbridge said, "she's just stopped for tea!"

Driving home, Amanda felt the wriggling impatience of dissatisfaction. She had been disappointed in the day and as the journey ended she admitted that Rhys's absence had been the main reason. Philip was excellent company but it was Rhys with whom she wanted to share her search.

Unable to calm her restless thoughts, she took out her notebook and read the names again. Sheila and William Beynon. Were they her great-grandparents? She stared at the names, willing them to reveal something. If only she had a photograph, that would at least give a focus for her tumbling thoughts and endless questions. Tired at last, she slept, to dream, not about Sheila and William Beynon, but of Rhys, magically finding a huge loving family for her, arranging them, presenting them like a bouquet.

When Amanda visited her brother, they met not at the flat which he had now vacated, being unable to pay the rent for an extended period, but in a café in the same area. As she listened to Roy's plans for the future, she felt her spirits rise. He really did seem genuine in his resolve to start afresh and forget the troubles of the past.

"See, Mand," he explained, "I'd fallen into the trap of always looking back. That way you never stand a chance of changing. I'm so much in the habit of blaming everything on what's long gone, I haven't allowed myself to get away from it. I've 'shackled myself willingly to a heavy load that's holding me back', that's how Gillian's dad put it, and it made sense."

"You know I'll help you in any way I can," Amanda said. In spite of many previous dashed hopes, there was something about her brother that made her believe that this time it would be all right. She went home bursting with the sensation that everything in her life was beginning to sort itself out beautifully.

Gillian had never been to the cottage now owned by Amanda, but, knowing she still lived in the bedsit, she wrote to her there. In the letter she explained that Roy had some debts which she feared might lead him back into crime and asked if Amanda, bearing in mind her own good fortune, would be willing to help.

Angry at the inference that she was selfishly enjoying her good fortune and forgetting her brother, Amanda called to see Roy at the market where he still did odd jobs and earned the occasional tip.

"If you want money, I'd prefer you asked me yourself," she said angrily when she found him helping to pack away the remains of a shoe-repair stall.

"What you talking about, Mand? I haven't asked for money. I'm doing all right here with this and that."

She took out the letter and waited while he read it. Anger suffused his face as he handed it back.

"I didn't know Gillian had written, honest, Mand. I don't know why she did. I don't owe anyone anything, although Dave came round begging for a few pounds last week. Forget it, off her head with worry about me she is. Afraid I'm going bad again if I'm a few minutes late home."

Amanda watched him. He was trying to laugh but he couldn't hide his anger. Something was up, she knew him well enough to know that.

"Look, I can help a little, perhaps a couple of pounds each week? It isn't much but it will buy a few meals, or help toward the rent of a room. I can't do more, not until the ownership of the cottage is settled." She was receiving rent for Firethorn

Cottage and besides, she still felt guilty about the condition that she was not to allow him to stay.

"I don't want it, Mand," he said with that forced smile that didn't reach his eyes.

"Please, Roy, I'd be happier if you'd take it."

He shrugged agreement and kissed her. "Right then, that's agreed and thanks. I'm lucky to have a sister like you, Mand, don't think I don't know it."

During the weekends, Amanda worked at preparations for Christmas, searching out a play for the children to perform, gathering ideas for cards and small gifts for them to make, displays to cover the walls. One Friday, needing a break, she telephoned Mrs Falconbridge and suggested going to Red Cliffs Bay for lunch on the following day.

"I'd love to and please, dear, call me Catrin."

Stopping the car by the now familiar hedge, Amanda looked expectantly at the front door but no Catrin appeared. She walked around to the back but there was no answer to her knock. Opening the door, she called.

"I'm here, in the kitchen, Amanda dear," Catrin answered.

Amanda saw at once that Catrin was unwell. She was sitting in her favourite chair covered with a crocheted blanket.

"What's the matter! Why didn't you tell me you weren't well?" Amanda cried in alarm.

"I thought I'd be all right by the time you got here. I do so hate worrying people."

"What about your famous two knocks on the wall?" Amanda demanded. "I think Philip will be disappointed that you didn't call him."

"It's only a heavy cold, but perhaps I oughtn't to go out for lunch."

"I should think not! I'll get something from the chemists to make you feel better, but first—" She picked up the small hearth brush and gave two loud knocks on the wall.

Philip came within seconds and was surprised to see Catrin wrapped up and obviously ill.

"What is it? Your cold getting worse?" He turned to Amanda. "She was out in the garden an hour ago!"

Amanda drove to the small row of shops that served the village and in the chemist bought Beechams powders. Next door at the greengrocer's she bought some fresh farm eggs and a couple of lemons. Unseen for the years of the war, lemons still seemed a bit of a luxury, she thought, smelling their fresh scent as she hurried back to the cottage. At the grocer's where she bought a fresh loaf, she was given some off-ration butter after explaining about Catrin being unwell. "If anyone asks, tell them it's only the scrapings of the wrapping paper," the grocer told her with a wink.

They were coaxing her to eat a lightly poached egg and thin bread and butter when Rhys walked in.

"What's going on here?" he asked, taking in the friendly scene.

"It's Catrin, she isn't well," Amanda began. "Philip and I are getting her some lunch."

Without needing to say another word, Rhys showed his disapproval. Amanda felt antipathy like an electric current passing between the two men. "Philip has been very helpful—" she began in an attempt to ease the tension.

"And Philip is just going!" Philip put down the tray he was about to hand to Catrin and with a wave went to the door. "Philip has to get HMS Land-Lubber out of the dock at two-thirty."

Amanda smiled at his reference to her conviction he was a sea captain and not the driver of a bus and was about to explain the joke to Rhys. A glance at his angry face stopped her.

As the door closed behind Philip, Rhys said softly, "Why did you send for Philip and not me?"

"I presumed you were still in London," she said. "Besides, it was quicker. He comes in answer to two knocks on the wall."

Tight-lipped, he went to his aunt. "I think you should be in bed," he said, and without waiting for a reply he picked her up and carried her to her bedroom. Amanda followed with the tray. Catrin said nothing, she just smiled at them with a quizzical look in her bright eyes.

47

"I'll sit in the kitchen," Amanda said as Catrin began to eat. "I'll stay a while, so call if you need anything."

"Thank you, dear."

Rhys followed her downstairs and she sensed his continuing disapproval. "I'm afraid she caught a chill when we went to the churchyard," she told him. "Philip and I were crawling around searching for the name Beynon and Catrin stood waiting. I remember she did look cold."

"What were you thinking of, allowing her to get chilled? Too busy exchanging jokes with Philip, I suppose."

"You suppose wrong! It was your aunt's idea to go and she is quite capable of telling me when she's had enough and wants to go home!"

He turned to look at her as though surprised at her outburst. "If Philip is helping you, you won't need these." He took a few pages of notepaper from his pocket. "I went to look up some records and found a few items of interest, but I was obviously wasting my time."

"No, Rhys. I'm very grateful, really."

Ignoring his bad humour, Amanda opened the pages and saw dates to add to those already noted. She began to tell him about the sketchy plan she had drawn.

"I know it's mostly based on guesswork, but *if* Sheila and William were my great-grandparents, then I have to be a daughter of one of their grandchildren."

"Obviously. But there must be other families called Beynon. Why presume it's this one?"

"Because it's Aunt Flora's family. She was the daughter of Sheila and William. I must be part of her family or why would she leave me the cottage?" Disapproval was slowly leaving his face and she smiled at him. At once the frown returned. "So," she went on, "if we accept Sheila and William, my mother was the daughter of either Flora, who so far as is known had no children, or the illegitimate daughter of Tom, who didn't marry. Or, if the story about a third child is true, then my grandmother went to America."

"Which begs the question, how did you and your brother end up in Children's Homes in Cardiff?"

48

"And the trail ends. I don't even know the third child's name."

"I do. I have her name and that of her husband."

Amanda looked at him, her eyes shining. "You have? Rhys, please tell me!"

"Flora and Tom's sister was Gwen."

"Gwen." She repeated the name, savouring it, trying to build it into an image of a person whom she would know as her grandmother. "It's my second name too," she said, her eyes shining. Rhys came to stand behind her leaning over her shoulder at the piece of paper he had placed on the table.

"Gwen married someone called Ryan Talbot and they had a son who died and a daughter called Sian Talbot."

"My mother might have been Sian?" Then she added with disappointment wrinkling her face, "No, Gwen's daughter Sian can't be my mother. Her name is Talbot. If I believe the rest, my name is or was Clifford."

"Her single name was Talbot: she married, presumably, if she had you and Roy."

"Oh, it's hopeless. I see my way through it then find another closed door. Now I'm looking for a woman whose name might have been Talbot possibly living somewhere in America!"

"Don't give up," he said, turning her to press her gently into his shoulder. "We're bound to find out the truth now we've made a start."

They stood together for a long moment and Amanda's thoughts were no longer on the information he had brought. The fresh clean smell of him was like an exotic perfume and she was possessed by an urge to bury her face against his neck, to move so their bodies were moulded together. She wondered if he regretted having to move as much as she did.

An hour later she left and he stood on the pavement watching until her car was lost to his sight.

Besides phoning, Amanda went once more to see Catrin. On a Sunday morning, she woke to a beautiful clear day. The forecast was good and she rang, suggesting they go for their postponed lunch. This time the front door opened and Catrin, warmly wrapped in a thick jacket and tweed skirt, stepped out to meet her.

"I'm so glad you're well again," Amanda said, helping her into the car and tucking a blanket around her knees.

"I'm well, and hungry enough to eat a horse, dear."

They ate at the Red Cliffs Restaurant, on the rocky headland, which being rich in iron ore gave the place its name.

"We used to picnic here years ago," Catrin said wistfully. "When there were small nephews and nieces to use as an excuse."

"You don't need an excuse," Amanda laughed. "We can come whenever you like and picnic just like you used to."

"With a bonfire and smoky tea? And sandwiches with real sand?"

"Of course. And if it's children you want I can supply a classroom-full."

After lunch they strolled in the mild air along the cliff top before returning to the car. A mist was beginning to settle over the sea, sliding down from the land that had been warmed by the late autumn sun.

Amanda was concerned at the slowness with which Catrin walked. "I hope you haven't overtired yourself," she said anxiously.

"I'll be glad to be back," Catrin admitted, "but I have enjoyed this afternoon."

"So have I. Thank you for coming with me."

"Will you do something else for me before you leave?" Catrin asked when they were back at the cottage. "Go and see Rhys? I've made a cake for him, and a few potato and cheese pasties with the last of my cheese ration. Oh what a treat it will be if rationing does finish next year. I'll go out and buy the largest slab of cheese I can carry and pounds and pounds of butter."

"It has been a long time, hasn't it? I can hardly remember not having to use ration books, or not having to queue for anything a bit special."

"Will you take them to him? He's going away again tomorrow and he'll find them useful."

50

Amanda's heart gave a little skip at the prospect of seeing Rhys, but she answered calmly enough. "Certainly. I'll go now shall I? Then I can come back and spend another hour with you before I have to leave."

The mist had thickened and the trees lining the lane were shrouded with it. It hung around the branches, moving slightly in the cooling moist air. When she reached the bungalow the front door stood open and a beam of light shone across the garden. She closed the gate behind her and looked around, wondering if Rhys had perhaps gone for a walk, perhaps to post a letter, leaving the door open for his return.

Voices murmured on the calm air and she looked towards the stream at the side of the house where vague figures were emerging from the mist.

"Rhys?" she called, walking towards the dimly seen figures.

"Coming!"

The ghostly shapes drew nearer and she recognised the tall slim figure of Rhys followed by others. The group were soon recognisable as a young woman and two children.

"Oh, it's you, Amanda. How would you like to meet two of your future pupils?"

He introduced the woman as Mrs Heather James and her two children as Helen, who was five and Jane, a shy four-year-old. Amanda bent down at once to talk to the little girls.

"How lovely to meet you before I start working at Mill House School. I won't feel so strange with friends waiting for me on my first day, will I?"

Helen, an outgoing, confident child, began to chatter happily to Amanda, but Jane was unable to answer her questions. She slid behind her mother's skirts and was obviously uncomfortable at the attention. Amanda didn't press her, although she was included in the brief conversation.

"Heather and I have been helping the girls collect gravel and weed from the stream to put in a fish tank," Rhys explained.

"They hope to find frogspawn in the spring," their mother explained, "and they can't bear to see the tank empty."

"Good idea. It's surprising what you can find when you put

some weed in a tank. All sorts of tiny creatures emerge. I'll bring a book next time I come so you can start identifying some of them."

The trio left and Amanda handed Rhys the box of food.

"Will you come in for coffee?" he asked.

Amanda hesitated. She wanted to accept. The thought of spending time with him was tempting but she shook her head. "I have to leave soon and I promised to spend the last hour with your aunt."

"I'd like to talk about the two girls," he said, and, presuming she would follow, went through the door, closing it against the now chilly afternoon. He led her to the kitchen, which was so very different from the one in Firethorn Cottage. She compared its functional and modern units with the cosy unefficient lines of Catrin's. But Catrin's worked well without modern improvements.

Rhys acted true to form. He took out coffee, percolator, milk and a tin of biscuits and left her to it. "I won't be a moment," he said as he disappeared. "No sugar in mine."

"Will I ever be invited here without having to prepare my own?" she demanded. But there was a chuckle in her voice.

"Poor thing. So put-upon!"

As they drank coffee, Rhys talked about Heather James's two girls.

"Helen is a bright little thing, but her sister Jane seems quiet for a four-year-old," he began. "I see them often and Jane doesn't make the progress her sister did. She walked late and talked late and never shows that spark of mischievous curiosity most children have."

"Some children seem content to observe for a while."

"But she's afraid of meeting people."

"Nervous of people or afraid of leaving her mother?" Amanda asked.

He shrugged. "When she starts at Mill House School, will you give her some extra thought?"

"My first task will be to study the children and consider their special needs. But of course I'll watch Jane and see she doesn't fall behind the others. That's a big danger with a shy child, she refuses to compete and quickly loses ground." She took another biscuit. "Are they special friends of yours?"

"Remember when you drove me to collect some photographs? That was Heather's husband, Haydn. He and I have been friends since we were at school. You're sure to meet him soon."

Thinking of the drive back to the bedsit where a pile of work still awaited her, Amanda regretfully stood to leave.

"Pity you're leaving again so soon," she said as she shrugged into her coat. "I don't think your aunt is really well yet. Lucky she has Philip next door. He'll see she's all right."

"Oh, yes," he said strangely, "good old Philip."

Amanda was still wondering about Rhys's obvious dislike of Philip Morgan when she reached home. Philip was kind and he certainly watched over Catrin. Rhys should be grateful as he was away so much, but he was not. There was always a hovering tension when Philip was mentioned. She thought that she would ask Catrin the reason, one day.

The weeks leading up to Christmas were busy ones for Amanda. Besides the handwork and decorations she made with the children and their normal class work, there was the Carol Service, the Nativity Play, and a Christmas Fair to raise money for much-needed equipment. There was sadness in the busy days too as she reminded herself that it was the end of her time there. Excited as she was about starting in the school in Tri-nant, she would be sorry to leave a place where she had been happy.

Besides the varied activities in school, there were visits to her brother.

Roy's apparent determination to start a new life away from his previous friends cheered her. Having convinced the authorities and those prepared to help him, he was getting a lot of help and encouragement.

"Pity you can't let me stay, Mand," he said every time she saw him. "I miss you and we're the only family we've got. It seems right to be together. Moving away from the familiar haunts would be just what I need, too. Tri-nant would be a wonderful fresh start."

"You know it's impossible, Roy," she told him, guilt churning her stomach and making her feel sick.

"But if you could find me a room in the village. At least we'd be together. You're all I've got, Mand." He turned away and added quietly, "I saw Dave again the other day, but I avoided getting back with him, afraid I am, mind. Afraid that if I stay around here he'll persuade me to get involved again."

Steeling herself, determined to resist this form of blackmail she shook her head. "No, Roy. I need a fresh start as well as you. You've brought my life into disrepute too, remember. I need this new beginning as much as you. And there's Gillian, she seems very supportive and her parents like you. How would she feel about you moving away?"

"It's only eight miles, Mand, and Gillian understands the pressure I'm under. She wants me to succeed and if that means moving away from the temptation offered by the people around me, then she's all for it."

"If you could look around for a better job you'd soon be secure."

"You make it sound so easy."

"Listen to those trying to help you and keep away from Dave! The rest will all happen if you really want it to. No one is a failure at twenty-five. You can start again and really make a success of things."

Roy nodded and assured her he would really try, but her confidence that he had changed had slipped considerably.

She called on Catrin briefly to return the African masks and deliver the books she had promised Heather James's girls, but the weeks went by so fast she had little time to spare. After a particularly hectic day which because of the Christmas Fair lasted from eight in the morning until almost nine o'clock at night, she reached home to find the developed photographs had arrived and she searched through them to see how successful her 'burglar' snaps had been.

It was difficult to recognise Rhys in the ones taken through the window but the shot of him standing at the door was excellent. A surge of pleasure welled up in her as she studied the picture. His face was serious and she remembered his

54

curiosity at the flowers she had left for Catrin. She propped
the picture on a shelf, and went to run a bath.

She had thrown her school bag and the items she had brought
home carelessly on the couch. She was too tired to sort them
out. They could wait till tomorrow.

As she began to undress there was a knock at the door.
Slightly irritated, she opened it to find Rhys there. "Rhys! What
a surprise. Won't you come in?" She led them into her solitary
room with an embarrassed wave of apology, conscious of the
chaos of books and half-made Christmas decorations strewn
about the room.

"I've just come in," she murmured.

"Not from school, surely?" He looked at his watch and
Amanda explained.

"We held a Christmas Fair this evening, it's been a long
day. I'm not usually this untidy." She picked up a waterfall
of books and invited him to sit.

"Have you eaten?" he asked.

Amanda looked at him quizzically. "Are you going to invite
me to cook for us both?"

He smiled to show he appreciated the teasing and shook his
head. "I thought we'd go out, unless you're too tired?"

"Give me time to bathe and change."

Leaving him studying her collection of books, she took her
fresh clothes and went along the corridor to the bathroom.
Twenty minutes later she was ready and sparkling, all thoughts
of a lazy evening forgotten.

Rhys took her to a restaurant near the edge of town where
the speciality was French cuisine. When they had ordered she
said, "How is Catrin?"

"It's Catrin I want to talk about."

"She's all right, isn't she? She was cheerful when I spoke
to her last."

"Cheerful, yes, but I don't think she's well."

"How can I help?" Amanda said at once, concern showing
in her expressive eyes.

"What plans have you made for Christmas?"

"None. In fact, I've refused invitations as I want to spend

the time preparing for my new post. I've some thinking and planning to do after talking to the Head and I have cards and posters to make."

"Aunt Catrin and I wondered if you'd spend the two days with us. Either at my place or hers – yours, I mean," he smiled.

"I'd love to!" A wide smile showed her pleasure. "But it's a family time. I wouldn't want to intrude."

"Aunt Catrin asked me to invite you."

"Oh." Amanda couldn't help the tiny gesture of disappointment at the implication that it was not his idea to share Christmas.

"And I thought," he continued, "as you're on your own, you might like the notion of spending Christmas in the village that will one day be your home."

"That was thoughtful of you," she murmured, disappointment still strong.

It was raining when they left the restaurant and Rhys took her hand as they ran to the car. Laughing at their discomfort, she shook her hair free of the thin, useless scarf hurriedly thrown across her head and pushed it into a pocket.

"Straight back to your fire, I think," Rhys said, opening the car door for her.

"How I'd love to be heading back to the real fire in Catrin's kitchen," she sighed.

"You surely won't keep the open fire when you move in?"

"I might change my mind but at present I don't think I'll alter a thing. I love everything about it."

"I'm glad. Although I wish Aunt Catrin would make some plans. I can't think why she doesn't at least start enquiries about a place to live. Whenever I ask, she just smiles mysteriously and says, 'something will turn up'!"

"You make me feel guilty. But surely you understand how much I want to live there? Besides being a place to live, it's a link with a family I didn't know I had."

"Then you'll come for Christmas?"

It was still raining when they reached the bedsit and they went in and thankfully closed the door against the unpleasant night. Switching on the gas fire Amanda was again confronted by the shamble of books and papers. "I think I'll leave these till the morning. Would you like some coffee?"

"Yes, but first, about Christmas. Will you come?"

"Thank you, yes, I'd love to."

"The cottage or my place?"

"You choose."

"I know you like the cottage but I think you should spend your first Christmas there next year, when it's really yours."

"Fine," she smiled. "I'll come early Christmas morning."

"No, you'd better come early Christmas Eve. There'll be shopping to do. You'll be cooking dinner so you'd better choose what we buy."

"*I'll* be cooking dinner? You're inviting me so I can cook?"

"A good rest is just what Aunt Catrin needs."

"Of course," she said, staggered by his suggestion. "And what I need is a couple of busy days!"

"I thought so." He ignored her sarcasm entirely.

While she sat suffering a mild panic at the thought of providing a full dinner for three people, Rhys seemed immune to her reaction. He looked around the room perfectly relaxed as she made coffee for them both, until he saw the photograph of himself.

"When did you take this?" He picked it up and studied it critically.

"Oh, do you recognise him? It's a photograph I took of a thief raiding Firethorn cottage!"

He laughed as she described creeping through the bushes, watching his suspicious antics.

She enjoyed watching him sitting across the room from her, so relaxed and at home, filling a gap in her life of which she hadn't been aware.

Already she was looking forward to Christmas with growing delight. But the happiness was tinged with worry. She had rarely cooked for more than two people and had never tackled a full roast dinner in her life.

Four

During the last frantic days before leaving Haversley School, Amanda felt genuine regret. She had enjoyed happy relationships with all the staff and there was the dissatisfaction of leaving the children only one term into the school year.

"Things rarely work out tidily," Catrin said when Amanda phoned her. "And just think how long you might have waited for another vacancy."

"I'm not complaining," Amanda assured her friend. "But I still hate leaving with my job only partly done."

In between school activities Amanda searched through cookery books with a fervour bordering on desperation. She had never attempted a roast meal, managing as she did on a tiny table-top cooker. How was she going to produce a traditional meal for three? She tried to keep her fears from Catrin. If Rhys's idea was to give his aunt a few restful days there was no point in ruining his plan by admitting her worries. But if I don't ruin the plan, Amanda thought miserably, I'll probably ruin the dinner!

"Will Rhys expect roast potatoes?" and "Will he want brandy sauce with the pudding?" She tried to make the questions sound like casual enquiries about his likes and dislikes. Catrin was not fooled for an instant.

"I expect you'll find it awkward, cooking a complicated meal in a strange kitchen," she said one day. "But don't worry, dear. Between us we'll make sure Rhys doesn't starve. I'm not going to sit and be waited on whatever he thinks. We'll do it together, won't we?"

Amanda wondered if her sigh of relief was heard at the other end of the phone.

When term reached its effervescent close, Amanda was waved off by the children and the staff and, hurrying home more emotionally drained than she had expected, she began to pack the few parcels for Tri-nant.

Cards were arriving with each post and she hung them on lines of string across the walls. One was from Gillian and Roy and she felt rather hurt that it had been written by Gillian and not by Roy himself. With a family of just two, she deserved a personally written card, didn't she?

She put the card in her bag to take with her. Catrin and Rhys knew she had a brother and she had to mention him from time to time, and build up to the moment when they would be introduced. That situation she would delay as long as possible, at least until Roy was established in a steady job. Having kept his prison record a secret from Catrin and Rhys this long, it was impossible to confess it, so she hoped it would remain hidden in the past, a disastrous period of his life never to be repeated.

The telephone rang before she had finished packing presents and it was Gillian. "Thank you for your card," Amanda began, then unable to resist, she added, "How nice for my brother to have someone to write it for him."

"He didn't want to send one at all," Gillian said sharply. "He has to get out of the flat at the end of December and he isn't feeling very Christmassy."

"He's lived there rent-free since I moved and he's had weeks to find somewhere else."

"He's still hurt at your refusal to give him a home. And owning a house and making up some story about not being able to take him in, well, with him being your only relative it seems very hard."

"If you've phoned to make me feel guilty then you can forget it! Roy has been in and out of prison since he was fourteen. Every time he was released he came to me, disrupted my life then got himself arrested again. Nothing I have done has helped. Nothing! I just feel that this time, if he stood on his own feet instead of looking for someone to lean on, he might succeed in doing something with his life!"

"He won't manage alone. You know that deep down, although it might ease your conscience to pretend different. Roy needs help and if you, his only sister, won't give it, then I will."

"Then all I can say is good luck! You'll need it!"

Amanda was about to put down the telephone when she realised Gillian was crying.

"Gillian? What's happened? What's wrong?"

"He's been arrested again. He didn't want me to tell you, he didn't want to spoil your Christmas! Now I've been sacked because they think I helped with information. If you'd been kinder this wouldn't have happened, and you know it. He's trying desperately hard to stay out of trouble. It's all your fault, hurting him like you did!" It was Gillian who replaced the receiver.

Amanda was distressed by the news and shaken by the accusations and, after staring at the silent phone for some moments, she rang Catrin. Not to tell her about the interview but to calm herself with talk about her forthcoming visit. Rhys was not in London as planned but in Snowdonia hoping for some winter photographs to complete his brochure project. Catrin told her he still expected to be back late on the evening of the twenty-third.

"The realisation that he could get the photographs a little earlier made him suddenly decide to leave," Catrin explained. "He's always been that way. Impulsive, unable to stay in one place for long. That's why he hasn't married," she went on. "Where would he find a girl to put up with his wanderlust?"

"Is it wanderlust or his job? He could hardly make films without travelling," Amanda said reasonably.

"Did the job create him or he create the job?" Catrin mused. "I think he chose a career that would allow him to continue his restless ways. He was always a wanderer. No, anyone who loved Rhys would have to be able to cope with his constant disappearances." She paused and said softly, "She would have to be an angel."

Amanda listened and wondered if she were being warned not to become too involved. She must have made it transparently clear that Rhys was one of the reasons for her frequent visits to the cottage at Tri-nant.

"This is the 1950s," she said airily. "People don't think of marriage as inevitable today. It's no longer the highlight of a girl's life to find a man and marry him. Money is less for women but, with talk of equality, that will change. Equal pay for an equal job will become a reality, won't it? It's over a year since it was discussed in parliament so something must happen soon. Even before it does, with a reasonable job a woman can keep herself, and being 'kept' used to be one of the main reasons for marrying, wasn't it?"

"Oh surely not, dear," Catrin argued. "I would have been financially secure without my husband but I loved him. Falling in love might be a drawback to this growing interest in equality, but you wait till you feel Cupid's arrow!"

"I've felt a few," Amanda admitted with a chuckle. "But so far the wounds have been superficial."

"Don't you want to marry and have children?"

"As I've believed myself alone apart from a brother I rarely see, a family is something I've longed for. But I'm happy with my life at present. I love my work and the thought of living in Firethorn Cottage makes me content."

Amanda spoke defensively, afraid Catrin was doubtful about her growing friendship with Rhys. After she had replaced the phone she wondered why she had been so sensitive. Was there a seed of hope in her heart that Rhys might consider her to be a woman who could 'cope with his constant disappearances'? Who could be 'an angel'?

At Gillian's home, Mrs Harris was consoling her daughter, and, somewhat doubtfully, promising her support for Roy. Mrs Harris was small and plump like her daughter and she was always adorned extravagantly in bright jewellery. She habitually wore short skirts and big jumpers which emphasised her rather dumpy shape, but she was pretty and lively and was extremely well liked.

Besides her jewellery, she had a sparkle in her smile and in her bright, friendly eyes. She loved her only daughter dearly and although she had reservations about encouraging a friendship with a thief, handsome and charming though he was, she promised to help make Roy's eventual release a second Christmas.

"We'll buy you a dress that's real fetchin'," she said. "A nice cheerful red. And we'll get a chicken to roast and make a real do. Save some presents too, shall we? And have a proper party with crackers and paper hats?" Her pretty face glowed as she saw in her mind's eye the splendid 'welcome home' she would arrange.

With very little time before the holiday engulfed all chances of getting news about her brother, Amanda spent the next day learning as much as she could. She didn't apply for a permit to see him, convinced that he would be well served by Gillian. She couldn't face more accusations, so she avoided asking Gillian for news but depended on the Probation Service, Roy's solicitor and the court. It seemed likely he would spend Christmas in custody. Well, she sighed, it wouldn't be the first time!

On Christmas Eve, Rhys was waiting for her at the bungalow with his aunt, and he showed her into the dining room where an attractively presented lunch awaited them. A buffet of small sandwiches, quail's eggs, salads, pickles, jam tarts and some delicious biscuits.

"What a relief! I'm starving and was afraid I'd have to prepare lunch," Amanda said, glaring at Rhys with a pretence of anger. "But this is wonderful. How did you do it? You only got back last night, didn't you?"

"I thought it would be quicker if we're to get our shopping done."

Leaving Catrin to pack away the remains of their lunch they went to buy what food they could find to last throughout the following three or four days. With meat, bacon, cheese, butter and fats still rationed it wasn't easy. But there was an air of optimism as everyone believed it would be the last Christmas of food rationing. 'If it doesn't end in 1954, I'm going to emigrate!' was a regularly repeated joke.

They had to queue for practically everything they needed, with shops even running out of vegetables as the time to close drew near. Amanda watched for signs that Rhys was losing patience but he seemed unaffected by the tedium of the constant waiting. It augured well for the holiday that Rhys was in a happy mood and so obviously pleased that she was there.

Most of the shopping was done in the crowded market and Rhys even admitted to enjoying the bustle and the pushing as they gradually succeeded in getting everything on their list.

"I know most do their shopping well in advance," he said as they struggled to push their way into a café for a welcome cup of tea. "But to me it isn't Christmas without a few hours of this agony."

Amanda thought of her own past Christmases when she bought only the same as on a normal weekend. "I usually spend a few hours with friends and that's about all," she said.

"Your brother doesn't share it with you?"

"He usually has other arrangements," she said, unable to keep the bitterness out of her voice.

"It might be different when you find your family. Have you learned anything more?" he asked.

"Not really. These past few weeks haven't given me much time to think about it. End of term is always frantic. I keep looking at passers-by though, and wondering if they are related to me. Foolish I know, but I might be standing next to someone at a stall, without knowing they're a cousin or an aunt. It's strange."

"Well, Aunt Catrin will be happy to be a deputy aunt until you find one of your own," he said.

"She's been very kind."

"Oh, here's someone who isn't a relation but could become a friend." He waved and Heather James pushed her way through the over-full café followed by a man Amanda was introduced to as Heather's husband Haydn. He was almost as tall as Rhys but fair and extremely slim. His light hazel eyes appraised her briefly as she shook his hand, before his attention returned to his wife.

Rhys ordered more tea and cakes and soon the four people were adding to the lively chatter that surrounded them. Rhys had to lean over her, his arm around her shoulders, to talk to Haydn. Amanda found his nearness intoxicating. She thought this was going to be one of the most wonderful Christmases imaginable.

"Was lunch all right?" Heather asked then.

"Perfectly fine," he replied. For a moment, Amanda didn't realise what had been said, then she glared at Rhys, outrage making her soft blue eyes glow. "You mean Heather made lunch? But you led us to believe—" She burst out laughing. "You really take the biscuit for cheek, Rhys Falconbridge!"

"Did I give the impression I was responsible for that delicious spread?" he asked innocently.

"Sorry if I spoilt your story," Heather smiled. "I should have been primed."

Haydn laughed with her and, seeing them side by side, sharing the fun, she had the impression of a gentle man, a kindly man for whom Heather and their children were everything.

Amanda noticed that all the time they were there, Heather kept glancing at her watch. She wondered if it was anxiety about her daughters. Heather James did seem a very tense mother.

As Heather gathered together her shopping in preparation to leave, a woman pushed her way past the other tables and stood in front of Amanda.

"Gillian!" Amanda said. "What a surprise. What are you doing here?"

"Looking for you!"

Amanda looked alarmed. "Is something wrong?" she asked, thinking at once of her brother.

"I think so! You could have permission for a Christmas visit to see Roy but he tells me you haven't applied for it."

"I'll come outside, Gillian, we can talk there." Amanda was afraid Gillian would say more than she wanted her new friends to hear, but Gillian refused to take the hint.

"Your only brother in prison over Christmas and you can't be bothered to go and see him!" she blurted out.

"Gillian!"

Rhys stood up and made way for Amanda to join Gillian. "You go and talk to your friend and we'll meet at the car in ten minutes, all right?" In a daze she collected some of their shopping.

She heard Rhys say casually, "Nothing to worry about, Heather, your new teacher isn't from a criminal background. It's only a traffic offence, isn't it, Amanda?" She nodded miserably, adding a new lie to the lie by default, and followed Gillian out of the restaurant.

They drove home in silence and as Rhys turned off the engine she said miserably, "You knew about Roy being in prison?"

"We knew. It was Philip Morgan who found out, according to Aunt Catrin, although she seemed rather evasive when I questioned her. He used to be a newspaper reporter and sniffing out facts is second nature to him. We were waiting for you to tell us but you obviously don't yet trust us enough."

"It wasn't a lack of trust. I wanted a fresh start, away from the worry of him coming home, making a mess of my life then being hauled away again, back to prison. First there were the remand cèntres, then prison. He's probably going to serve his twelfth prison sentence and I'm tainted by it. What's even worse, he's involved Gillian who's been so good to him, and both of them blame me! I need to put it all behind me and have a fresh start as much as a criminal does."

"It makes a bit of a mockery of you searching for family if you can't cope with one brother," he accused, softening the remark with a smile. "Don't be ashamed for someone else's actions. You can't take on other people's problems."

"How can you know what it's like! I'm trying to make a life for myself and he seems hellbent on ruining it. I was almost engaged to a man called Edmond, but after Roy's most recent arrest for a string of robberies, not one, mind, a whole string of them, well, Edmond didn't want to see me again."

"He couldn't have loved you if he was put off by your

brother's behaviour." He drove through the gate and stopped the car.

"He *did* love me and our plans were ruined by Roy's activities. How could you understand? You in your safe secure life? It's easy to accuse me of not caring, but what good has caring for him ever done?"

"I didn't mean to accuse you of not caring. I think you care too much and—"

Ignoring his words she jumped out of the car and walked back to close the gate.

She was relieved to see someone walking along the road, someone she could talk to and ease the bitter disappointment of the shopping trip that had been ruined by Gillian.

"Philip, a Happy Christmas to you," she called gaily. "Who's your furry friend?" she asked, pointing to the rather large dog walking beside him.

"He belongs to old Mel Griffiths," he said. "Laid up he is with a touch of lumbago, so I offered to walk Ben for him."

Rhys came back for a second load of shopping, gave an exclamation of impatience and walked back into the house. To compensate for his rudeness, Amanda stopped and talked to Philip for a while. "That's very kind of you," she said.

"Not really. I like a walk and Ben's good company. I hear you're staying with Rhys for Christmas?"

"Yes. Catrin and me. What are your plans?"

"I'll stay home. I'll probably eat at the hotel on Christmas Day, just to make a bit of difference."

"But that's a pity. I'd have thought you'd have plenty of invitations. You're always doing favours for people."

"Last year I spent a lot of time with Catrin. Rhys was in America and we were both on our own."

Amanda went into the bungalow feeling disappointed with both Catrin and Rhys that they could leave Philip out of their arrangements.

"Philip is alone for Christmas," she told Catrin. "It seems a pity when you and he are such good friends."

"He wouldn't have come if he'd been invited," Catrin explained. "He and Rhys aren't exactly friendly."

"If Philip is alone at Christmas or at any other time it's because he chooses to be," Rhys said from the doorway.

Amanda saw at once from his stony expression that now was not the time for further questions, so she changed the subject.

"We met Heather and Haydn James in town," she said. "They're coming to see us tomorrow, if they can tear the children away from their new toys!"

"That will be lovely, they're delightful girls. Jane will be in your class, won't she?" Catrin smiled.

"We also met a friend of mine, Gillian Harris. She told everyone loudly and clearly about my brother Roy being in police custody." Catrin looked at her quizzically, waiting for her to say something more. "He's a habitual criminal, a thief, breaking into houses and stealing money and anything he can sell." She took a deep breath and went on, "Oh, it's all right. Rhys reassured Heather that her children would be safe, that Roy's was merely a traffic offence, that I don't come from a family of criminals, although that might not be such a surprise!" Tears threatened and she waited for Catrin to ask her to leave.

"Put it aside, dear, let's not think about it until after Christmas. We'll enjoy these few days, then we can discuss what's best to do later, that is if you want to discuss it. It really isn't our business what your brother gets up to, you aren't his keeper or his conscience, you know."

"I wonder how she knew where to find me?"

"If this Gillian is a plump young lady with short fair hair about your age, then think I might have seen her knocking on Philip's door. He would have guessed you'd be stopping for tea at some time during the afternoon, and working out which café wouldn't have been difficult."

"Time to pull the curtains and raise the drawbridge," Rhys said, sliding the heavy velvet curtains across the windows. "Amanda, what are you cooking for dinner?"

"Me?" Amanda said with a startled look. "I thought my duties didn't start until tomorrow!" She winked at Catrin.

"Oh, well, if you're going to quibble about a few hours—" he said, pretending offence.

Amanda went into the kitchen where she had already found a tin of prawns, an extravagance that had cost Rhys a large number of food points out of the monthly allowance. She began preparing for a vegetable, prawn and rice meal she had once had on holiday. She piled the plates and they ate off trays near the roaring log fire, and sat talking until long after eleven o'clock.

They spoke of past times and Amanda asked Rhys about his American Christmas of the previous year.

"I was helping to make a documentary on unusual pets and, as it wasn't quite completed, I decided to stay on rather than come home and have to go back."

"Did you enjoy the American-style Christmas?" she wanted to know. "How does it differ from ours?" Usually, when she asked Rhys a question he enlarged on it and spun stories around his experiences, but this time he seemed reluctant.

"I prefer this," he said briefly. "America isn't a place where I've been happy."

Amanda's room was next to Catrin's and they agreed to call each other when they woke.

"Rhys will be up before either of us," Catrin told her. "He's one of those people who can't bear to stay in bed once he's awake."

Amanda thought she too would wake early, worrying about that goose she'd promised to cook!

She lay in the strange bed listening to the strange sounds, and knew she would be unable to sleep. It was useless trying to read, she wouldn't concentrate on a word. Worries about Roy and, by this time, belief in Gillian's accusations that she had let him down would certainly keep her awake. Slipping on a dressing gown she went quietly through the lounge to the kitchen. Taking a cookery book from the shelf she began trying to memorise the cooking times of the enormous bird. Tomorrow's dinner was another reason she couldn't expect to sleep. If only sausages were the traditional fare!

She looked at her watch. It was a little after one. She wouldn't need to start cooking until nine, but she had to do something towards it now. Anything to ease the agony of waiting and wondering if she would be able to produce the festive meal that most people seemed to achieve without effort.

She was so engrossed in her calculations she didn't hear Rhys come padding into the room in bare feet.

"That goose is for lunch, not breakfast," he whispered. "What are you doing up at this time of night?"

"I'm too restless to sleep," she said, trying in vain to hide the cookery book. "I was just looking something up. Cakes! I thought I might make some cakes for Helen and Jane. I brought some margarine and butter," she defended quickly. With rationing still in force there was no surplus for extra cooking.

"I think a cup of milky cocoa is what you need." He opened the fridge door and handed her a bottle of milk. "Make one for me, will you?"

"One day you'll invite me for a meal without my having to make it," she growled.

"I gave you lunch today, didn't I?"

"With a little help from your friends!" The usual banter was stiff and forced.

He revived the fire and moved the couch closer to its glow.

"I should have told you about Roy," she said as they sipped their soothing drinks.

"I can understand why you didn't. This place with its new address and the new job, it's a fresh start for you, isn't it?"

"I didn't intend abandoning him. But I hoped that by the time I introduced him here, he would be settled in a job and making his way in the world without having to steal. What an optimist! Everyone will know. Gillian might as well have used a tannoy system!"

"You mean she didn't?" He succeeded in making her smile. "Heather won't discuss it and neither will Aunt Catrin, so you can have your fresh start, so long as your one-time friend Gillian doesn't blurt it out too often."

"Am I being unfair to refuse to help him one more time?"

"No. And you should stop thinking you are."

They sat for a while in companionable silence, then the special magic that is Christmas led them to reminisce.

"There's something mystical about this festival," Rhys said quietly. "It brings back memories more readily than any other time."

"My happiest childhood memories are of Christmas," Amanda said, "although this will be the first time I've spent a traditional Christmas in a family home, apart from my own. I've never been a part of it before. There's been Roy once or twice, but he was usually out, sharing someone else's day."

"That's sad."

"I didn't think so. It was what I was used to. Although I confess I did feel miserable sometimes, glancing through windows at crowded rooms, at families having fun." She looked at him, his eyes shining in the flickering light from the fire. "Have you ever had a really sad Christmas?"

"I've seen friends go through bad times and, as it was this time of year, the memories remain."

"I don't think I've ever felt really sad, I expected so little, unaware of how wonderful it could be."

"There won't ever be any more sad Christmases for you. From now on you'll never be alone or without friends," he whispered.

She was drawn to him and leaning towards him their lips touched gently but with such tenderness she wondered if he had been misled by the intimacy of the fire-lit scene and imagined for an instant she was someone else. He whispered her name then, his lips touching her cheek and her heart lifted with joy knowing it was her, Amanda Clifford, who filled his mind. His arms held her and their second kiss lasted until the room filled with its magic.

Slowly he released her and looked down into her gentle eyes, darkened with love. He kissed her again, playfully, on the tip of her nose and said, "Bed for you, young lady, or you'll never be up in time to cook my goose!"

She returned to her room but this time it was not the thought of the dinner that kept her awake.

At seven she again crept into the kitchen and made a few

small cakes. At least sugar was no longer rationed and she could ice them to make them more edible. While they were cooking she began preparing the vegetables. The house was silent and there was that inexplicable air of expectancy that pervades the atmosphere when there are surprises to unfold.

She had just finished peeling the potatoes, counting them carefully to make sure there were sufficient, when a sound made her start. She watched as the door slowly opened, expecting to see Rhys. But it was Philip standing there, dressed against the cold of the early morning in corduroys and a thick, weatherproof jacket which made him look even larger than usual.

"Philip? What are you doing out so early?" She stood back for him to step inside.

"I'd forgotten about Catrin being here instead of her cottage. I've brought her present," he explained. He handed her a paper carrier containing several brightly-wrapped gifts. "Put these under the tree for me, will you?"

"Thank you. There are some gifts for you but we left them at the cottage. Will you go in and fetch them or wait till we get back?"

"I'll wait. Tell her I'll light her fire ready for her return, will you? But I won't look at the presents until then."

"Happy Christmas, Philip."

"A Happy Christmas to you, Amanda." He leaned forward, put a hand on her shoulder and kissed her cheek. "Enjoy your visit. I'll see you before you go back, won't I?"

Behind them the door opened and Rhys stood there.

"If I might come in?" he asked sarcastically.

"Philip has brought presents for Catrin," she explained.

"I see. Well, if that's all—?" Rhys glanced pointedly at the door then at Philip. Philip left with a casual wave.

"That was so embarrassing!" Amanda said. "Why do you have to be so rude to him?"

"I can't stand the fellow, and you'd be wise to give him a wide berth!"

"Why should I? I don't know anything that justifies such

treatment. I refuse to dislike someone because you say I should!" Amanda said angrily. "I'm sure Catrin doesn't share your views."

"If you're going to be entertaining visitors, don't you think you should get dressed?" He glared at her and left the room.

"Oh dear," she muttered. "Not the best start to the day."

She needn't have worried. When they next met he was cheerful and perfectly relaxed. Amanda had bathed, and had dressed in a turquoise dress, specially bought to wear on Christmas Day. She found Rhys and Catrin in the kitchen preparing a light breakfast.

"When we were children we weren't allowed to open a single present until we'd eaten. And that was the only morning of the year when I wasn't hungry!" Catrin said.

Unwrapping the presents was fun and Rhys watched Amanda, marvelling that it was the first time she had been a part of such a happy, family occasion. She had a scarf from Philip, a book on garden birds from Catrin and Rhys had given her a delicately carved family of harvest mice.

"It's beautiful!" she gasped, stroking the polished wood as if the animals were real. "Where did you find such a treasure?"

"Haydn James makes them," Rhys explained. "I thought you'd like an ornament to start your new home."

"Thank you." She kissed him lightly on the lips in the way she had thanked Catrin.

Catrin beamed at them. She was utterly content to be sharing the holiday with two of her favourite people, she told them.

"Now for dinner." Amanda walked with some trepidation towards the kitchen.

In fact everything went well. With Catrin's guiding hand the goose was perfectly cooked and the vegetables miraculously all ready at the same time.

At three, when they were still at the table, there was a knock at the door.

"Good heavens! That will be Heather and Haydn and the girls!" Rhys gasped. "I hadn't realised the time!"

Dishes were stacked and the table cleared as the James family removed their coats. Kisses were exchanged and Amanda sat near little Jane and her mother.

Throughout the afternoon Amanda tried to coax the little girl to talk to her, but each time she asked a question, her mother answered for her and she saw Heather's arm tighten around the child as if reassuring her she wasn't expected to reply.

"I don't know how she'll manage when school restarts," Heather said anxiously. "She was most unhappy there. She hates leaving me even for a few seconds."

Amanda shook her head, silently asking Heather not to put negative ideas in Jane's head.

"I'm a new girl too, remember," she said. "I'm depending on Jane to help me on my first day."

When the visitors had gone, Amanda asked Rhys to give her some background. "Heather seems particularly close to Jane," she said hesitantly. She knew how fond Rhys was of the family and was afraid of offending by appearing to pry.

"Helen has always been confident and strong. Jane needs extra care," was all he said.

"Has she been ill? Or away from her mother at any time?"

"Only briefly, when she was a baby."

He was answering her questions but Amanda felt a reticence. It was as if the spoken words were used to hide something. She remembered a drama teacher once saying that dialogue disguised thoughts as well as revealing them. She guessed this was what she had meant.

Five

Boxing Day was free from cooking worries as they ate well but simply on cold meat and salads. After lunch Rhys suggested a walk.

"I think we need to freshen ourselves after all this food, don't you?"

Catrin shook her head.

"You speak for yourself, I'm content to sit here," she replied.

"Are you feeling all right?" Amanda asked anxiously.

"Of course, dear, but I don't feel the need to go galloping about like you young things."

Amanda was not fully convinced.

Rhys collected their coats and took Amanda up on the hill behind the bungalow which overlooked both the village nestling in the valley which hid the stream and, in the distance, the sea. Both were invisible that day, lost in the haze of the winter day. She looked down at the few visible roofs and chimney pots in the sparsely populated area and said, "Somewhere down there is someone who knew my family. Someone I have to find."

"We will, I'm sure of it." He put an arm around her and she was comforted by his assurances and flattered by his concern.

The mist was thickening, the best of the day already gone.

"Not the best time of year to see the view," Rhys smiled. "We'll have to come again later when the weather is better."

"It's in the summer I'll really get the know the place," she agreed.

"You think you be happy living in Tri-nant? You won't miss your present home and friends?"

"Having a place of my own is worth uprooting myself for."

"You'll be uprooting Aunt Catrin too, unfortunately. She doesn't seem to be making any plans. She refuses even to discuss it, insisting that something will sort itself when the time comes."

"Does she think I won't live in the cottage d'you think?"

"Perhaps she thinks you'll change your mind about living in Tri-nant."

"I won't change my mind."

She wanted to make her home in Firethorn Cottage and be able to walk from room to room and wander out into a garden that was her own. But most of all, she admitted silently, it was the thought of living where she would see Rhys and perhaps become a part of his life.

"When does Roy come out of prison?" he asked as they made their way back down the hill.

"He hasn't even been sentenced yet, but I suppose it will be a few months. He might not bother to let me know. Gillian seems to have taken full responsibility for his welfare. His recent letters have been full of lightly-veiled reproaches and I hear Gillian's voice in them. Perhaps blaming me makes Gillian feel even more noble. I hope she won't be badly hurt."

Rhys said very little when they parted at the end of her brief visit. Their time together ended so casually it was hard to believe the middle-of-the-night kiss had ever happened. The Christmas holiday had begun badly, with the interruption of Gillian's appearance and her outburst, and it had ended unsatisfactorily, like a book with the last page missing, she thought sadly. And with no hope of a sequel.

The bedsit seemed cold and impersonal when she stepped inside. The cards had sagged or fallen and there were a few pieces of wrapping paper and glittering string left from her present wrapping. It made the place look very sad, the morning after a party that had never happened. The thought of living there for ten more months was hard to take.

75

She looked through the post that she had neglected before leaving for Tri-nant and opened one from Eric Green, Roy's Probation Officer. It explained that if he received a non-custodial sentence, he intended to take a room with the parents of Miss Gillian Harris. Amanda put the letter on her desk intending to reply, but the following day, Monday, she telephoned instead.

She was angered by the tone of the man's voice and wondered irritably what story Gillian had told.

"You have inherited a house I understand, Miss Clifford, but have chosen to rent a single room so you are unable to accommodate your brother."

"That's right. I can't accommodate my brother. Every other time I have done so but this time I cannot, and, in case you've been misinformed, Mr Green, I do not take possession of my inherited cottage until next year!"

"I'm sorry, I didn't mean to imply—"

"Oh, didn't you! Well let me make this quite clear, Mr Green. I have given up expecting my brother to go straight and if Gillian thinks she can persuade him when I could not, she's welcome to try."

Temporary relief followed her firm replacement of the receiver but remorse quickly followed. She wouldn't have abandoned Roy, she would have helped him as she had always done, apart from having him on the premises, but it had been spoilt by Gillian feeding him discontent like giving a baby milk and he had taken it willingly. Now, after all the years she had tried to support and help him, she had been painted blacker than black.

Taking out wrapping paper and string, she parcelled up the new clothes she had bought for Roy. New shirts, underwear, jumpers and two pairs of slacks. He was always glad to start afresh. His favourite shampoo, shaving cream and soap were the luxuries, helping to rid him of the scent of the place, making him feel human again. Childishly, she hoped Gillian hadn't thought to do the same, as she wrote her brother's name and addressed the parcel care of Gillian Harris, to await his next bout of freedom.

The rest of the holiday was spent in preparation for the new school and visiting friends, but there was no joy in any of it. Distressed at the thought of Roy's disloyalty, and reminded of her loneliness, aware of the lack of someone with whom to discuss it, she constantly looked at the photograph of Rhys and wished the loneliness would end.

Two days before term began she went to see Catrin. She shouldn't go too often, she knew that the more she went the more miserable she'd be at returning to her bedsit, but she determinedly hid her unhappiness. She did not want Catrin to know how she felt and become uncomfortable at staying on at Firethorn Cottage.

Philip was there when she walked in. He was fixing a plug to a table lamp.

"Ah," he said, "just the young lady I want to see."

"Philip has news for you," Catrin smiled. "I think you'll be pleased."

"About my family?"

Philip nodded. "It isn't definite but I've heard rumours that a woman who lives about two miles from here is a possible cousin, God knows how many times removed. Probably too distant to be any use."

"I don't care *how* distant!"

"I'll take you there if you like," he said, digging into a pocket and handing her a piece of paper bearing an address. "I know the place, a friend of mine lives near. That's how I heard of her. This friend said her parents once lived in Tri-nant, although he didn't think she had any relations left."

"What's her name?" Amanda asked excitedly.

"I can't remember. But," he warned, "I know it wasn't Beynon."

"That doesn't matter. She's probably married and changed it." She hugged Philip and her eyes shone with the excitement of it.

"Oh, this is very nice," Philip laughed, his arms wrapped around her as he swung her off her feet. "I'll search even harder if this is my reward!"

Over his shoulder she saw Rhys enter the room and at once

she rushed to show him the piece of paper. "Look, Rhys, Philip has found someone who might know my family. He's offered to take me to find her, isn't it wonderful?"

Rhys took the paper from her and nodded. "I know the place. I'll take you tomorrow morning."

"Yes, that's fine by me," Philip said with a shrug of dismissal as Amanda turned to see his reaction. "I'll be working so I wouldn't be able to go until the weekend."

Amanda was surprised at the lack of ill will on Philip's part. How could he tolerate Rhys's rudeness without retaliating? She was extra-gushing with her thanks to Philip for finding the address, to compensate for Rhys's ill manners.

"Don't expect too much, mind," Philip warned. "There's nothing certain about it."

When Philip had gone, Amanda showed by her attitude how angry Rhys had made her feel. He appeared not to notice and she was soon forced to abandon her attempt to make him feel ashamed. But she still wondered why a seemingly well-balanced man like Rhys could be so strong in his dislike of someone as well-intentioned as Philip.

Before she left Tri-nant that day, she went to see Heather James. If she were to be accepted as a friend she had to be honest. It was time to explain about her brother Roy.

"I know I appear cruel refusing to give him a home when he comes out," she admitted, when they sat with a cup of tea and a flat slice of fatless sponge cake. "But I had decided not to take him in this time, even before I'd heard about the cottage being mine. I explained to Gillian that with my place to treat as home, he had no real incentive to get out and find a job and a room. I made it too easy. I thought she agreed, but he has charm, my wayward brother, I'll give him that."

"I do understand and I'm sorry you have this problem," Heather said. Eyes cast down she added meekly, "I wouldn't have had the strength to do what you did though. I would have given in under moral pressure. I admire you for doing what you did."

"And you don't blame me?"

"No. I wish I could be as determined," Heather admitted.

"Don't try and change. I think most would be glad for you to stay just as you are," Amanda smiled.

"Oh, it's nice being considered to be sweet and gentle," Heather said in a burst of confidence. "The helpless woman has a definite attraction. But being sweet and gentle can ruin lives you know, as much as criminal brothers can. Better to be firm and honest really, even if it makes a few enemies. Otherwise, you can ruin lives for others and yourself too."

Amanda waited for Heather to explain, but she stood up as if regretting having spoken and said nothing more.

The following morning Amanda rose early, excited by the prospect of visiting the mysterious woman who might or might not be a relative. At nine o'clock she was ready to leave. The phone rang and it was Rhys telling her he was unable to take her.

"Amanda, I'm sorry. I have to go back to take more footage. The stuff we've got isn't good enough."

"It's all right," she said, trying to sound unconcerned. "I can go on my own. Or with Philip," she added provocatively. "He'll be free at the weekend."

"No. Wait for me to take you," he said firmly. Before she could argue or ask why, he finished the call.

Disappointment and frustration ruined her day. She sat and glared unseeingly into space and wondered why she wasn't ignoring his demands and going on her own. Because you want him there to share it, she admitted sadly.

Leaving very early to drive to Mill Lane School for her first day, she left the car outside the cottage and called on Catrin.

"Good luck, my dear. I'll be out this afternoon, but come and have a snack with me at lunchtime, will you? And let me have your first impressions?"

At the school, a group of children were gathered, obviously waiting for her to appear. Helen and Jane stood near their mother and Helen waved excitedly, pleased to be the one to recognise the new teacher, important in her little group. Amanda waved back.

Shy little Jane stood beside her mother and Amanda went over and took her hand after greeting Heather. "I'm glad you're coming with me, Jane," she said. "Thank you for waiting for me."

She saw the child's face pucker and the mouth became a pout as tears threatened, but Amanda went on talking cheerfully and asked Jane to carry one of her bags. Soon, Amanda was moving away from Heather, Jane looking up at her with the beginnings of trust as they reached the classroom door. Each time Jane glanced back at her mother, Amanda coaxed her on.

While the children began to line up in the playground, Jane helped Amanda unpack her bag in the classroom.

"We won't be able to do this every day," Amanda explained, "but for today, I'm glad of your help."

When Amanda had her children gathered around her to begin introductions, she was surprised when a glance out of the window showed Jane's mother still waiting there alone, all the other parents having gone. She knew the child was anxious, but where did the anxiety stem from, the child or the mother? At lunchtime she discussed it with Catrin.

"I suspect the need is in Heather more than Jane," she suggested.

"It's possible, dear. Very often the mother needs the child to want her so badly, she won't allow the little one to leave."

"Have you come across similar cases?" Amanda asked, aware of Catrin's previous career.

"Oh yes. There was a mother who had a four-year-old whom she still nursed in a blanket. She was persuaded to bring the child to a nursery class and was gratified when the child screamed and wanted her to stay. But when she was told the child settled happily within five minutes of her leaving, she didn't bring him again. At five he was still treated like a baby, carried around and not allowed to run about. I was told the poor woman had lost her other children and her husband in an accident and was terrified of being left alone."

"Is there something in Heather's experience to account for Jane being so clinging? Helen isn't treated the same."

"Heather's had her problems." Catrin wore a closed-up expression and, afraid of being thought too inquisitive, Amanda refrained from further questions.

She was relieved when the first day was over. She was more tired than usual, being anxious to learn the new routines and begin to know her class. Jane was her constant companion and she did not mind. It was a step in the right direction for her to attach herself to someone other than Heather. She learned from other teachers that the previous term had been spent with Jane just sitting in a corner on her own, firmly grasping a toy brought from home.

With Helen one side of her, a proprietory hand on her handbag strap, and Jane holding tightly to her other hand, Amanda walked out of the school gates.

She searched among the lively crowd for Heather and saw that Haydn was with her. Helen ran to them with a joyous shout. Jane let go of Amanda's hand and burst into tears.

As Amanda approached them, her heart gave a skip when she saw Rhys was also with them.

"Hello," he smiled. "I thought I'd come and see how your first day went."

She was so pleased she almost hugged him as most of the children around her were hugging their parents. He took her heavy bag and they walked to the end of the road, where the group had to separate to go their respective ways. When they were alone, Amanda smiled up at him.

"Thank you for coming to meet me. Catrin is out this afternoon and I didn't relish walking out and driving straight home to my empty room."

"Do you have to go straight back?" he asked, pulling her arm through his. "I thought we might have a snack and go to find this mysterious relative of yours."

"Oh, Rhys! Could we?"

"We could try."

"I thought you'd be away for a few more days," she said as they reached the gate of the bungalow.

"I should be, but I was afraid you'd become impatient and I didn't want you looking for this person alone," he said. "The woman could be dishonest and try to diddle you out of your life savings, or she could insist that the cottage is really hers. I think you'll have to tread very carefully."

81

"I hadn't thought of anything like that," Amanda admitted solemnly.

They found the house without difficulty and Amanda's fingers began to fiddle with her gloves and handbag as her nervousness mounted.

It was bitterly cold, the air harsh and still, as if pausing to decide whether or not to snow. She began to shiver as she waited in an agony of suspense while the door was unbolted and opened.

The woman who answered was young; in her early thirties, Amanda guessed, and very beautiful. But her expression stopped the question on her lips. The woman was staring at Rhys at first with disbelief then with undisguised delight.

"Rhys! Darling! You've found me!" she said in a high, childlike voice with a strong American accent.

Rhys stepped back and in a tight voice, said to Amanda, "There's obviously been some mistake. This is Jessica Maybury, an actress. Jessica, meet a friend of mine, Amanda Clifford."

Jessica did not hear his words. She didn't acknowledge Amanda in any way. She was staring at Rhys, her beautiful blue eyes wide, her arms outstretched in a theatrical way and he backed further away.

"But darling, Rhys. I don't understand." She lunged elegantly forward and hugged him, moulding her body against his. "How did you find me?" She reached up and kissed him firmly and with groans of pleasure, fully on the lips.

Amanda watched and knew for the first time the miseries of jealousy. The young woman was so lovely, her slim figure emphasised in a fitted dress that was clearly expensive. Her long, reddish-brown hair swung around her shoulders shining with health and expert grooming. Her eyes were closed in ecstatic pleasure and, even though she was not close, Amanda could see the long lashes, fallen on the perfect cheekbones.

She stood back as Rhys and the woman discussed their unexpected reunion. Wave after wave of dismay flooded her mind as she saw the companionship of Rhys being taken away from her.

82

She tried pretending it was the loss of a cousin that was responsible for her disappointment but knew it was this beautiful woman from Rhys's past that was causing the real pain.

She forced herself to look at Rhys's face as Jessica Maybury pressed her lovely face to his. Was it her hopeful imagination, or was Rhys less than pleased at the meeting?

Jessica invited them in for a drink, the invitation being waved at them both, but Amanda was ignored by the woman, who poured a whisky for Rhys.

"Not for me," he said firmly. "I rarely drink during the day, you ought to know that."

Jessica put down the drink and smiled at him.

"Of course. How silly of me." She put her head on one side and smiled up at him through unbelievably long lashes. "Tell me, darling. How did you find me? Was it difficult to follow my trail?"

"We came here looking for Amanda's cousin," he explained. "I had no idea you were here. As far as I was aware you were still in America."

"I needed a vacation, you had talked about this area, so . . ." she finished vaguely.

"So you're not the person who has roots here?" Amanda put in, not wanting to sit any longer in embarrassed silence.

"I'm American," Jessica replied tartly. She did not look at Amanda as she answered, her eyes never left Rhys. Amanda became more and more uncomfortable. She could hardly offer to go and leave them to talk as she had to wait for Rhys to drive her home. Besides, she thought rebelliously, I don't *want* to leave them!

She felt dowdy and dull and quite unable to compete with the lovely creature, but something in Rhys's face gave her hope. No, she would wait and see what Rhys said about her when they were alone.

"I hope you enjoy your stay," Rhys said rather formally. He seemed ill at ease and Amanda presumed it was her presence at such a personal moment.

"Perhaps we could go now, Rhys," she offered. "You could come back and talk to your friend later?"

Both people turned to look at her as if they had forgotten she was there. Amanda walked to the door and stood, waiting for Rhys to join her. The atmosphere was stifling, and she knew she had to end this scene. Opening the door she stood in the freezing air wanting to run away and forget she had ever met Rhys. It was a long time before he joined her and her teeth were chattering with cold and misery.

When he at last came out, Jessica reached up and kissed him again, long and lovingly. Amanda refused to watch. If the kiss had been his idea she didn't want to know.

"What an amazing coincidence," she said brightly when they were once more in the car.

"No coincidence," he said grimly. "Jessica doesn't depend on such vagaries, she has the knack of making things happen."

"She couldn't have known we'd call, surely?"

"She knew I lived in the area. It was only a matter of time before she arranged for me to 'find' her."

Amanda was confused and she waited for him to continue.

"We met in America while I was filming a commercial for American television. It was for an animal sanctuary. I filmed some of the more unusual pets that had been rescued, and Jessica held the animals and looked glamorous."

"I see," Amanda said, although she did not.

"When I left America she wanted to come with me. But our lives would never have mixed. I'm always travelling and so is she. What would have been the point of taking a brief relationship any further?"

"It would have been difficult," Amanda murmured, hoping Rhys wouldn't see how near to tears she was.

She couldn't remember ever having been so depressed. She had begun to accept she was falling in love with him and here she was, listening to his confessions about his ex-love like a magazine agony aunt!

"I'm sorry it didn't work out," she said, thinking that at least she understood his unhappy American Christmas.

He stopped the car and turned to her, his face mysterious in the darkness. "I'm sorry too. Here I am talking about a fleeting attraction and not giving a thought to your disappointment."

"My disappointment?" For a moment she couldn't think what he meant, her mind was so full of his meeting with Jessica.

"You were hoping for a cousin?"

"Oh, that? It doesn't matter. I've resigned myself to the truth. It's too long ago and the family was too small. It has died out and I've been following a false trail."

Catrin was home and they went in to tell her about their wasted journey. Rhys said nothing about knowing Jessica Maybury and Amanda followed his lead.

"Never mind, dear," Catrin patted her hand affectionately. "There's still a chance someone in the village will know something."

"Perhaps." She shrugged disconsolately and Catrin looked at her shrewdly, guessing that Amanda had lost more than the hope of finding a cousin.

She wondered if they had argued, or if Rhys had just realised they could never be more than friends. Either way, Amanda was subdued and unhappy.

Amanda didn't see Rhys in the weeks that followed. She tried not to think of him or imagine what might have been. It was a blessing to have the new job on which to concentrate, and the dreams of Rhys loving her, and of finding a family, were both locked away in a corner of her mind.

Jane was slowly accepting her as a person to trust. She was beginning to open her shell and take notice of some of the fascinating discoveries the classroom offered. She spoke very little but instead of staying in her corner, had begun to edge nearer and nearer to the group, especially when it was story time. Amanda made sure she had a view of the pictures and the puppets she frequently used, and was included in the happy communal activity.

She learned the date of Roy's release from prison from the Probation Officer, Eric Green. She didn't give him the chance to be rude, just asked for the date and time. Then she wrote to Roy at Gillian's parents' address wishing him well and asking

85

him to arrange a time and place where they could meet and catch up with each other's news. She had written to the prison regularly but had not received a reply. His allowance of letters was presumably going to Gillian, she thought with sadness. His most recent time out of prison had lost her a friend and a brother. It was frightening as well as hurtful to think she might lose touch with Roy altogether.

After school one Friday, she posted another letter to him and knocked on Catrin's door. It was opened by Philip.

"Come in," he said, "Catrin's making pancakes. We hoped you'd call." He was wearing old, shabby trousers and a jumper with holes in it. He apologised for his untidiness. "I've been winter-pruning the apple trees," he said. "Catrin called me in for pancakes and tea." He washed his hands and sat at the table as Catrin came from the stove, flushed from cooking.

"Tuck in," she invited. "They're best eaten warm." She joined them and they sat companionably in the fast fading light.

"How did you get on with the enquiry?" Philip asked. "Learn anything, did you?"

"No luck," Amanda groaned. "The woman was an actress from America, her name wasn't Beynon and she said she has no family here."

"Ah," Philip said, nodding wisely, "but we all know what actresses are for changing their names!"

"She would have remembered her own name when I said it," Amanda argued. But, she wondered, had she actually used it? The woman hadn't listened to a word she said anyway. She had been too busy looking goggle-eyed at Rhys!

"Why not go there again?" Philip suggested. "Perhaps if we asked the right questions, the right answers will pop up? My newspaper sources definitely reveal that she has connections in the area."

Yes, Amanda thought, Rhys was her connection, not a family called Beynon. She did not mention Rhys recognising the woman; if he hadn't admitted to knowing her it was best she said nothing.

"It wouldn't hurt to talk to her again," Catrin coaxed.

Amanda was filled with dread at seeing Jessica Maybury again yet at the same time curious enough to agree. She wouldn't want Rhys to think she was prying though, but as her reason was a genuine one and supported by Philip and Catrin, wasn't a second visit justified?

"Let's go now." Philip stood and collected Amanda's coat.

"You're more enthusiastic than Amanda!" Catrin laughed. "Be careful you don't unearth a few skeletons of your own!"

Like Rhys had, Amanda thought uneasily.

They went in Amanda's car. She had sold the Austin and treated herself, spending almost four hundred pounds on a brand new Ford Popular. Philip's only transport at that time was an ancient bicycle.

As she parked she saw there was a light in the window and suffered panic at the thought that Rhys might be there. But she was reassured by realising there was no Landrover outside. The door was opened quickly, as if Jessica was expecting someone. Amanda stepped back and left Philip to explain.

"We're looking for someone called Beynon," he began. "It's a long time ago but we thought you might be able to help us?"

Amanda saw the woman stiffen as if the name had surprised her. She glanced at Amanda and recognition dawned.

"Beynon? There's no one of that name here." She turned to Amanda. "Weren't you the woman who called here with Rhys?"

"Yes," Amanda said, then gabbling somewhat in her haste to get out what she wanted to say before the door was shut, she added, "I understand someone connected with the Beynons who once lived in Tri-nant was here. She might be called Sian Talbot and would be about forty years old."

"That lets me out for heaven's sake!" Jessica snapped. "I'm nowhere near that age!"

"I'm sorry, I wasn't suggesting—"

"Why do you think I can help? What d'you want with her anyway?" Her American accent was strong as she added, "What in hell are you pestering me for?"

Amanda hesitated and Philip answered for her. "Someone

we know is looking for her family. We thought this Sian Talbot might be able to help."

"Sorry, I don't know anything about any Talbots or Beynons." She disappeared inside and Philip and Amanda looked at each other as the sound of the slammed door echoed around them.

"Did we touch a nerve then?" Philip wondered.

"She doesn't fit anyone we know about. She's only about ten years older than me."

"Oh, I think she's more than that. Could she be a cousin, a decendant of Tom?"

"She'd have said, surely? And if she's from America, how could she be expected to know about someone so long ago? Oh Philip, it's hopeless. Let's go back and report our failure to Catrin." They got into the car with Philip in the driving seat. He started the engine but didn't immediately drive away.

"Get married, have lots of children and start a family of your own," he advised. He put a hand on hers. "Are you open for offers?" he asked softly. In the glow from the fascia his eyes had that piratical glint in the ruggedly handsome face; that hint of recklessness which made her curious about his past, but she wouldn't encourage him to talk about marriage and children. That would mislead him into thinking some interest was implied.

He was charming but he made no demands on her heart. She enjoyed his company but he didn't pull at her emotions like Rhys, although in many ways he was more considerate. It was a difficult moment and she decided to treat it humorously. "Would you expect to be waited on in true chauvinistic style?" she asked lightly.

"Never," he said with mock severity.

"Would you complain if I ruined the dinner?"

"I'd eat every scrap."

"Would you tell me I'm wonderful, even when I'm not?"

"Constantly."

"I'll put you on my list."

It was late when Amanda reached the bedsit and for the first time she had found the journey long and boring. It might be an idea to find accommodation in the village. There was no difference between a bedsit here or there. It would be further away from Roy when he was released, but distance could be measured in more than miles.

It would certainly shorten her day and make it easier to involve herself in village life. She decided to place an advertisement in the post office window.

Perhaps I'll advertise for a family too, she thought foolishly. There's no chance of my finding one. As for beginning one of her own as Philip had suggested, first she'd have to fall in love. Rhys was the only possibility there, and Catrin had made it clear he was not the type to settle and raise a family.

She picked up the photograph of Rhys. Inheriting the cottage had led her to many new friends. Besides Rhys, there was Catrin and Philip, plus Rhys's friends the Jameses. So why did she feel more lonely than ever before?

She counted out the possibilities on her fingers. Her brother no longer needing her had left a void. The faint chance of finding someone of her own had made her dissatisfied. The attractions of Rhys Falconbridge had woken her from her passive acceptance of what life held. Better if that solicitor's letter had never found her, she thought as she settled unhappily to sleep.

Six

R oy was accepted into the Harris household like a long-lost son. Gillian's story that he had been abandoned by first his mother then his sister had truly aroused her family's sympathies. The fact that he had been in and out of prison since a child had been hurriedly brushed aside, a result of no one caring.

"Cuddles," Mrs Harris said firmly. "If you're lacking in cuddles when you're little, you can't never be happy!"

The room he was given was at the back of the house with a window looking out over wasteland on which an old hut stood, a relic from the war when it had been used for civil defence exercises. Other houses backed on to the square of untidy grass on which people walked their dogs, children played and courting couples promised each other the moon.

To Roy it was heaven, sweet-scented and luxurious after the weeks spent in prison. The greatest joy, as always after a spell inside, was having a room to himself.

Plump Mrs Harris bustled around making sure he lacked nothing, searching for ways to please and surprise him. Roy was not very tall but as she was a little under five feet she had to stretch up to hug him. Hugs he would never lack while he was living under her roof, she constantly reminded him. He loved it.

Although he was still hurt by Amanda's refusal to give him a bed, he couldn't help being glad she had not. She had never been able to completely hide her disapproval. She had not been an enthusiastic cook either, and Mrs Harris seemed determined to fatten him into a portly young man to match her plump young daughter, Gillian.

The Tangled Web

Mr Harris did his bit to make sure Roy felt at home. He worked on the railway as a porter and on his days off he would encourage Roy to work with him on jobs about the house, to make him feel a part of it. He looked at Roy proudly as he tended the garden, chopped wood and, with Mr Harris's help, mended an old bicycle given to him for his use.

He didn't work Roy very hard, always saying, "Now steady on, boy, don't go at it bald-'eaded, there's all tomorrow not touched yet." Roy was the son he never had.

Roy had said goodbye to Dave when they had parted at the café near the prison, and he was really determined not to fail. With his debt to Dave paid off and a couple of hundred pounds hidden for when he felt able to collect it, he knew he stood a chance of keeping out of prison, especially with Mr and Mrs Harris treating him like a deserving case and Gillian treating him like the lead in a romantic film.

His determination to forget his life of crime grew and was partly thanks to Gillian for her support. A greater part of his new-found strength was a childish wish to blame Amanda for not giving him the right encouragement on past occasions. He had to prove he was not weak but lacked the right kind of help. Twice in the first week he succumbed to temptation, each time a purse resting on the top of a shopping bag he considered fair game. It would be a lesson for the owners and lessons had to be paid for.

The orderly routine of the Harris's houshold was balm after the regime of prison but after only a couple of weeks it began to pall. He couldn't admit it to anyone but himself, but he needed excitement and a use for his particular skills.

Staring out of his window late at night he almost unthinkingly began to plan a night's work. The self-destructive need to take a chance and try one more night of daring break-ins was strong and sometimes when his need of that foolish excitement frightened him he would cringe under the blankets and wish Amanda were there to talk to. Gillian, sweet as she certainly was, couldn't understand this need to dare, to try and beat 'them', to come home with some stolen item and laugh at his own audacity.

91

He would have been all right if Dave hadn't found him, he was sure of that. Pity he had taken to calling into that particular café each day after going down to look for work.

Dave had a rough idea of where his friend was staying and having located the Labour Exchange, had guessed with startling accuracy the exact café among several in which Roy would choose to while away the afternoon. He stood at the corner one morning and waited for the arrival of Roy, all the time watching the crowds for the opportunity to pick up something of value. Like Roy he was adept at grabbing a woman's purse from the top of her shopping basket.

He missed Roy as he came around the corner and entered the Labour Exchange but saw him on the way out. He was looking pleased with himself.

Roy had found a job. Only washing-up in a café, but it was approved by his Probation Officer and the employers knew about his record so there was a good chance of sorting his life out. He thought he would stay for as long as he could with the Harrises; it was cheap, they certainly looked after him, and Gillian was in love with him and gave him the adoration he needed.

Optimistic thoughts danced in his head as he left the Labour Exchange and turned to go back to the Harrises. No cup of tea and an idle afternoon today. He was excited at being able to tell Gillian his good news. She was so enthusiastic and it was flattering how proud she was of his smallest achievement.

The smile faded as Dave moved away from the wall he was leaning against and called to him. But his confidence remained high. He could cope with Dave's persuasion, easy. They'd have a bit of a confab then he'd run off to tell Gillian his good news.

"Hi there, Dave. What you doin' round here then?"

"Looking for you, boy, looking for you."

"I thought we'd agreed not to see each other again. I've got Gillian, see, and she doesn't like me meeting up with pals, you know what women are like, jealousy I suppose, Dave."

"I'm in trouble Roy, and I need your help to get out of it."

"If it's money, well you know I can't do nothin'. I pay

Gillian's mother and that about finishes me off. Sorry mate, but I can't help, honest."

"I owe the bookies and you know how rough some of them can play. Got to have fifty by Saturday and you're my only hope."

"Fifty? I couldn't find fifty fags!" Roy laughed.

"This is serious stuff, Roy my old mucker. I told them if I can't raise it you're my partner, see, so you have to help, right?"

With such a threat, it didn't take long for Dave to rouse enthusiasm for 'one last go' in Roy. Dave played on the man's need for the excitement as well as his fears of being attacked for debts for which he was not responsible.

"A job washing up?" Dave sounded horrified. "You've been had, mate. That's not a job, it's a damned insult!" After two cups of tea, laced with slyly-added alcohol, Roy agreed with him. Within fifteen minutes, he was already planning how he would get out of the house and over the waste ground. Dave stopped him.

"I've got a better plan. This time we have to have a sound alibi. I've sorted all that out. Now, tell me again about this girl of yours."

Much later, when their plans were made, Roy walked over the ground they intended to work, storing in his mind every ally-way, every short cut, the gardens with broken fences, the weak hedges where he could push through and disappear.

When he went home he invited Gillian to go to the pictures to celebrate his fortune in finding a job.

"It's only washing-up in a rotten old café, love, seven in the morning till five at night with a couple of hours off during the day. But it's a start. And they know all about me so there's no fear of something being said and ruining it all."

"I was going out with Mary," she said doubtfully.

"Great, love, bring her an' all." Then he started to complain about a stomach upset, running to the lavatory several times with desperate urgency. He assured Gillian it was all right and nothing would spoil their celebration.

There were only two seats together and Roy insisted Gillian

sat with her friend. It couldn't be better. It was working beautifully. Going to the toilet was amusing as such things often are and he waited until the girls were involved in the film before darting out of the side entrance through the fire door, leaving it slightly ajar and going to where he planned to meet up with Dave.

Dave was waiting in the doorway of a derelict house and, taking the stuff from him, Roy ran as fast as he could to the garden shed where they were hiding it. Dave returned to the dancehall and looked for the girl he had danced with four times.

Neither had been missed. Each would have someone swearing they couldn't have been away long enough to rob houses. The police would begin to think there was another thief working the area.

Roy was puffing a little when he returned to his seat but that was put down to his stomach upset and regretfully he agreed when Gillian insisted they went home early.

Their system was so successful they were unable to resist trying it again. One robbed a couple of houses, the other stashed the stuff away so he wouldn't get caught with it on him, and both were absent for less time than was needed for a burglary. They both had an alibi of sorts, sufficient at least to add doubt to the police when they were questioned. After a couple of times they didn't bother to use the cinema plan, going out at night was so easy, and with the unsuspecting Harrises asleep Roy began to enjoy his return to 'what you do best' as Dave put it.

It was on their sixth foray that they hit trouble. This time Roy was in the cinema alone and got out the same way as before, some time after starting an argument about where he was sitting. He walked into three houses through unlocked doors while the occupants were watching television. He only stole money. No point taking risks on other property, he'd never talk his way out of anything like that.

Coming back with the intention of starting another fight to make sure he was remembered, he darted through the garden of Seventeen Wall Street, down the alley-way which would take him out into Davis Gardens, and around the corner to the picture house. But something was wrong. The end of the alley-way was blocked and voices warned him there was something wrong. The was a crowd of people gathered there, and flashing lights warned of some official activity, an accident perhaps. What filthy luck, he complained silently.

He moved away and went back on himself before walking as casually as he could down the main shopping thoroughfare and into the side gate of the cinema. The door was locked and it was almost time for the film to finish!

Desperately listening and hoping not to hear the National Anthem being played, he climbed up on to the low roof of the toilets, and squeezed himself into the small frame. He only just succeeded in getting through. He reached his seat just in time to trip someone who was hurrying out early, trying to avoid standing to attention during the Anthem. An argument led to a few blows being struck and he heard someone say he was the man who was causing trouble earlier. Making sure a few people would remember him, he went out still arguing. Satisfied his alibi was safe, he went home and told Gillian that he was getting too fat.

"I won't be able to get myself out of tight corners if you and your Mam feed me up any more," he said, adoration and appreciation for his supper in his blue eyes.

He found out later that the cause of the blocked alley-way was an object suspected of being an unexploded bomb.

"Blimey, Dave," he laughed. "A bloody bomb and nearly nine years after the war. That Hitler was determined to be a flamin' nuisance, wasn't 'e, eh?"

Amanda had several replies to her advertisement for a room. She collected them one lunchtime and when she saw Heather James waiting for Helen and Jane, she showed her the addresses.

Looking through them, Heather gave her opinion on each.

"That one would be small. This one is a rather boisterous family, I don't think you'd get much peace. The third I don't know. Perhaps Mrs Falconbridge will recognise the name.

95

"I'll ask her. If she doesn't know, Philip probably will."
Amanda saw Heather's expression change when she mentioned
Philip and she asked, "Don't *you* like Philip either?"

"No. He isn't a very nice man. I knew him well, once."

Amanda guessed there was a broken romance there and
asked no further questions. But she was puzzled by the intensity
of the dislike some held for the man. She had always found him
kind and thoughtful.

"He should never have come back here!" Heather said
vehemently. "I'd avoid him if I were you!"

"Not easy when he'll be my neighbour at the end of the
year," Amanda reminded her.

It was bitterly cold that February, and every day children and
parents injured themselves on the treacherous roads. Hurrying
down the road from school, Amanda slipped once or twice on
the icy surface that hadn't thawed for several days and she
intended to ask if Catrin needed anything to save her going
out in the dangerous conditions.

Catrin was at the gate when Amanda came in sight of the
cottage and it was clear she was not well. She was leaning on
the gate as if depending on its support. Her head hung low and
she looked very tired.

"Catrin? Are you all right?" Amanda ran the last few yards
and helped her along the path and into the house.

"I'm a bit tired, dear, that's all," Catrin replied. "I've been
standing for a while, hoping you'd come." She shivered inside
her coat.

"You shouldn't stand around in this weather. The tempera-
ture is so low the school playground is unusable. You should
stay indoors. Look, I've brought us a couple of buns to have
with a cup of tea." Bustling her inside Amanda was concerned
at the slowness of Catrin's steps. She made her comfortable
in a chair near the fire and handed her the crocheted blanket.
"Keep your coat on for a while," she instructed. "What were
you thinking of, standing out there in this cruel weather?"

"I didn't want to miss you, dear."

"Then you should have phoned the school. The Head doesn't
mind taking a message."

"Was that your advertisement in the post office?" Catrin asked.

"Yes. I think it would be better if I live nearer the school, for after-school activities for one thing. I've had a couple of replies, look." She gave the letters to Catrin who ignored them completely.

"I have a better idea. Why don't you move in with me? There's plenty of room."

Amanda smiled at her. She had thought of it of course, but she didn't want to suggest it in case Catrin was embarrassed by having to saying no.

"I'd love to live here with you," she said, kneeling beside her friend. "But are you sure? Is it really what you want?"

"I'd be glad of your company, especially when I feel unwell."

"I wish you'd think about it for a while though. You'd lose your privacy and the freedom to do with your day as you wish. To a certain extent that's impossible to avoid, although I'd try not to disrupt your life too much. But will you talk it over with someone – Rhys or Philip, preferably both – before offering me a room?"

"I'll ask their opinion, yes."

"If you still think it's a good idea a week from now, we'll discuss it fully. And thank you."

After a brief talk about school and other matters, Amanda drove back to town, a bubble of excitement threatening to burst out in a shout of delight. Since first seeing Firethorn Cottage she had longed to live there. Waiting for the year to pass was agony and this was a perfect solution.

She had hardly taken off her coat when the phone rang.

"Amanda?" Rhys said. "Are you busy this weekend?"

Her heart sang at the sound of his voice. "Oh, nothing important," she said casually.

"I need an assistant for a couple of days," he explained.

"I might have guessed it wasn't for the joy of my company!"

"I'm taking some film of dippers, so could you be ready for an early start?"

"What d'you call early?" she asked in trepidation.

"I'll collect you on Saturday morning at four."

"Oh, that's marvellous! D'you mind if I'm still asleep?"

"Not at all. The walk will wake you."

"A long walk?"

"Only about three miles. Oh," he added, "you will bring sandwiches and a flask, won't you?"

In fact it was three-thirty when Rhys arrived. She answered the door still tousled from sleep and he made coffee while she completed her preparations.

The drive through the lanes was eerie. They saw no sign of life in the buildings they passed. No lights shone through curtains and they didn't meet another vehicle.

"Do you often come out this early?" she asked, when they had been driving about thirty minutes.

"I work shifts in a way," he smiled, showing a glint of white teeth in the darkness. "If I want to record something at dawn I have to be in place well before the sun begins to show. In fact, I've spent days and nights in a hide to get the footage I want, on many occasions."

"What are you hoping for today?"

"Wait and see. I'm sure you'll enjoy it."

"It's certainly different from my usual Saturdays!"

Leaving the car in a farmyard, she was guided through a gate and across a field. She followed blindly, holding a scarf around her face as some protection against the icy air. There was no moon and the shadows thrown up by the occasional light from his torch were distorted, blending with objects they passed and confusing her eye. He stopped, and in that strange hush of the darkest hours she heard the sound of a stream.

"Almost there," he whispered. "Hold my hand and keep right behind me so you don't fall into the water. I don't want this to be a wasted journey," he added unsympathetically. "The hide isn't far now."

The stream became louder and Amanda realised they were walking on the precarious edge of the bank. Thank goodness the earth was being held firm with frost, she thought. A canvas structure covered with branches and dead leaves emerged out of the darkness, into which they crawled. There was very little room, and she presumed it was probably intended for one person.

"Kneel beside me," Rhys whispered. He bent forward, his arm on her shoulder, his face close to hers, guiding her to look through the observation slit. The water was close and just visible, moving like dull metal with an occasional glint of white.

"See where the stream falls over those rocks?" he whispered. "Tucked underneath is the nest site of a pair of dippers."

"They can't be nesting this early? It's only February."

"It's almost finished," he assured her.

"Can I have some coffee?" she asked, but he shook his head.

"We might be lucky enough to see a fox or even a badger but they'd smell coffee, mistrust it and stay away."

They knelt very still and Amanda found it difficult to concentrate on the thought of seeing a pair of dippers, beautiful birds though they were. Rhys's cheek was warm against her own and the glow was invading every part of her body. She moved slightly and his grip tightened.

"Not too uncomfortable, are you?" he asked.

"No, I'm fine," she replied, wondering if he could hear the beat of her heart so close to his own.

"I'll just check the camera," he said, moving slightly away from her. He seemed satisfied all was well and returned to his original position.

Amanda wondered whether his nearness was of necessity or whether he wanted to feel her moulded against him. Although the light was gradually increasing she couldn't see his face to read his expression but hoped it was as satisfying for him as for her.

The sky lightened, the banks of the stream were no longer black but shone brown, touched in places with patches of ice, and with a strengthening outline. The water became lighter too and shone dully in the wakening day. They saw a water rat go down and touch the water as if testing to see if it was too cold for a bathe. He strolled on, hoping for an unwary insect or small animal to fill his empty stomach.

"Watch that rock near the nest," Rhys whispered. "They'll land on there any moment now."

Amanda watched and beside her equipment began to hum quietly. A small brown bird with a white breast and reddish-brown underparts landed where he had said, bobbing with what looked like impatience. In no more than seconds, an identical bird had joined it. She had seen dippers before, strolling in and out of a stream turning over stones looking for food as if the water didn't exist. But never this close.

She was enchanted to see them greet each other with a loud and cheery song. They stood facing each other as they sang, very close, so their beaks seemed to touch in a kiss. After a moment they flew off and soon began returning regularly with nesting material. She was dreadfully cramped but she didn't move until the machine beside her was shut off.

"That was magical!" she whispered, and in the restricted space she hugged him. "Thank you for letting me come."

His arm reached around her and his lips touched hers in the friendly darkness. He looked at her, his face mysterious in the closeness of the hide. "You really enjoyed it? Being cramped and cold and having to wait perhaps for nothing? Didn't you hate it?"

"It was worth everything to see them bid each other good morning." But she was thinking more of his lips so close to her own than the kiss of the dippers.

"Coffee next, I think. We'll take a chance on missing a sight of Mr Fox!" His words brought her down to earth.

She fumbled in the bag she had brought and they struggled to make themselves comfortable in the confined space.

"I didn't design this for two," he said, pulling her to lean against him as they sipped their coffee.

"I think it's perfect," she said boldly. "More room would be a terrible waste." She heard him chuckle.

"What next, more photographs?"

"I might get some extra footage if something interesting turns up but it isn't really necessary if you've had enough."

"I'd like to stay."

For two hours they waited, Rhys watching through his camera lens as the birds flew back and forth, resting occasionally to stand bobbing on the rock above their nest. It was eight o'clock when they began to pack up.

"Now you'll realise why I invited you," Rhys said, pointing to his equipment. "I've left all this stuff here for a week but I need to take it home today."

"Oh, Rhys; and there's me thinking you wanted me for my fine intellect, not my muscles!"

"I rarely invite anyone to join me," he said seriously. "If they're bored it ruins the day."

"No chance of that." She held up a hand to be helped from the tiny hide. He didn't release her when she stood beside him but pulled her closer. Her arm slid around his strong back and she stretched up to meet his kiss. He stared at her, a soft, loving expression in his eyes.

"Amanda, if only we could—" Words were on his lips but he hesitated to speak them. She held her breath. Was he going to tell her she was important to him? That Jessica Maybury was not a threat? He shook off the moment of intimacy with a laugh that sounded forced.

"Good heavens, girl! Your nose is like an iceberg!"

Feeling rejected and wondering why, she began to collect the equipment he wanted her to carry back to the car. Her magical time had ended.

The uneasiness lasted until they were back at the farm. There the once silent place was filled with activity, with people hurrying to and fro, a tractor moving off and machinery whining in the distance. A couple of men waved to Rhys and he called a friendly greeting.

"I have an idea this morning was a successful one. I'll take the films to Haydn straight away and tell him to hurry. I'm impatient to see what we've got."

"Does Haydn do all your work?" Amanda asked, anxious to return to their former comradeship.

"Most of it. I develop some stuff just to keep my hand in, but Haydn is much better than me. He's a professional, I'm the amateur."

"It's mostly films you make, but you take stills as well, don't you?"

"I'd like to write a book one day, on wildlife of course, but I can't decide on a subject. Bugs maybe. They've always had bad press."

"Why not write about all you see on your stream? You could include bugs as well as the better-known creatures."

They had reached the outskirts of a village and he stopped the car and stared at her, excitement deepening the colour of his eyes.

"I think that's it! A book about my stream! It is mine, at least, the part of it that runs through my garden. I'll discuss it with my agent on Monday!"

Amenda felt vibrations of excitement flowing out of him. He smiled at her and restarted the car, then he became vague and she knew he was already working out ideas in his lively mind.

"Do you mind if we drop these films off before I take you home?" he asked.

"The day's my own," she smiled. "Shall I go with you or stay with Catrin until you've finished talking?"

"Come. Heather will be pleased to see you."

Returning to Tri-nant they passed close to the house where Jessica Maybury lived and Amanda mentioned calling a second time.

"She wasn't at all helpful. I think she was expecting someone else and was afraid we'd be in the way."

"We?" Rhys queried. "Who went with you, Aunt Catrin?"

"No, it was Philip's idea." She saw at once he was displeased.

"Why Philip? Wouldn't Aunt Catrin have been more suitable?"

"She wasn't keen to go. And I thought Jessica Maybury was the type who might open out more readily to a man," she said with a hint of asperity. "I didn't think she'd be as keen to help a woman!"

"Did you learn anything?"

"She reacted to the name, then closed the door firmly in our faces."

"That's odd."

"A detective might have learned more but I had the impression she wasn't interested enough to help."

"Why should she if she isn't involved?"

"No reason, but most people at least hear me out."

"Perhaps you were right, the moment was inopportune."

"Perhaps." Amanda was not convinced.

They drove through the slowly wakening village, where the shops were preparing for business. A delivery van was dropping off crates of vegetables at the greengrocer's. They passed a van smelling so strongly of fish it didn't need to advertise its business on the side. There were few people about.

When they reached the James's house next door to the Cwm Gwyn Arms, Heather was pleased to see them. After Amanda and Rhys had explained to her how they had spent their morning, she handed Amanda a book on birds and they settled down to talk about her experience with the girls.

"And you didn't have breakfast?" Jane asked, her eyes round with concern.

"We had coffee, sandwiches and biscuits. Not the usual breakfast is it? And we ate it in a camouflaged tent right on the bank of a stream."

"Can we do that one day, Uncle Rhys?" Helen asked.

"Not at four in the morning, I hope," Amanda laughed.

When the six of them were sitting round the large table, Heather asked Amanda about her search for accommodation.

"Did you have any luck with those addresses?"

"New accommodation? What's happened, have you been thrown out of your bedsit for unruly behaviour?" Haydn teased in his gentle way.

"She finds it a long way to drive every day," Heather explained.

"I didn't know you were moving," Rhys said with a frown.

"I spoke to Catrin – at least, she saw my advertisement and spoke to me – and she's offered me a room."

"Aunt Catrin offered?" Rhys looked suspicious. "That's odd. She has always refused to share with anyone. You aren't trying to put her out are you?"

"Of course not!" Amanda answered in surprise. "As if I would! The cottage is mine in October but if Catrin isn't ready to move out then I'll wait until she is!"

"I'm sorry, I spoke without thinking."

"I should think so too," Heather said. "Just for that you and Haydn can wash the coffee cups."

Amanda was grateful to Heather for brushing aside the hurtful remark but she wondered why Rhys had been so rude. She doubted if he ever spoke without thinking, so why had he reacted so unkindly to her news? Was it because she would be living next door to Philip, she wondered?

As Rhys was driving her home he brought up the subject again and Amanda was immediately on the defensive.

"What's the real reason for wanting to move in with my aunt?" he asked.

"One reason is because I happen to be fond of her and I enjoy her company. The other is because I think she needs someone there to keep an eye on her. Now, are you going to make that into something utterly selfish?"

"Then it's nothing to do with Philip?"

Amanda laughed. So that *was* the reason for his rudeness. "Why should Philip have anything to do with my decisions?"

"It was he whom you called when Aunt Catrin was ill, and he whom you chose to go with to see Jessica. You must admit you show him a great deal of interest. Especially as you know I'd prefer you stay away from him."

"It's none of your business," she retorted indignantly. "But as for moving in with your aunt, it was *her* idea, *her* suggestion. Ask her if you don't believe me. I didn't agree but asked that she discuss it with you."

"Just speak to me about things that concern her in future, please, and not Philip."

"If you're around," she retorted. "But there's no way I'll refuse Philip's help if Catrin needs it."

"If you're looking for reliability then you won't find it

in Philip Morgan," he said. "That's one attribute he sadly lacks."

Amanda said no more. She wanted to howl. The day had been so wonderful, starting out in the darkness of early morning and watching the delightful antics of the dippers. Why did it have to end with a quarrel, and about Philip, who was not that important?

"Philip doesn't matter enough to quarrel about." She spoke her thoughts aloud. "Can't we talk about something pleasant before we part?"

"When are you moving in with Aunt Catrin?"

"If she agrees after thinking it over carefully, then perhaps during half-term. It's only a few weeks away."

"Tell me when and I'll help transfer your things," he offered.

She almost assured him there was no need, she had so few belongings in the bedsit, but, afraid he might take it as a snub, she thanked him.

"Make it the Thursday. That will give you plenty of time at each end for packing and unpacking," he suggested.

They were talking like strangers, formal and stiff. She was filled with despondency as she let herself into her room and listened to his car moving away from her.

Despondency was the word to describe Gillian as she sat on Roy's empty bed staring at the used notes in her hand. She had found them when placing some freshly-washed socks in his drawer. So, he was stealing again! She had sensed it for weeks but tried not to believe it. Her plump face was deeply saddened by what she considered her failure. If she had shared his bed, ignoring the fear of her parents guessing, he wouldn't have wanted to go out at night.

Where was he now, she wondered. What poor unfortunate was he robbing this time? Intending to sit and wait for his return, she made herself comfortable against his pillow and sat there staring at the open window, only a faint rectangle in the blackness of the night.

* * *

Eight miles away, Roy was staring at a window from the outside. The partly open window of Firethorn Cottage. It would serve Amanda right, he thought, and a gleam of temptation showed in his blue eyes. So far as Amanda knew she was his sister and yet she was treating him worse than she'd treat an unpleasant stranger. Serve her right if he robbed the cottage she refused to share with him.

He began to examine the walls for a way to climb up, his mind overcoming the difficulties, planning his entry, working out his route through the rooms. But he turned away. No, he'd leave the old lady in peace, he'd go for the bungalow down near the stream. It was empty and, hidden away like it was, he'd have plenty of time to find out where the owner kept his cash.

Seven

There was uproar the following morning when Amanda went to school. Four houses in the village had been robbed, mostly of money but some keepsakes, souvenirs and small items of jewellery that were of little real value but were irreplaceable had been lost.

Of all the outraged mothers hovering around the gate comparing what they knew, only Heather looked at Amanda quizzically, obviously wondering about her brother.

Angrily, Amanda told her in a whisper, "I hope you aren't thinking Roy had anything to do with this! He wouldn't be so stupid!"

"Who's Roy?" a small voice asked and Amanda smiled at Helen and assured her that it was someone she didn't know.

"Isn't Roy your big brother?" the child asked and Amanda's eyes darkened with concern. How much had Helen overheard when she had explained to Heather? And more important, how much had she told other people?

Heather did nothing to discourage her daughter from talking about Roy, and continued to stare at Amanda with undisguised suspicion. Amanda felt close to panic. Once more Roy had entered her life and threatened to upset it.

It wasn't until later, when school was finished, that she learned that Rhys's bungalow had also been burgled during the night. He had been in London and arrived home to find the back door forced and money he had left in a drawer missing. Some of his ornaments and carvings from his travels had been carelessly thrown around and damaged, presumably as the thief searched for money.

"It looks like whoever broke in seemed to want me to know

107

he's angry with me," he said, sadly dropping some of them into the ash bin. "But who that can be I can't imagine. I don't think I've deliberately harmed anyone in my life."

Amanda thought of Roy. Had he become more bitter, more resentful of others having more than he? Greedy, daring, but harmless was how she would have described him.

"At least that lets Roy out," she said with relief. "He has never shown anger or violence."

"Let's hope he stays that way," Rhys replied, looking at her enigmatically, implying perhaps that people can change.

When Roy had arrived home the previous night he had been shocked to see Gillian sitting on his bed waiting for him.

"So, your resolution didn't last long, did it?" she said sadly as he negotiated the small window and dropped silently down.

"Gill, love, I've only been for a walk. Lovely night it is, come and look out of the window."

"It's no good, you might as well tell me. At least forewarned is forearmed."

"But Gill—"

"Tell me, Roy. All of it." So he explained about the burglaries, using anger over his sister as an excuse for his lapse.

"Truth is, Gill, this would have been my last anyway. I was greeted by an old man at the last house. Creepin' down the stairs I was, so quiet you'd never believe, and there he stood looking at me real hard, like some headmaster with a stupid pupil. There was a lolloping great dog beside him, the poor thing was so old if he'd barked he'd have fallen over. Well the old man demands to know what I'm doing. Well, I had to laugh. There I was, in his house with a small bag over my shoulder creepin' down his stairs in the middle of the night and he asks what I'm doin'. Funny really, don't you think?"

"What did he do?"

"Only tried to have a go at me. Poor old sod. I could've snapped him like matchwood."

"You didn't—?"

"No, never hurt no one in my life, you know me better than

that. But the thing is, he saw my face. I'm not worried mind.
He probably couldn't see further than the end of his nose, I saw
the mark where his glasses rested clear as clear. No, I doubt if
he'd recognise me again, but I decided it was enough and that
was definitely the last time. Scary really. Twice it's happened.
Twice I've been caught by someone in the house and in the
same village each time." He shuddered. "Gives me the creeps
it does, they never sleep! No, never again."

"If only I could believe you, Roy."

"You can, love. I promise. Just don't say nothin' about this
and you'll never have a moment's worry ever again."

Rhys arrived promptly on the Thursday of half-term to help her
move. Catrin had been insistent that it was what she wanted, so
Amanda was concerned to see suppressed disapproval showing
on Rhys's face.

All her possessions were packed in boxes and labelled, so
it didn't take long to load the Landrover and her Ford Popular.
Looking back at the empty room she felt only slight regret at
leaving. It had been her home for a short while, but the news
that she owned a cottage had caused it to lose any charm it
might have had.

"Aunt Catrin has promised to have lunch ready, so you'd
better hurry," Rhys called as he put the last box into the car.

She was mildly angered by his abruptness. Why should he
spoil this for her? He had helped her willingly enough, but
there was an air about him of something not said.

"You still think it's wrong for me to move in with your
aunt, don't you?" she asked. "It isn't for ever you know. If
she changes her mind for whatever reason, I'll move out. I
don't intend being a problem for her."

"That's up to you and Aunt Catrin." His voice was calm but
Amanda knew that something about her move was the reason
for his edginess.

"You don't think we'll get on together?"

"Who are you referring to, you and my aunt or you and
Philip? He's the real reason you're moving, isn't he?"

That nonsense again. "What a preposterous idea!" she

109

laughed. "We've mentioned this ridiculous idea before. Why should I want to live next door to Philip so urgently?"

"He's an attractive man and you're an unattached female, there's nothing odd about that is there? It's only strange that you aren't honest about it."

"Rhys, I *am* being honest! Why should I lie to you? I wanted a room nearer the school, I advertised and Catrin offered me one. I also think it's an idea for her to have someone with her, she hasn't seemed well recently."

"That's considerate of you."

She looked at him, wondering if there was sarcasm in his words. "I like Catrin. I did from the moment we met. You don't have to know someone for years before you know they'll be a friend. Don't you make instant decisions about people sometimes?"

He looked at her, the expression in his eyes softening, as he returned the smile. "Of course. Although a first impression can be wrong," he warned. Amanda guessed he was referring to Philip again.

"In that case you allow the friendship to fade. But it's better to be disappointed occasionally than to miss something wonderful."

He helped her into her car and they set off in stunted convoy to install her in her temporary state as lodger at Firethorn Cottage.

A smile lit her face as she turned the final corner and came to where the cottage stood, mellow in the pale sun, waiting for her. Although only a lodger for the next eight months, she was coming home. Rhys and Catrin picked up on her excitement and they all laughed like children as her boxes were taken up to her room.

When Rhys had gone down for the final load, Amanda looked out of the window into the wintery garden. Daffodils were showing their spears of green, some with buds stretching up toward a cold sky, already showing a petal or two of golden yellow. Snowdrops nodded sleepily under the trees. A few polyanthus and a pansy or two had defied the frost to open their faces. Against the background of bare, cold earth, there was more than a hint of spring among the leafless trees.

She felt rather than heard Rhys come and stand beside her. She turned and smiled at him.

"What are you dreaming about?" he asked softly.

"About the thrill of being in a house that's my own, and how I'll add a few more shrubs next year and—" She stopped suddenly. "I don't intend doing anything to make Catrin think I'm anxious to be rid of her, so I won't even mention new shrubs to her."

"I wish she'd make some plans for October," Rhys said.

"Don't worry, she has plenty of time. As long as she needs, believe me."

"I do."

She leaned back, her head resting against his shoulder and looked up at him with a smile.

"In case you're wondering why I don't invite her to live with me at the bungalow, I can't," he told her. "My life is so irregular and I don't want commitments or obligations. Do you understand?"

Amanda moved away from him instinctively. The softly spoken words were a warning to her not to expect more than friendship. Her colour increased as she wondered if her pleasure in his touch had been too blatantly shown.

"We'd better go down," she said with a forced smile. "I don't want to keep my landlady waiting on my first day."

"So you *do* think I should consider inviting her to live with me!" He held her from leaving. "I thought you'd understand."

"Oh, I do," she said airily. "I can see how important it is for you not to have any restrictions. You need to be as free as the birds you like to photograph."

"If I tried to live my life around someone else, my work would suffer. I love it too much to risk that. If I had someone warning me not to be late for dinner, or insisting I kept a social date when I needed to be elsewhere, I'd be unhappy and the person making the demands would be unhappy too. I've seen it happen."

They went down to lunch and Amanda was over-bright, determined Rhys wouldn't see how his words had hurt her.

"I have to leave directly after this," he said as Amanda brought in the coffee. "I have an appointment at three-thirty."

"Thank you for helping," Amanda said. "Some things are much easier with two."

"Some things are," he repeated and Amanda realised how easily a simple phrase could be misconstrued.

Catrin looked at them quizzically and Amanda forced a smile.

"Can I ask another favour, Rhys?" she asked.

"Of course." He looked at her warily.

"Don't look so worried," she was forced to retort. "I want to set up a pond and wildlife display in school. Would you mind if I searched the stream and its backwaters for frogspawn and other things to fill it? I'll return everything to the stream later of course."

"Why don't you take some of the children? I'll get permission from the farmer and you can walk through the garden and out into the field behind the house."

"That's a good idea, thank you."

When Rhys had gone, Amanda congratulated herself that she had handled a tricky situation very well. Catrin, however, was not fooled.

"Have you and my nephew had a disagreement?" she asked.

"No, but I think he's afraid that, living near, I might take up too much of his time."

"That would be a good thing if you ask me," Catrin said firmly. "Dashing about, never finding time to relax and enjoy life. You've been good for him."

That was not his opinion, Amanda thought sadly. I've definitely been warned off!

Roy was finding life tedious. Ever since the police had practically forced their way into the Harrises home the night of the first robberies, and followed up the raid with another only days later, he had been treated with less than cordiality.

112

The third visit, when he had been actually arrested and questioned, finally ended the Harrises dream of turning him from a hardening criminal into a respected citizen.

The cause of the trouble had been Dave. Caught practically red-handed after breaking into a small shop and stealing a television and a couple of radios, he had insisted that Roy would supply an alibi. Unfortunately, although Roy would have helped, he was unable to as he had been home, playing whist with the Harrises.

His room at the Harrises' had been searched, the house too was subject to a very thorough examination. They were visited many times by various policemen and although he had not been charged, the Harrises' euphoric, noble feeling in helping someone desperate for a chance had vanished like a puff of steam from a kettle. They had fervently believed that a good home and caring people and enough of Mrs Harris's cuddles would be enough to keep him from re-offending. The attitude of the police showed them how little they thought of his chances of going straight.

Now the Harrises' neighbours were talking and the realisation Roy was bringing their home into disrepute had frightened them, made them aware of the dangerous situation he had brought to them.

They no longer tried to be friendly, obviously wishing he would leave but lacking the nerve to tell him. Instead of fussing over him and trying different ways to please him, showing him how much he was trusted, they were practically keeping him a prisoner.

"It's out of one prison, into another," he grumbled to Gillian one evening in early March, when they sat on the couch trying to talk without being overheard by her parents. "They won't even let us go to the pictures on our day off. Washing up all the week in a grotty little café and then home to suspicious looks and accusations."

"They were frightened, Roy. They've never had anything to do with the police before, you see, and it unnerved them."

"They knew I was just out of prison, didn't they? They must have guessed I'd be a prime suspect for anything that happens.

The police didn't proceed with their enquiries, did they? That's because they couldn't prove I'd done it! Because I hadn't," he emphasised. "And there's your Mam and Dad acting like I was tried and found guilty. It's so unfair, Gill."

"You can't blame them. You did lapse, didn't you, Roy? That time I waited up for you to explain that money? Those robberies where you were seen by that old man?"

"All that started because I went for a walk. Ask Amanda, she'll tell you I've always done that when I'm restless. I just went out for some air because I couldn't sleep. Insomniac I am, and what a bad thing that is for someone trying to go straight. Temptation never leaves me, you know. Every day I have to fight it off and all on my own too. If I could get into bed with you beside me, Gill, I'd never want to go out at night, believe me!" He kissed her, watching to make sure he wasn't observed by the two listening to The Archers, which had passed its eight hundredth episode, and whispered, "Blimey, Gill, what a thrill that was, coming back from my wanderings that night and seeing you waiting for me on the bed. I told you your Mam and Dad were heavy sleepers, didn't I?"

Encouraged by her smile as she remembered their kisses and making up after his confession, he went on, "It won't always be like this, Gill. The police'll get fed up of looking for me every time something happens."

"I suppose they will forget you eventually, and find someone else to hound. Then our life will be free of these embarrassments. Sorry about Mam and Dad, but they didn't expect midnight bangs on the door."

"They should have. Dammit, the Probation Officer made it all very clear, tried to warn them what it would be like and all they did was smile and convince themselves that they'd make everything all right and be able to boast about how they'd saved a lost soul!"

"All right, they were told, but the police coming at night was still a shock. They didn't really expect it to happen."

"That's what got to my sister, you know. I'm beginning to understand how she felt, now I'm on the straight."

"Would you like to go and see her, now you feel less bitter towards her?" Gillian asked.

He shook his head. "I don't have the money. After a couple of trips to the pictures and paying your Mam for my keep, and it's little enough she asks for, bless her, well, it doesn't leave much for bus fares and visiting."

"Perhaps in the summer. It'll be a pleasant day out for us then."

But Roy didn't intend to be staying with Gillian and her miserable parents when summer came. He was free, he had money and he had plans.

Storms prevented Amanda from moving far from the cottage over the following days. The wind lashed at the trees and threatened to take the door off its hinges every time it was opened, like a ferocious animal venting its spite on everything in its path. Rain filled the gutters and poured down the paths.

On Sunday it abated, leaving a tranquillity that made the ferocity of the past days seem impossible. Amanda gathered up broken branches and twigs from the garden and tied up fallen shrubs. Then she decided a walk would be a good idea after days of being indoors.

"I expect the stream is flooded," she said to Catrin. "I'll go and search along the banks for frogspawn before it rains again. I can still take the children later."

Carrying one of Catrin's buckets and wearing a pair of wellingtons belonging to Philip, much to Catrin's amusement, she set off for Rhys's bungalow. She knocked on the door more from politeness than for the need to tell Rhys what she was doing. She had made up her mind she would trouble him as little as possible.

To her surprise the door was opened, not by Rhys, but by Jessica Maybury, looking very glamorous and casual in a fur-trimmed negligee.

"Rhys is away at present," Jessica said in a bored voice, "Can I give him a message?"

"No, it doesn't matter," Amanda said, conscious of her ridiculous appearance. "I've come to collect a few things from the stream. I won't disturb you." She turned away and made for the back of the house as quickly as she was able in the ridiculous wellingtons.

She was angry. So that was why Rhys had been at such pains to explain that she shouldn't become too interested in him! He needn't have bothered. She was perfectly happy to ignore him completely!

She threw the bucket onto the grass near the stream and glared at it. Why had she decided to make a pond for the school? It was a silly idea. These children weren't townies who would never have the chance to discover such things for themselves.

Tempting as it was to return home and forget the whole thing, she walked on, squelching through the muddy edge, searching along the high-water mark where the damp conditions were likely places for the jelly-like spawn.

Among the debris left by the swollen stream she found a few of the speckled mounds and put them in her bucket. She forced her mind to stay away from Jessica Maybury but could not resist glancing back as she headed for the gate.

Standing in the window watching her, the figure of the young woman was clearly seen and Amanda thought she was wringing her hands as if in anxiety. Does she want me out of the way before Rhys comes back? Amanda wondered. Well, she can wait.

Dawdling, glancing occasionally at the watcher at the window, Amanda walked through the shallower parts of the stream, collecting a few pieces of wood here, a couple of handfuls of weed there. A couple of large stones were lifted and carried under her arm; they would be needed for the baby frogs to rest on later.

When she eventually reached the gate, Jessica opened the front door and called, "What did you say your name was?"

Amanda unwillingly walked back. "Clifford. Amanda Clifford. But I might be related to the Beynon family. I just don't know."

Jessica looked her over, a curious expression on her lovely face. There was more to be said, but Amanda wondered irritably how long she was expected to stand, holding a muddy bucket and a couple of rocks, while Jessica decided whether or not to say it.

"You're from round here?" Jessica asked.

"I might be." Amanda shrugged. She began to experience a growing impatience. She wasn't sure she wanted to discuss her situation with Rhys's girlfriend. She nodded a vague goodbye and began to leave.

"Just a minute. Maybe I *can* help."

"Help me? How?"

Jessica stared as before but still seemed unwilling to speak.

Amanda gave a loudly audible sigh. There was no way she wanted to be here talking to Jessica when Rhys returned. She still smarted with embarrassment when she remembered how clearly he had told her he didn't want her. Another confrontation, especially in front of Jessica, would ruin the pleasure of moving into the cottage entirely.

"You're looking for relations, aren't you?" Jessica said eventually.

"You've already told me you don't know anything."

Amanda's simmering anger was suddenly dissipated as she saw real distress on the woman's face. There *was* something to say. Breathlessly she waited. Jessica began twisting her hands together nervously.

"I'm distantly related to the Beynon family and you might be a member of the family too." The words seemed to choke her and Amanda frowned.

"Why didn't you tell me before?" she asked.

"The connection – if there is one – is very distant."

Putting down the messy bucket, Amanda stepped nearer. "Could you remember some names, or dates, anything that might give me a lead?"

"Tell me about yourself," Jessica asked, ignoring the question. "How old are you?"

"Twenty-three."

"What do you do, you're a teacher aren't you?"

Amanda nodded. "About the names, I've drawn a complete blank. My only hope is Aunt Flora's sister, Gwen, who lived in America. If you know of any cousins it would help."

All the time she spoke, Amanda felt the words were not being heard. The woman shrugged and, still without responding, went towards the doorway. "Sorry," she said as the door closed on her. "I don't think our families are connected after all."

Amanda picked up the disreputable bucket and walked away. She was fuming at the off-hand way she had been treated. But as she approached the cottage the anger again died. There was something odd in the way Jessica had studied her. Anxiety had been visible in the lovely eyes and in the twisting hands.

"If there's anything to learn it's unlikely she'll tell me," Amanda said to Catrin and Philip later, when she had told them of her strange encounter.

"Sorry to say it, dear," Catrin said, "but this woman might simply be what we used to call a nosy parker, just curious about you and wanting to find out more."

"And nosy parkering is something at which I was once an expert," Philip said, "so I'll see if I still have the touch."

Amanda looked puzzled until Catrin elaborated. "Philip was once a very successful news reporter. Until about five years ago in fact."

"I still have a few contacts," he said. "A phone call or two wouldn't hurt."

"Why did you change from a news reporter to a bus driver in a small Welsh village?" Amanda asked.

"It's a long story," he said. "I've told Catrin most of it and perhaps one day she'll tell you."

Catrin looked sad. She did know most of the story and this was why she had such sympathy for Philip and also why Rhys, who knew only a part of it, resented him so much.

"I'm sorry," Amanda said at once. "I didn't mean to pry!"

"You weren't. There's a deal of difference in being interested and being—"

"A nosy parker," she finished for him and they all laughed. The subject was dropped but Amanda remained curious.

Philip was an enigma and, although he didn't attract her in the way Rhys did, she liked him and couldn't help wondering why he had left his chosen career.

"It was a combination of several things, I believe," Catrin told her later. "His wife couldn't cope with the constant absences and they parted. Then they realised his wife was pregnant and he gave up the career he loved and tried to make a success of his marriage. It didn't work and he left, taking the child with him for a month or two when his wife was ill. The child went back to her and there was Philip, having lost not only his wife, his home and child but his work as well."

"Where is his wife now?"

"That's something he'll never talk about."

"What a pity he gave up his job."

"I think he's content now. He's well liked by most of the people in the village and seems to have accepted his new life. A man like that needs a very special woman. A special kind of love."

Amanda's thoughts immediately turned to Rhys. "Rhys dislikes him, doesn't he?"

"They knew each other years ago, but – well, you know how impossible it is to persuade a man to talk, yet we chatter merrily all day."

"Yes," Amanda said, "and it's well past time for supper!" She knew Catrin was being evasive and didn't want to risk that one question too many that can cause embarrassment, so she went out and clattered the dishes and sang a cheerful song.

That evening she wrote one of her regular letters to Roy. She didn't receive any in return but went on writing, giving him news of her new class and the various people she had met. Each letter ended with a list of questions about him to which she begged a reply, but weeks passed and none came. She felt guilty at not inviting him to come and see her, but she knew he could easily ruin everything if he became a regular visitor and news of how he had spent most of his youth was revealed.

From mutual friends, she gathered he was still living with Gillian Harris and her parents and she hoped it would turn out

119

to be the pivot that turned him away from crime. There were more juvenile than adult criminals she had read, so some of them must change, she thought hopefully.

The pond display in school was a great success but she didn't suggest taking the children through Rhys's garden to explore the stream. She averted her eyes each time she passed his bungalow. If Rhys and Jessica were having an affair she would rather not watch it happen.

She still pictured Jessica watching her as she scrabbled about in the stream; a still figure apart from her twisting hands, looking glamorous yet melancholy in the fur-trimmed negligee. Just thinking of the contrast with herself clambering about in muddy water filled her with embarrassment.

A few weeks passed without a sign of either Rhys or Jessica until on a Sunday morning in late March, without warning, they both arrived.

"You remember Jessica?" Rhys said. "She's been staying at the bungalow when I've been away."

"Yes, would you believe, the chimney pot was blown down during those frightfully scary gales and took some slates off my roof. I was petrified, wasn't I Rhys darling?"

Amanda disappeared into the kitchen to make coffee. Rhys and Catrin had automatically led Jessica into the lounge and turned on a fire for her. I'm a person for whom the kitchen will do, she fumed to herself. But Miss High and Mighty Maybury mustn't be offered anything but the best! She slammed the coffee pot onto the table and glared at it. "I hope your coffee spills all over you," she muttered.

"What are you doing, talking to yourself?" Rhys asked, entering the kitchen without her seeing him.

"I'm telling the coffee to hurry up," she said angrily. "Don't you ever talk to inanimate objects?"

"All right," he laughed, putting up a hand to ward off an imaginary blow. "I only asked!"

She handed him a bag of biscuits and pointed to a plate. "Open these, will you, while I get the cups."

"Does Jessica make you so angry?" There was amusement in his voice.

120

"No. Why should she? It's just that Catrin and I were just going for a walk and now we'll have to postpone it."

"Aw, what a pity," he teased.

She pushed past him, taking the tray of cups into the lounge where Catrin and Jessica were sitting in uneasy silence. When she returned to the kitchen, Rhys was sitting in Catrin's favourite chair near the fire.

"What have you been doing while I've been away?" he asked. "Have you learnt anything about your family?"

"Oh, I think I'll forget it," she said. "I appeared from nowhere and the stories about gooseberry bushes are true after all."

He chuckled and reached out to take her hand. "I missed you while I was away. Did you miss me a little?"

"Yes. I had to collect bugs and things and you could have carried my bucket." She was using humour to ease the hurt of seeing him with Jessica.

"I did have a report of someone creeping about in my garden one day."

"That was me, looking like an abandoned boot." She gestured towards the other room and added, "And her in there looked like she'd just got back from a beauty parlour."

"She probably had. That's where she spends a lot of her time!"

"She's very beautiful," Amanda admitted painfully.

"So are you. Even in someone else's wellingtons."

She turned to look at him. His face was serious, no smile to show he was teasing. He pulled her gently towards him and kissed her. She looked into his eyes and saw reflected there a longing as strong as her own. She moved towards him again, her lips reaching for his, then a peal of laughter reached them from the other room. She jerked away from him, the reminder he was not alone shocking her from the moment of love.

"Hadn't we better return to your girlfriend?" she asked.

His grip on her tightened. "Amanda," he said urgently. "Why are you so distant? I've been away, aren't you glad to see me back?"

"Jessica is waiting for her coffee." She tore herself away and began attending to the percolator, but her hands shook and he took it from her.

"Careful," he said, "you'll be spilling it in someone's lap if you don't calm down."

"That's fine, as long as it's the right lap!" She was disconcerted to hear his chuckle as he followed her from the room.

"I understand you and Rhys worked together in America?" Catrin was saying when they entered the lounge.

"That's right," Jessica said. "Rhys was filming a documentary about unusual pets. I was the assistant who held the animals. It was made to make money for some animal sanctuary. Rhys called it Beauty and the Beast, wasn't that lovely of him?"

Depends which way round he meant it, Amanda thought wickedly, but she smiled politely.

"What are your plans for the future?" Catrin asked. Jessica shook her lovely dark brown hair and looked at Rhys.

"That rather depends," she said mysteriously, "doesn't it, Rhys, darling?"

"Jessica can either return to the States and take a small part in a stage play or stay here and do some advertising to be shown in the cinema. She hasn't made up her mind, yet."

Amanda watched the silent messages Jessica was passing and wondered what to believe. Rhys was not showing signs of a close involvement with their lovely visitor, but there was definitely something between them.

Rhys stood to leave and Amanda was relieved that the uncomfortable visit was over. Catrin tried to talk of everyday things as their coats were gathered, aware of the uneasy mood.

Amanda watched as Rhys and Jessica walked off towards the bungalow, Jessica holding Rhys's arm possessively. As they passed out of sight with a final wave, Philip appeared and walked towards their open door.

"So, the great Miss Jessica Maybury meets her public," he said.

"You've learned something!" Catrin's words to Philip were statement not question and she was smiling at Amanda.

Amanda was still watching the corner around which the couple had disappeared. She forced a smile and tried to show interest as Philip said, "Come on, don't you want to hear what I've discovered?"

"Of course. But let's go inside, it's freezing."

Once Philip began to talk, Amanda had no difficulty in concentrating.

"Jessica Maybury's real name is Sian Talbot. Her mother was Gwen Beynon, your Aunt Flora's sister. Her father was Ryan Talbot. She was born here in Tri-nant and so far as I can learn, she is probably early to middle thirties. What about that then?" His pleasure in passing on the information for which she had been searching showed in his smile and his sparkling eyes.

"So she must be related to me! But why did she lie?"

"Afraid of giving away her age to Rhys no doubt. Or perhaps she has an unsavoury background she's trying to run away from. Who knows? I doubt she'll tell us."

"She says she's American and thirty years old."

"And that's what Rhys probably believes."

They discussed the news for a long time but it seemed to bring Amanda no closer to a solution. In fact they were now further away than ever, if Gwen's daughter was no longer a possibility as Amanda's mother.

"There must be a branch of the Beynon family separate from Aunt Flora's immediate family that we've yet to discover," Amanda said sadly. "But how can we find them? We haven't got a single name to give us a start."

"We'll have to go back further than Sheila and William Beynon, to your great-great-grandparents." Catrin said.

"Or what about an illegitimate child, brought up by some one other than Gwen?" Philip suggested.

"Give up," Amanda said. "I was made of gingerbread and baked by the fairies."

Eight

Catrin and Amanda set out on their belated walk and their feet took them past Rhys's bungalow.

"If the Landrover's there, shall we call on the way back and tell him what Philip discovered?"

"If you like. But let's not make a plan, just see how we feel later. We might come back a different way." Amanda was determined they should!

Skirting the school grounds they made their way across a field to join up once more with the stream. The ground dropped away below them and in the distance they could see the silvery gleam of the sea.

"Shall we turn back now?" Amanda asked, "or are you able to walk a bit further?"

"I'd like to walk around and back through the village on the other side. There's a catkin tree where we might collect a bunch to decorate the hall."

"If you're sure it won't tire you?" Amanda asked doubtfully, thinking that they would have to pass Rhys's bungalow after all.

"I feel fine, dear. Don't worry."

Amanda watched her companion as she climbed over the stile and jumped down lightly into the field which led them back to the road. She was amazed at how much Catrin had improved since she had moved in with her. Perhaps she is simply more relaxed, knowing someone is there, Amanda thought. But whatever the reason, she isn't the same person.

Rhys was standing at his gate when they reached the bungalow.

"I saw you coming," he explained, "and I thought you'd appreciate the offer of a cup of reviving tea."

Amanda looked anxiously around for a sign of Jessica's presence as she entered. The room looked much as usual, nothing feminine lying about.

"Jessica isn't here." Rhys seemed to read her thoughts. "And," he went on, "that makes you the favourite for making the tea."

"I thought there'd be a snag!" she said, disappearing into the kitchen, ignoring his first remark.

When she returned with the tray, Rhys and his aunt were looking out of the window.

"It's amazing how spring-like everything is," Catrin was saying. "The trees are ready to burst into leaf and the birds are already pairing up." She pointed to a pair of bullfinches on the branch of an apple tree waiting to plunder its new shoots.

"I'm already busy with preparations for the Easter Bonnet Parade," Amanda told them, glad of a safe subject. "So don't talk to me about spring arriving. In our classroom it already has!"

"So that's why you've been asking for unwanted hats."

"Most mothers will make one for their own child but there are always a few who won't bother, so I make a few to save disappointments. I can't risk a child being missed out of the parade."

"What about the boys, don't they have any fun?" Rhys wanted to know.

"The boys are in charge of refreshments. All the children will help to make cakes and the boys will offer them around."

"If I'm free I'll come and take photographs for the school scrap book," Rhys offered and Amanda was delighted. He took out his diary. "What date will it be?"

"Good Friday is April the sixteenth but we want the Parade on the ninth."

"I can't promise, I—"

"I know," Amanda tried to sound off-hand, "you can't complicate your life with any commitments!"

"Nonsense, dear, Rhys isn't afraid of commitment. But

he does need friends who understand his work. Not like poor Philip," she added with a surreptitious glance at her nephew. "His wife couldn't accept his constant travelling. She loved him without appreciating his need to do the work he enjoyed."

Amanda's heart began to race as she watched Rhys's face cloud over. "Time we were leaving," she said firmly. "I have work to do and you'll be glad to get home and change out of those shoes, won't you, Catrin?"

Catrin looked surprised at the acerbity in Amanda's voice, but she rose without another word.

Amanda decided to stay on at school one evening, to make the extra hats for the Easter Bonnet Parade. She told Catrin not to expect her for tea.

After seeing the children safely out of school and into the care of a parent, she was about to return to her classroom when she noticed Heather and the two girls waiting for her.

"I'm staying on for a while," she explained. "I want to work on the hats."

"Five minutes to hand the girls over to Haydn and I'll help," Heather offered.

Amanda huddled inside her coat as Heather hurried Helen and Jane to where Haydn was waiting at the turn of the lane. The weather had turned icy and she was glad when Heather reappeared and they could run for the warmth of the classroom.

Heather was clever with her hands and after being told what was required, she deftly transformed old hats into flower-covered bonnets. Heather and Haydn had already promised help on the day and the two young women chatted happily about the arrangements until the hats were completed.

Amanda surveyed the colourful collection. "I doubt if we'll need any more than these. Most mothers will supply their own creations. We've just made sure none will be forgotten."

"You're very thoughtful, Amanda," Heather said. "And you've been wonderful with Jane. She's so much happier since you came."

"Thank you," Amanda smiled. "She's a delightful little girl."

"I wonder if Rhys will take pictures? He doesn't seem to know where he'll be at any time, does he? I couldn't live with that, could you?"

"It depends. If I were married to a man whose job took him away but I knew he came home to me as often as he could, because he wanted to be with me, then I think I could cope." She was staring into space, thinking of Rhys, and when she looked at Heather she saw the woman was upset.

"It can be very lonely when you're left for weeks and you imagine your husband having fun without you," Heather said quietly.

"There are marriages that survive long separations though." Then, to comfort Heather she added, "So much depends on how a man treats his wife. If he's insensitive to her problems, well, I can see how impossible it would be."

"Rhys will never marry. He seems to have the best of both worlds, an aunt to spoil him and the freedom to do as he pleases." Heather spoke harshly and Amanda wondered with alarm whether she were in love with Rhys.

"Why do people think of marriage as the end of freedom? Being with someone you love isn't a prison, is it?"

"It can be!"

"Was it, for you?" Amanda spoke softly. She knew she was treading dangerous ground and was afraid the question might be considered an impertinence. Yet she sensed the other woman's need to talk.

"Yes. I was left on my own with a small child and I felt trapped. I'm so lucky to have found someone like Haydn. He'd never leave us."

"Is it wise to be so dependent on another person?"

The scared look that had left Heather's face while she made the hats had returned and Amanda cursed herself for causing it.

"Haydn helped me face up to leaving my husband and he promised to stay with us. Jane isn't Haydn's; she was born soon after I'd left my husband you see," Heather went on. "I think that's why she's been so clinging."

"Her confidence is growing. She'll be fine. By the way,

she'll be having a reading book soon, but don't tell her just yet."

"Haydn will be pleased, he spends a lot of time with her. Helen picks things up quicker than Jane."

"Children catch worries quicker than the measles," Amanda said with a laugh. "So try not to show your concern." Taking a chance on being rebuffed she asked, "What did your husband do, Heather?"

"Oh, let's not talk about him any more!" Tension showed in Heather's thin face and clouded her eyes. "Haydn looks after us now."

"Sorry, I had no right to question you." She wondered about Haydn. Had he given up on any plans for a life of his own, so Heather could be secure? What could he have done that was so terrible, this ex-husband she never named?

When the two women left the school it was raining. Cold icy rain that seemed to burn the skin on their faces and made their foreheads ache.

With hurriedly shouted goodbyes, they went their separate ways, Heather to the house next door to the Cwm Gwyn Arms, and Amanda to Firethorn and a welcome cup of tea.

She slowed as she passed the bungalow. The place looked dark and empty. The garage doors were closed and curtains covered the windows. But she no more than glanced in case she were wrong and Jessica was watching from the darkened room. Rhys had been away for a few days and she wondered vaguely when he would be back.

Her question was answered when she reached the cottage.

"I've had a call from Rhys, dear," Catrin said. "He's coming home tonight and I promised to turn on the heating and put a casserole in the oven." She looked at Amanda pleadingly. "I don't feel like going out on a cold evening like this, but I did promise."

"You are definitely not going," Amanda said. "It's freezing cold and raining and you'd be soaked. No, I'll walk down later."

"Thank you, dear." Catrin smiled sweetly. "I hoped you'd say that."

For the first time, Amanda felt she had been manoeuvred into something. She looked at the guileless face of Catrin and wondered about her illness before she invited her to come to live at the cottage, and about the stiffness which miraculously cured itself. She shook her head impatiently. She was imagining things. What could Catrin gain out of pretending to be ill?

"The casserole is already cooked so if you could take it down about ten o'clock?"

"I need to go before that. The place will be so cold."

"For you and me perhaps. But Rhys sleeps in the most uncomfortable places. Tents!" She shuddered expressively. "Ten o'clock will be fine."

By that time the rain had stopped and, dressed warmly, she set off for the bungalow. Before she entered, she knocked, half expecting that Jessica would be waiting for Rhys too. The place was dark and empty. She turned the heating on and set the meal to warm in the oven. It was late, but she put a match to the log fire and waited until it was cheerfully burning. Then she prepared to leave; there was nothing else she could do. As she stepped outside, headlights dazzled her and she closed the door instantly. If Rhys was with Jessica she didn't want to meet them!

In the darkness of the hall, almost without thinking, she stupidly decided to hide. Once they were inside she could slip out without them knowing she'd been there. I'd never make a criminal, she thought wildly, thinking of her brother in similar circumstances. Her heart was racing with guilt and the fear of being seen, as she slipped into the dining room and watched the hallway through the partly-opened door. Why was I such an idiot? she asked herself. I'm really stuck now I've committed myself to hiding in this ridiculous way. It's too late to show myself.

A figure was visible outside the door, silhouetted by the glare of an outside light. She made a move as if to go and open the door but again, courage failed her at the thought of seeing Jessica. No, her decision was made. She would have to remain hidden until Rhys was inside and hope to make her escape later.

Rhys came through the door bringing the cold fresh air with him and dropped a pile of equipment on the floor beside the telephone. He picked up the receiver and dialled, glancing around casually while apparently waiting for his connection and Amanda slowly pushed her door closed.

"Hello," Rhys said loudly. "Is that the police? I want to report a burglar – yes, here, now – the address? It's—"

"Rhys, it's me!" Amanda burst out and snatched the phone from his hand, expecting him to be shocked, angry, in fact any reaction but this. He was laughing.

"How's that for owns back?" he said, hugging her. "I saw you at the door as I drove in and guessed you were still inside."

"But the police—?"

"My thumb was on the bar, don't worry. What are you doing here?"

"Catrin asked me to come and put a casserole in the oven. She said you need a hot meal."

"What I need is this." He put a hand behind her head and pulled her towards him. His lips met hers, gently at first then with a deep longing that almost overwhelmed her. She clung to him, wanting to stay close for ever.

He seemed tense when he released her.

"Come and help unload the car," he said gruffly. Amanda knew the remark was a shield to hide his desire for her and the affect of their kiss. "Then you can tell me what you've been doing while I've been away." He helped button her coat tightly and tie her scarf, and every touch and gesture was a caress. His eyes held such longing that she wanted to throw herself into his arms, but she pretended unconcern.

There were several loads to be brought in and the biting wind cut through the coat and made her shiver.

"I'm sorry. I shouldn't have asked you to help in this weather. I didn't want you to leave," he apologised. "Come in and warm yourself." He led her towards the huge, crackling fire.

The scene looked tempting. A man for whom she felt a growing love, a cosy fire and an intimate glow from a lamp illuminating the settee. She shook her head. She would soon be out of her depth with this man.

"I'll see you tomorrow," she said. "Catrin will wonder where I am."

He began to argue, then picked up his car keys and collected his heavy sheepskin. "Very well. But I insist on driving you. It isn't far but it's late and I don't want anything to happen to you."

It was only a few silent moments before the car stopped outside Firethorn Cottage. "Give Aunt Catrin my love and tell her I'll see her tomorrow, will you?" He took her hand as she reached for the door. "Amanda, I missed you. I'm so glad you were there to welcome me home."

"I'm glad you're back," she whispered in a small, tight voice.

He kissed her lightly and stepped out to open her door.

She walked to the gate, conscious of a fierce urge to run back to him. This won't do, she told herself. I'm making an impossible situation for myself if I give in to this. Denying herself the painful pleasure of looking back, she went into the house. Leaning against the inside of the door she listened with something approaching despair as the car drove away.

"Back so soon, dear?" Catrin called. "I thought you'd have stayed and talked to Rhys for a while."

"How could you have thought that?" Amanda asked. "You said he wasn't expected back until much later."

"Did I say that? Oh, I must be getting muddled."

Amanda looked at the innocent face with its halo of white curls. Catrin getting muddled? No chance of that! She had known exactly what she was doing when she sent her to the bungalow at the time Rhys was expected. What is she up to, she wondered? First warning her that Rhys was not a candidate for marriage, then throwing them together.

She herself must have made a mistake. Or perhaps Catrin

had forgotten what Rhys had told her. But another look at the gleam in her friend's blue eyes and she was completely confused. There was more to this lady that she had suspected!

She told Catrin about Rhys frightening her by pretending to call the police.

"But why did you hide, dear?"

"I thought—" Amanda was about to lie but changed her mind. "I was afraid I might embarrass Rhys if there was someone with him."

"By 'someone' you mean Jessica Maybury?"

"Or someone else."

"Jessica Maybury is no longer in the area. There wasn't an affair you know. I think Jessica hoped there would be, but Rhys doesn't like vain women and they don't come much more vain than Jessica!"

Amanda's thoughts kept her awake most of that night. Her relationship with Rhys was growing. His pleasure at seeing her couldn't be denied. But where would it lead? She thought of Heather's description of the impossibility of living with a man whose work took him away for long periods and wondered if she would be able to cope, and whether she'd be given the chance to find out.

A week before the Easter Bonnet Parade, Rhys was at the cottage when she returned from school. A tray was set with cakes and tea and he looked as if he had been there for a while. Amanda greeted him with shyness, convinced she had been the subject of conversation. The momentary shyness faded as Rhys offered her the chair closest to the fire, and began talking about his visit to London.

"I've spoken to my agent to discuss the book about my stream," he said, "and he thinks it's a good idea."

"I'm glad. Have you decided how to arrange it?"

"Not the seasons. Nor 'A day in the life of . . .'. I want something different," he frowned.

"Collect your favourite pictures and an idea will come," she advised.

"I think you're right. It's like a friendship. It isn't until it grows that you know what sort of friendship it will be."

He was looking at Amanda as he spoke and she wondered how he saw their relationship growing. Nothing in his handsome face gave a hint of his thoughts. Shyness returned and made her turn away from his scrutiny.

"Will you come and look at some photographs?" he asked her. "I'd bring them here, but there are boxfuls. Why not come tomorrow after school, and have tea?"

Some devil in her made her decline. "I have some work to do after school," she said. "Finishing touches to the bonnets."

"Ask Heather to help, then you'll be able to do both," he said, handing her the phone.

The Easter Bonnet Parade was to be held outside if the weather allowed, but judging from the cold winds that prevailed, and after several severely icy and snow-bound weeks, it was more likely to be in the school hall. Amanda had asked the children to bring the hats before the actual day so she could check them and make sure they fitted. Heather came with the two girls as Haydn was out, and they set out the hats on desks and tables in the school hall, which soon looked like a small garden. Half an hour later she looked at them and was satisfied she had done all she could to make sure the day was a success.

At the corner of the lane she waved goodbye to Heather, Helen and Jane and explained she was going to look at some of Rhys's photographs. "Catrin is meeting me there and Rhys has promised tea, which probably means I'll have to make it," she laughed.

"You might be surprised," Heather said. "Rhys is capable of producing an excellent spread at times."

"You're right. I would be surprised! In fact, I bet you an evening of minding Helen and Jane that you're wrong."

"It's unlikely we'd collect," Heather said at once. "We never go out without taking them."

"What a pity," Amanda looked at Heather thoughtfully. "I'd have thought a few hours out of the house on your own would be refreshing for you both."

"The girls are all I need."

Amanda was frowning when she left the threesome and walked towards the bungalow. Love and care she could understand, but Heather seemed afraid to let the children out of her sight. It was approaching the end of Jane's second term, yet Heather was at the gate long after school had started and was always out there long before the time to collect her, standing where Jane could not fail to see her.

Amanda noticed that Jane aways sensed when her mother arrived and she would leave whatever she was doing and wander towards the window, giving a tiny wave to the lonely figure standing near the fence.

Rain, wind and even snowstorms didn't prevent Heather from waiting long unnecessary hours each week, so Jane wouldn't think she had been forgotten. Amanda puzzled over the reason. Heather's insecurity had caused the child to become anxious; she was sure the problem was with Heather and not her younger daughter.

The door of Rhys's bungalow stood open but there was no reply to her call. She walked through the garden and there they were. Catrin stood behind a camera which was fixed on a tripod and Rhys was holding up an arm as if around someone's shoulders. As Amanda watched, Rhys called, "Ready?"

"Perfect!" Catrin called. Then she left the camera and ran to Rhys, slipping into his widespread arm. A camera clicked and they both laughed.

"There, you see? Taking your own photograph is easy." He saw Amanda and called her over. "Come and see what Aunt Catrin's been doing."

The intricacies of delayed camera work were explained to her and she surprised him by understanding a lot of what he said.

"I have learnt a little about the subject," she reminded him.

"You could both be very useful to me," he said as, with an arm around each of them, he led them inside.

To her surprise, tea was prepared. Teacakes ready to toast,

sandwiches neatly arranged, and scones, thick with jam and cream, temptingly displayed. "And before you accuse me," Rhys said, "I did it without help!"

When they had eaten, Rhys spread out a number of photographs for them to study. Amanda could see he had an expert eye for blending the colour of the subject and the background. Portraits of birds, fish, reptiles and flowers living around the stream in endless variety.

"I wouldn't want to discard any," Catrin wailed.

Handling them with care, Amanda put them into three separate groups.

"Morning, noon and night?" she suggested. They discussed the possibility for some time, and it was almost nine before the pictures were finally put aside.

"Come and have a drink?" Rhys suggested. "We just have time."

Catrin shook her head. She closed her eyes as if tired. "Not me, my dears, but don't let me stop you from going. I'll stroll back and prepare for bed."

Amanda was about to say she too would go home, but Rhys forestalled her.

"We'll take you home first, Aunt Catrin. Then Amanda and I will go to the Cwm Gwyn Arms."

Amanda looked hard at Catrin. The sleepiness had vanished from her eyes. She smiled at the woman and was rewarded with a twinkle-eyed wink. Startled, Amanda stared, but the beguiling expression was back as Catrin smiled wearily up at her nephew, who was holding out her coat.

"Thank you my dear. I'm sorry to be such a spoilsport, but I do get suddenly very tired, sometimes." She looked so innocent Amanda began to wonder if she had imagined that wink!

"What are you playing at?" she whispered as Rhys went to start the car.

"Propinquity, that's all."

"What does propinquity mean, Rhys?" Amanda asked when they were sitting with their drinks.

"This." He moved closer and put an arm around her tightly. "It means nearness, or kinship I think. Why?"

"Oh, nothing. It just popped into my mind." Catrin, she thought, you're a very crafty lady. She was unable to hide a smile.

"What are you smiling at?" Rhys asked.

"Oh, something Catrin said earlier," she replied vaguely.

A voice they recognised called from the doorway and Amanda looked up to see Haydn. Collecting more drinks from the bar he came and joined them.

"Not interrupting anything, am I?" he asked.

"Of course not!" Amanda answered quickly. "We were discussing Rhys's book."

Amanda sat back while the two men became very technical. She asked an occasional question and the time to leave came too quickly.

"Why didn't Heather come with you?" Amanda asked as they were leaving. "I've offered to look after the girls if she wants to go out and there must be others willing to help?"

"Thanks, but Heather won't leave them. I pop out for an hour now and then. It would do her good to have an evening out though. Perhaps when the girls are older."

"Any time she changes her mind," Amanda offered, but knew it was a vain hope.

Rhys drove her home but didn't go inside. "Say goodnight to Aunt Catrin for me," he said. "I won't see you for a while but I hope to be back for the Easter Parade."

"Thank you for this evening, Rhys. I enjoyed it. Catrin did too; pity she was so suddenly tired." She said the words pointedly, wondering if he had guessed the fatigue had been arranged so they could go out alone.

"I hope she isn't ill," he said.

"I've invited her to the Easter Bonnet Parade. She wouldn't dare be ill and miss that!" Amanda said.

"I'll see you both there." He kissed her warmly, his arms holding her tightly, before walking back to the car and driving away.

Amanda watched until a bend in the road hid the lights of the car from her sight and went indoors to tell Catrin about the visit to the Cwm Gwyn Arms.

"Catrin, you must know why Heather is so over-protective with Jane," she said, as they sat beside the dying fire with a milky drink. "It's surely more than a broken marriage? They're happy now aren't they, Heather and Haydn? Helen doesn't worry her so much. It's little Jane. Jane never visits friends or invites friends to tea like her older sister. And from what I gather, she is never allowed out to play."

"The child might not want to. No mother treats her children exactly the same. Each child has its needs and the mother acts according to the individual child."

Amanda shook her head. "The trouble is with Heather, not Jane. But there's no way I can find out. Heather clams up when I try to discuss it. You must know, Catrin. Can't you tell me?"

"Ask Rhys, dear. He and Haydn are friends; he'd explain better than anyone else could."

Amanda nodded but she knew she wouldn't speak to Rhys about it. She had tried, but that invisible barrier was around the subject, whoever she asked. Rhys and Catrin must surely know but for some reason neither would talk about it.

On Sunday afternoon, Amanda took her camera and went down by the stream in Rhys's garden. An hour later she was lying on the bank on the unbelievably cold mud, half hidden by a hide used occasionally by Rhys. Her camera was pointed at the water where a small trout searched the bottom in the clear stream.

Out of the corner of her eye she saw a flash of bright blue and knew instinctively it was a kingfisher. She lay still. Perhaps she would be lucky and get a shot of the elusive bird. She watched, hardly daring to breathe, willing it to return.

Rewarded after a very long wait when she was about to give up, she aimed the viewfinder and clicked until the bird had vanished. The trout had long gone, but she was more than happy with the afternoon.

She slowly wriggled out of the collection of wood and leaves that had kept her hidden. When she stood up she realised with a shock that she was not alone. The light was fading and in the deepening shadows, she saw Jessica watching her from beneath a tree.

"It's you!" Jessica was obviously disappointed. "I saw someone under the dead wood and thought it must be Rhys."

"Rhys is away," Amanda said stiffly.

"Oh, well. I don't suppose he'll mind my using the house. I have the builders in and I can't possibly stand the chaos for another day."

Amanda didn't reply. She couldn't tell Rhys's girlfriend not to stay. It was obvious Jessica had a key. She collected her bag and camera and nodded to her. "If you'll excuse me I have to go. I want to take this film for developing."

"Why d'you bother?" Jessica asked in a bored voice.

"What d'you mean? I bother because I'll be able to use them at school if they're good enough."

"You won't impress Rhys by crawling about in mud." Jessica followed Amanda past the bungalow. "Rhys goes for glamour, not mud-larking."

"I'm not trying to impress. I do what I like doing."

"And you like being a teacher?"

"Very much."

"Don't you want more out of life than that?"

Amanda turned to glare at her interrogator. Jessica stood leaning against the corner of the bungalow and Amanda had to admit she made a beautiful picture with her rich red jumper and dark green skirt, her light brown hair falling softly to her shoulders.

"At present I am completely happy doing what I do. When my work no longer fulfils me, then I'll look for something else."

"Oh, I see, you're just hoping for marriage like most young girls. Well, let me warn you, Rhys isn't the marrying kind."

"So I understand."

"But," Jessica said, smiling a dazzling smile, "I think I'm about to make him change his mind."

Amanda adjusted her shoulder bag and smiled back sweetly. "Then I wish you luck. You'll need it!"

"Perhaps I won't stay here after all. I think I'll join him in

London. The big city is more our sort of place than muddy streams."

"Hardly worth you bothering. He's coming back to photograph the children on Friday."

"You're sure, are you?" Jessica lifted her skirt and tiptoed daintily up to the road. Amanda clumped behind her in Philip's wellingtons, feeling far from feminine.

On Friday, as the time of the Parade drew near, Amanda was feeling apprehensive. There was no sign of Rhys. Jessica had obviously succeeded in keeping him away.

"Lucky I own a camera," she said to Catrin and Heather, who had come to help dress the children. "I was afraid he wouldn't make it."

"He'll be here," Catrin said confidently. But Amanda remembered Jessica's words and was not so sure. A second disaster was the non-appearance of the person who was to give the commentary as the children walked across the stage one at a time to display their bonnets. As it was her idea, it was Amanda who was expected to take the woman's place.

Giving last-minute instructions to the excited children, she left them and walked towards the stage trying to sort out a few ideas for describing the parade. As the Head finished his welcome to the audience, the door opened and the tall figure of Rhys entered.

Her heart lifted with joy. So Jessica had failed to keep him away. Mixed with happiness at seeing him was a nervousness. How could she give a humorous send-up of a fashion show with him watching her? He was bound to compare her to Jessica, a trained actress. Then she looked at the huddle of children beginning to push their way into the hall. This was their special day, not hers. She must forget her own problems and do her best, for their sakes.

Rhys sidled his way past the closely packed chairs to the front of the stage, where he could get an uninterrupted view of the participants. She smiled a welcome and began.

In gentle mockery of a fashion show, she described the hats and gave the name of each model who would then pirouette for the audience. Rhys took photographs of each child and some of the parents. The youngsters reacted to the mood and began posing for him, much to everyone's amusement.

After everything had been cleared away, Catrin went home declaring she was again the victim of sudden tiredness, and Rhys took Amanda out for a meal. While they waited for coffee, Amanda showed him the photograph of the kingfisher, which unfortunately had come out as little more than a blur of blue and green with only the front of the bird clearly shown.

"When did you take it?" he asked, not displeased with its effect.

"The day I spoke to Jessica. Didn't she tell you?" She waited for his reply, hoping they hadn't met, but guessing from his face that they had.

"She didn't mention it."

"She didn't? I thought she'd have delighted in telling you I was in your garden lying in the mud for hours and ended up looking like part of the bank. The contrast between us was unbelievable!" She tried to make it a joke.

"She came to the hotel I always use, but didn't stay long. I was busy and Jessica hates being ignored."

His reply pleased her enormously.

Nine

Roy knew Mr and Mrs Harris wanted him gone, but with Gillian still supporting him and proclaiming his innocence he felt confident enough to spend his savings on a car. Not a new one like Amanda had chosen, but a second-hand Riley, long-bodied and impressive with its black shiny coach-built body and leather interior, its highly polished chrome and distinctive horn.

"Soon be well known this car will," he told Gillian. "Proves I'm not worried about the police watching me, doesn't it? Stop your Mam worrying about me then, won't it?"

They went for a drive, the three Harrises and Roy and he drove close to the village where Amanda lived, his sharp eyes always on the lookout for a likely place to 'do'. He sensed that Mr Harris had something on his mind and, afraid he was going to be told to go, he decided on a move to placate him. When they returned to the house, he hung up the keys on the draining-board hook and said generously, "Borrow it whenever you want, Mr Harris. It's for us all to enjoy, mind, not just me." His offer didn't work.

"Sorry, son," Mr Harris said, glancing shiftily between Roy and Mrs Harris. "Me and the missus have discussed it and we want you to leave. Not immediate, mind, we'll give you a few days to get somewhere else, but we can't stand the shame of it no more."

Gillian believed Roy was going straight, even though the police seemed to visit more regularly than the postman, and her mother was nervous and anxious for him to be gone. She pleaded in vain.

"Right then. I'll get out by the end of the week." Roy smiled

141

affectionately at Mrs Harris who was almost in tears. "But I can come and see you, can't I? And Gillian isn't forbidden to meet me, is she? I couldn't cope with losing you. You've almost become my family and that's a fact."

"Sorry, Roy," Gillian said later, "I've tried to change their minds."

"Once the police leave me alone they'll feel better about me." Roy put on his most lugubrious expression and hugged a tearful Gillian.

"Why are they hounding you?" she demanded the following morning after yet another visit from the local police. "Don't they understand that with our help you are keeping away from crime? They still come here demanding to know exactly what you were doing at the time of every crime that happens round here. This last one was miles out of town, how do they think you get there for heaven's sake? Your car is too noticeable for you to go anywhere without being spotted."

Roy hadn't told her about the old van he had the use of, belonging to Dave's family, which he used to enable him to travel far away from the places where he was likely to be a suspect. He also had the bicycle Mr Harris had given him. It was a war-time model, dull-coloured, and without chrome to shine and make him visible he could creep along the lanes in safety.

"I think I might go and see my sister, see if she'll take pity on me when I tell her I'm homeless."

"Mam won't throw you out without anywhere to go, you know that!"

"Yes, but Amanda doesn't!" *She doesn't know I'm not really her brother either,* he thought with a secret smile, *and he wasn't about to tell her!*

Amanda and Rhys were eating at a restaurant in Mumbles within sight of the sea, at a place where boats were still lying up waiting for the start of summer. From the window at which they sat, tall masts formed a forest, lit by the yellow street lights. Beyond, the sea glinted metallically and the shore lights in the distance formed a bright circle around Swansea bay.

"How old is Jessica?" she surprised him by asking.

"Don't tell me you're still trying to fit her into your family tree?" he smiled.

"No-o-o, but she hasn't been truthful. She didn't tell me her real name is Sian Talbot."

"It doesn't go with her glamorous image I suppose. If you change your name you hardly tell people the real one, that would defeat the object."

"I suppose the same is true about her age."

"She tells me she's thirty. So there's no way she can fit into your sketchy plan, is there?"

"I suppose not . . ." Amanda sounded doubtful and Rhys frowned at her. "But if she's the daughter of Gwen and and Ryan Talbot," she went on, "her real age is thirty-eight or nine."

"Hardly old enough to be your mother. And your name is Clifford, remember."

"I'm sure she knows something about me. She could help if she wanted to."

"Let's forget Jessica and her mysteries for tonight. What about a walk? It's a lovely clear night."

Dressed in an ancient sheepskin coat of Rhys's which he found in the back of the car, Amanda looked tiny. Rhys laughingly took her hand which had all but disappeared inside the sleeve, and they strolled through almost empty streets, aimlessly wandering and talking about the book Rhys was planning.

"I might want to include your photograph of the kingfisher," he said. "I haven't taken a better one."

"Luck," she said modestly.

"Patience," he corrected.

The following morning was bright and there was a breath of spring sunshine in the air. At ten, Rhys rang and suggested they invite Heather, Haydn and the girls and go on a picnic.

"It's a bit early in the year, isn't it?" Amanda queried.

"Nonsense;" Rhys scorned. "You can always borrow my coat again if you're such a cissy!"

Catrin was enthusiastic and at once began preparing food.

143

At ten o'clock they were on their way, two cars in convoy, the James family leading the way.

They settled in the shelter of the sand dunes on a bay from which deep cliffs rose tall to the moorland above. While Haydn set out the blankets and food, the girls searched the pools, and Amanda saw how afraid for them Heather was. She hovered near, her jaw stiff with tension, her hand ready in case one should falter.

"It's all right, Heather," Amanda said. "Rhys and I will stay near, and watch them every minute. The pools aren't deep. You go and sit with Catrin." Heather went, but with obvious reluctance.

"I wish someone would tell me why it is she's so afraid for them," Amanda said.

"They're good parents," Rhys defended.

"I agree, but Heather is so over-protective, especially towards little Jane. There must be a reason."

"There was some trouble when Jane was born, but it's Heather's story, not mine. She'll probably tell you herself when she knows you better."

"I don't want to pry," Amanda said stiffly. "But I am her teacher and if there are difficulties, I can help, if I know what they are."

"You have helped, enormously."

She looked at him, his hand ready to support as the girls dared to jump across a small pool. He was fond of them, that was clear.

Jane soon became bored with the pools and tucked her tiny hand into Amanda's.

"Time to eat I think," Amanda said. The two girls shouted agreement; Helen first, echoed by Jane, who was inclined to follow her sister's lead.

At three o'clock they gathered up their scattered belongings and returned to the cars. The day had been a successful one but Amanda guessed that Catrin would be glad to get home.

"If you aren't doing anything today, will you help with some typing?" Rhys asked. Amanda agreed, guessing it was work on his book. He stopped at his bungalow and ran in to collect some papers. Sitting in the car, Amanda saw the door opened for him, a swish of a red skirt briefly seen before the door closed behind him. Jessica was in residence again.

She took the papers in silence, hoping for a comment, but there was none.

Knowing the actress was with Rhys, Amanda made a greater display of pleasure at seeing Philip later that evening. She made him coffee, cut him some cake and burst into a lively description of their day out, but without mentioning Rhys's part in it.

"What are you doing?" he asked, glancing at the pages of neatly typed manuscript. "More homework?"

"No, some work for Rhys. But I've finished for today." She put it firmly aside.

"How are Helen and Jane?" Philip asked. "I understand Jane is a bit slow at school?"

"Not at all! She's slow to open out but there's definitely nothing wrong with her mind. I doubt if she'll ever be an extrovert, she only shouts or does anything lively when Helen gives a lead, but she isn't unhappy, or slow."

"She went on stage during the Easter Bonnet Parade," Catrin added. "She couldn't have managed that a few months ago."

"If only Heather wasn't so anxious," Amanda sighed. "I still think much of the trouble is with Heather and not Jane."

"Heather rejected the child at first," Philip said quietly.

"Heather? I can't believe it. She's devoted to the girls."

"It wasn't her fault," Philip went on. "You mustn't blame her. She had – marital worries."

Amanda waited for more but Philip stood up and walked to the window. There was a sadness about the droop of his shoulders.

"You can trust Amanda with the story, Philip, dear," Catrin said.

Philip turned to look at her and said quietly, "Heather was my wife."

Philip's words left behind a hushed silence. Disbelief made Amanda stare at Catrin, who nodded.

"Helen and Jane are your daughters?"

"Yes."

"And Heather rejected Jane?" Amanda couldn't take in what she was being told. "But why? What happened to make her not want her child?"

"The marriage had been difficult for some time." Philip said, returning to his chair. "Heather couldn't cope with my constant absences and irregular hours. Stuck in the house all hours, she felt the lack of fun in her life."

"Philip was a newspaperman then," Catrin explained. "Heather loved him but couldn't take the way he lived."

"Didn't she know about it before you were married?" Amanda asked.

"She knew, but the reality was harder to take than she'd imagined. Love doesn't conquer all."

"And Jane?" she coaxed.

"Poor little Jane came at the wrong time. Heather became depressed. She played records all day and half the night, hardly bothering with the girls. I gave up my job to see if it would help, but it was too late. We'd lost what we'd once had, and we decided it was best all round if we separated."

"I'm so sorry."

"It's worked out all right. For Heather at least. She and Haydn are much better suited. He works at home," he added with a harsh laugh, "so she doesn't have to spend much time on her own." There was bitterness in his voice and Amanda realised that although he appeared to be a contented man, driving his buses and enjoying his garden, he had bitter regrets over the loss of his family and his career.

It was much later that she thought about Rhys's dislike of Philip. Was his reason the distress caused to Helen and Jane?

"He saw the girls suffering and he can't forgive Philip," Catrin explained. "Haydn has always loved Heather; they were on the verge of marrying when Philip came on the scene. It was Haydn who came back and helped pick up the pieces when she and Philip parted. They came here, were accepted as a family and very few know the real story. They aren't married you see, dear."

146

"It's odd that Rhys is so against Philip though. He seems such a fair-minded man."

"Haydn is Rhys's friend. I doubt he's ever thought of there being another side."

Amanda woke very early the following morning. Being Sunday she had not set her alarm and the shrill demanding call of the phone startled her.

"Would you like to come and see some bats?" Rhys's disembodied voice asked. Still confused by the sudden awakening, Amanda said she'd love to.

"When?" she asked, looking at her clock in disbelief.

"Now. Can you be ready in ten minutes?"

"With or without sandwiches?"

"With of course. Why d'you think I'm inviting you?"

"Then you'd better make it fifteen minutes!"

Catrin was awake, having heard the phone. Amanda took her a cup of tea and explained the reason for the call.

Since moving in, Amanda had always cooked at weekends, and she asked, "Can you manage a snack at lunchtime? I've no idea how long I'll be. But I'll be back to cook this evening."

"Invite Rhys," Catrin suggested.

It was then Amanda remembered Jessica. "Perhaps he has other plans," she said, thinking of the glimpse of red skirt as Jessica opened the door to Rhys.

"Oh, his visitor didn't stay, dear," Catrin said brightly.

"How did you know I was thinking of Jessica?"

"I saw her too. But unlike you, I asked Rhys to explain. She'd been walking and had called to beg a lift home."

Amanda was not convinced.

Rhys arrived before she had packed the food and Catrin helped her fill two flasks.

"Knowing Rhys as I do, it's better to have too much than hope to be anywhere near a café." she said ominously.

It was still only four a.m. when they were on their way, driving through sleeping towns before leaving civilisation behind them and climbing into the hills of the Brecon range, then on and up, into the harsher mountains.

Rhys obviously knew the area well. He left the car near a small waterfall which flowed steadily out of the rock beside the narrow road. He fitted the rucksack of food and equipment on his back and added a couple of torches and a rope. Amanda too was draped in camera equipment, which, on Rhys's instructions, she fixed on her shoulders and across her body, leaving both hands free for climbing.

Their route took them over an innocent-looking river bed. A thin trickle of water flowed through the centre but debris on the banks showed how wide it could be after heavy rain.

The mountains seemed a long way away, and she guessed that the visit to the bat cave entailed walking several miles. Amanda wondered just how far she would have travelled before she saw Catrin again. Rhys's attitude to distance was unpredictable.

"I left some stuff here last time I came," Rhys told her as they puffed their way up a steep slope covered in places with treacherous scree. "There's so much needed that one journey isn't enough."

"Is that safe?"

"It's hardly a spot to attract passers-by."

"That I can believe!" Amanda said with feeling as they dropped into a valley to be faced with yet another climb.

The cave looked little more than a crevice and could easily have been overlooked, but once inside they had ample room to stand.

"There aren't any bats here, it isn't high enough," Amanda complained. "Where would they sleep?"

Rhys pointed to a low entrance to a second chamber. "We're going through there."

Leaving their baggage in the outer chamber they slid through to a much larger cavern beyond. The powerful torch showed a high ceiling and revealed dozens of the sleeping creatures they had come to see. While Amanda held a torch, Rhys climbed, with another light fixed to his hat.

"I've been helping a friend ring them for research purposes," he explained.

Amanda watched in facination as he lifted the tiny creatures off their perches, attached an identifying ring and hung them up again like tiny overcoats on pegs.

When they returned to the outside, the air was warm after the chill of the cave. Amanda unpacked their breakfast while Rhys did some filming and they ate, savouring the beauty of the slowly wakening scene before them.

Hill rose beyond hill, purple blue and grey and, in the valley, every green imaginable. Here and there an outcrop of grey stone, some sliding downwards like a petrified waterfall, others strong and smooth, defying the changes of centuries.

Trees grew out of rocky areas where green lichens showed bright, revealing the presence of water. Mist hazed the far distance and it was gradually being dispersed by the sun's welcome rays. Amanda thought she had never seen anything so beautiful.

She became aware of Rhys's attention and turned to see him staring at her, a smile on his face that made her heart lurch with joy.

"Beautiful, isn't it?" she said, her breath tight in her throat.

"Beautiful," he said, leaning forward and kissing her. "Very beautiful and desirable." He opened his arms and she moved into their welcome, wanting to stay there for ever. She knew she loved him and could be happy if he would only trust her with his love. But wrapped in the circle of his embrace, her heart knew no peace. Visions of Jessica taunted her. Warning words invaded her mind, reminding her of his reluctance to accept commitment. As she kissed him and felt his desire for her in the strength of his arms, a tear fell and soured the magic of the moment.

It was Rhys's plan to film the bats as they flew from the cave one evening to hunt for food. He set up some cameras ready, then they left the cave.

He walked ahead of her down the scree, showing her how to run across it, knees high, and she followed, obeying his shouted instructions.

It was still early and Rhys didn't head for home. Instead he took the car over some precarious roads, where the drop at the side made Amanda feel giddy.

"I don't think I'd like to drive up here at night," she said, looking at the toy-town sheep below them.

"It's unnerving at first but I'm used to it. I love the mountains and the hills. I respect them though," he added. "They don't tolerate fools."

"Will you have dinner with us?" Amanda asked when they were on their way home. "Catrin asked me to invite you."

"There's something I must do this afternoon, but if you don't mind me coming at the last moment, I'd love to."

He left her at the gate but didn't go towards home. Amanda was curious but tried to forget that he was going in the direction of Jessica's house.

When she opened the gate she heard voices from the garden. She expected to see Catrin and Philip. What she did not expect was to see Catrin up a tree!

"Catrin!" she called. "What are you doing up there?"

"Hello, dear. I didn't expect you back so soon. Where's Rhys?"

"He'll be here later. Now what is going on?"

"My fault I suppose," Philip came through the gap in the hedge. "I told her I'd paint her apple trees but I forgot, so she started without me."

"Look, dear." Catrin showed a jar of noisome fluid to Amanda who curled her nose in disgust. "I don't know what it does but Philip says its essential."

"Come down, Catrin, I'll attend to this," Philip said, taking the brush and jar. "I'll have it finished before you've set the table for tea," he said pointedly. "All right?"

Amanda felt grubby and Catrin hardly looked immaculate so they both went to tidy up before preparing tea for them all. Over the simple meal Amanda told them about her fascinating morning. Catrin was interested but Philip seemed subdued.

When Catrin left them, he said, "I bitterly regret giving up the work I did, you know. Specially when I see someone as animated as you, doing such interesting things. And Rhys following his career with such enjoyment. I had all that but I threw it away, for nothing. The moment will pass, it usually does, but at present I feel jaded, stale, unfulfilled."

"It was a good morning," Amanda said. "but I confess it was Rhys's company that made it so for me."

"You're fond of him."

"I know what you're going to say. He isn't the type to settle down and he wouldn't give up a promising career for love."

"I hope he wouldn't! It would be a terrible mistake."

"He might trust someone to accept his erratic life. Some marriages cope successfully," she insisted.

"Most do not. Divorce is increasing, and don't get the idea that divorce is an easy way out. One or the other will suffer. Men usually have to give up their children. Women become bitter in their demands for financial assistance. It's a mess. Best you keep out of it."

Amanda was aware of a growing pity for Philip, but she knew she could say nothing to help him. She couldn't criticise Heather, who was her friend. She took his hand and pressed it.

"You're still young enough to start again. Pick up the threads and build up your reputation again."

"No chance I'm afraid. It's a young man's game. I'm too late to try and get a job."

"You were good once," she coaxed, "so what about freelancing? Begin gradually, you won't have lost your skill."

"I don't think I want it badly enough. If I had someone to succeed for, someone willing to take a chance with me, it would be different."

Again Amanda had no answer. She was committed to Rhys whether he wanted her or not. She could not give Philip the hope she would change. She knew that whatever the future held for her, her love for Rhys was a permanent part of it.

When the knock at the door came, one lunchtime, Amanda ran to answer it, presuming it was Rhys with his arms full. Standing on the doorstep, smiling his charming smile and looking well pleased with himself, was Roy.

"Hello there, Mand. Thought I'd better not wait no longer for an invite; like. So, here I am. And is this the house we were left by some old auntie then?"

"Who is it, Amanda?" Catrin called. After the initial delight at seeing him, the realisation that he was here and she had to go back to school made Amanda want to close the door and reply, "No one". But Roy's foot was already on the hall mat and then he was walking through as if he knew the place and shaking hands with Catrin and admiring the furnishings as if he were a regular and important guest.

"Real brammer of a place this is, Mand. There's bucked you must be livin' in a place like this."

"Catrin, this is my brother, Roy. Roy, meet Mrs Catrin Falconbridge."

"So, we meet again," Catrin whispered to a startled Roy.

Alarmed that she should remember him, Roy stared at her, made speechless by the shock. He turned to his sister, wondering what would happen next. Amanda made the introductions, which Catrin coolly accepted as though they were complete strangers.

There was no time to sort anything out, as Amanda had to return to school. She tried to make him leave, suggesting he came back at the weekend when there was more time but he out-manoeuvred her with ease, saying he would be, "Happy to spend a couple of hours chattin' to this lovely lady, while I wait for you to finish sorting out the kids."

"Sorry, Roy, but I'll have to ask you to come back later," Catrin apologised. "I also have to go out, you see. If I'd known you were coming – but it's too late now for me to change my afternoon plans."

Unperturbed, Roy smiled at her, his warm smile already softening Catrin's heart. He really is a charmer, Amanda thought, watching him almost flirting with Catrin.

"There's a pity. Still if it's only for a couple of hours, I'll drive around a bit and come back, is it, Mand?"

She had no choice but to agree.

Outside he pointed to the Riley and told her proudly it was his. "Well known that car is, Mand, so there's no chance of me misbe'avin', is there? Not with a vehicle everyone notices."

A small boy was sidling around it, his fingers making marks on the polished metal and Roy glared at him and shouted, "Get away from there. Cheeky article! Come back again and I'll give you a real belter, mind!"

Laughing in spite of herself, Amanda waved goodbye, refusing a lift back to school, and hurried on her way. Whatever sort of villain he was, her brother was irresistibly likeable. Catrin had fallen under his spell within minutes. She was blissfully unaware that Catrin and her brother had met before, that Catrin had threatened Roy with a gun while he was attempting to rob her.

When she returned home after school she saw with irritation that her car had been moved down the road and Roy's stood close to the gate. Inside, Catrin had a table set for tea and Roy was ensconced in Catrin's favourite armchair.

"Come on, Mand, pitch in. We're starved, waiting for you to dawdle home."

"Thank you," she said sarcastically. With a lifted eyebrow she glanced at Catrin, expecting disapproval, but she was chuckling.

"Your brother is looking for a place to live, dear," Catrin told her, "and I've made a few telephone calls and found him a room with a family near the Cwm Gwyn Arms."

At once Amanda panicked. "I don't think that's a good idea, Roy," she began.

Open-faced, innocence pouring out of his clear blue eyes, Roy asked, "Why?"

She could hardly tell him she didn't trust him not to steal from her friends, or that she wanted to live a life of her own without being caught up in his.

"Don't worry," he said, with a cheeky glance at Catrin. "Going straight I am. And Catrin knows all about my sordid past."

"I, better than most," was Catrin's enigmatic rejoiner.

To Amanda's relief, Roy didn't visit Firethorn Cottage very often in the weeks that followed. He found a few casual jobs, gardening mainly, and seemed to be content to share the village but not interfere in her life. The only unpleasant surprise she had was one morning when she saw him bringing Jane James to school.

"What's happened? Where's Heather, and Helen?" she asked anxiously.

"Helen's got measles and with Haydn already off somewhere for the day, and Heather having to wait for the doctor, I insisted on helping by bringing Jane to school. She's already had it, see."

"And Heather agreed?" Amanda asked weakly.

"Friends we are and Jane is safe as 'ouses with me, aren't you, chicken?"

During the next few weeks, Rhys came with more typing but he said nothing about the arrival in the village of her brother, after an initial comment. From his conversations, Amanda knew he had obviously revisited the cave, but she had not been invited. One day after he had shared her and Catrin's evening meal, he stood up and told them, "I'm sorry but I have to eat and run. I want to get to the cave before it's too dark to see my way there."

"You're going to spend the night there?"

"It's the only way to be ready for when they fly out and in."

With a packet of sandwiches and a couple of flasks, Rhys set off as soon as the meal was finished. Amanda and Catrin shivered at the thought of the lonely cave to which he was heading but, discomfort and all, Amanda would willingly have joined him.

Out for a walk the following day, Amanda saw Heather and Haydn out with Jane. Roy was with them. Jane was holding his hand and was proudly carrying her reading book in the other. Heather was delighted with her daughter's progress but Amanda hoped she wouldn't pressure the child to catch up with some of the others.

"Don't forget to bring it back on Monday," she warned and Jane nodded importantly.

To Amanda's relief there were no burglaries reported. But, she told herself, Roy wouldn't be stupid enough to steal on his own doorstep. With trepidation she scanned the papers for reports of robberies in other places within a radius of ten miles, which was how far she thought he could travel on that bicycle he had brought with him.

Passing the bungalow one morning she heard an expletive and looked down to see Rhys kicking his car tyres angrily.

"Puncture?" she asked with a grin. "Kicking is one way of dealing with it, I suppose, but borrowing my car might be quicker!" She took her keys from her bag and threw them down to him.

"I have to be in Cardiff by eleven," he explained. "I won't be back until late though, are you sure you don't mind?"

"So long as you promise not to kick it!"

He thanked her and said, "I'll treat it like a baby."

So it was with deep shock that he felt the unbelievably loud scraping on the side of the car. He had been delayed, it was almost two a.m. as he approached the village and he was tired. He wasn't going fast, but he took a corner rather carelessly and didn't see the bicycle until he heard the scraping sound of it running along the side of Amanda's car. Her new car, he reminded himself in those first seconds.

He got out thinking he had bumped against the corner of a low wall but to his horror saw he had hit a cyclist. He ran at once to where a man was slowly getting up. Thank God he wasn't hurt. The man turned to face him and he saw he was wearing a balaclava which had been added to, so that the only visible portion of the man's face was his eyes and nose.

"Are you all right?" he asked.

The man grunted and hurried off.

"Shouldn't you get to a hospital to be checked over?"

Another grunt before the man heaved up his bicycle and, running with it, disappeared into the night.

With a torch, Rhys examined the car. The paint was badly scratched and there was a dent in the door. One of the headlights seemed out of line and, shaking with shock and with embarrassment at the thought of explaining the damage to Amanda's car, her new car, he drove the rest of the way home.

He didn't leave the car outside Firethorn but parked it in his drive. He would have to go straight to the garage in the morning and arrange for the damage to be put right.

Roy walked Jane to school the following morning and when she was safely inside, he waved to Amanda through the classroom window and set off for his first job of the day, digging out a pond for a cottage near the shops. He saw Rhys as he was coming out of his drive in Amanda's car and he waved. Then he saw the damage and gasped.

"What happened? Is Amanda hurt?"

Rolling down the window, Rhys assured him his sister was safe. "My fault and she doesn't know yet," Rhys admitted. "I misjudged a corner and hit someone on a bicycle. He ran off so I presume he was unhurt. It gave me a bit of a fright though and I'm very upset about doing this to Amanda's car."

"So long as no one's been harmed," Roy said.

Suspiciously, Rhys watched as the man walked away. Roy had a bicycle and was given to wandering about at night. He didn't really believe he had given up his criminal ways, even though the police hadn't been able to prove anything. That bicycle of his could get him quite a distance during the hours of darkness.

He studied Roy carefully but saw no suspicion of a limp.

That afternoon Rhys was waiting for Amanda outside school and he confessed to damaging her car. Heather and Jane were there, Haydn being home with Helen and her measles. After anger and criticism, and slow forgiveness, Amanda turned to walk home, leaving a very contrite Rhys to hurry off and call at the garage to check on the fate of the car.

As Amanda stood exchanging a last few words with Heather and Jane, she saw the smile fade from Heather's face. Turning, she saw the reason. Philip was walking towards them, old Mel Griffiths' dog at his heels. Jane went at once to talk to the dog but Heather pulled them roughly away, her eyes steely. Jane was obviously not allowed to know her father.

"I must be a little off colour," Philip said later. "I don't usually feel the hurt so badly any more. I know it isn't the girls' fault, they don't know who I am. I stayed right away from them until a few months ago when I moved here. But it's cruel to see your own children and have no part in their upbringing."

"But you gave them up, surely?" Amanda said coldly. "You had the choice?"

"No, I didn't. Heather was so ill, playing her damned records all day, refusing to talk except through a solicitor. She wanted me out of their lives completely and, instead of maintaining them financially, I was asked to go away and give up all rights of access. She had rejected little Jane and I had taken her, but then I was told Jane's place was with her mother, so back she went. Helen was not quite one year old. I might not have been much of a husband, but I loved them enough to do what I was told was best for them."

Amanda listened to his story. Had Rhys been wrong when he told her Philip had walked away and left his family without a thought? Was Heather's story the truth, or Philip's?

Rhys was standing at his gate and Philip gave her a departing wave and headed away from the bungalow, a lonely figure, walking someone else's dog. No wonder he spends so much time with Catrin, she thought sadly.

She ignored the look of disapproval on Rhys's face, avoided further mention of the accident to her car and asked instead about his most recent filming of the bats.

"I don't know yet, Haydn hasn't finished processing the film. I might have to try again later."

"Did you bring the equipment back?"

"No, and now I wish I had. I'll have to make another trip up there even if this film is satisfactory."

"Not in my car," she couldn't help saying with a grim expression. "Will your cameras and stuff be safe up there?"

"As long as there aren't any landslides, volcanoes or earthquakes it should be safe enough." He stepped out of his gate and asked, "D'you think I could invite myself for tea? Or am I firmly in the doghouse?"

"Catrin loves to see you. You know she'd be pleased."

"But I must start thinking of the cottage as yours," he reminded her. "It's the end of April, so in six months' time Aunt Catrin will have to find herself a new home."

"Has she discussed her plans?"

"She's always telling me she's leaving it to fate!"

"What about the house next door? Philip has only rented it for a year, hasn't he?"

"I don't know and I won't ask."

"Rhys, why do you hate Philip? You must admit he's good to Catrin. He's always fixing something or other. She only has to mention wanting something done and he's there to attend to it."

"Philip is kind for only as long as he wants to be. You can't rely on him. He should have stayed in Cardiff and never have come here." Anger quickened his pace.

"Surely you can sympathise with him wanting to see his children?"

"So you know about that."

"Yes, I know, and I understand how he must feel, seeing Helen and Jane and not being allowed to take part in their lives, or even talk to them."

"You've only heard his version."

"He does have one!"

"Did he tell you he tried to persuade Heather to have an abortion when Jane was expected? That's how much he loves his children."

"The marriage was already in difficulties, wasn't it? Heather was unable to cope with Philip's job or the prospect of caring for another child."

"When the argument is as strong as between Philip and Heather I suppose people believe the story they hear first."

"I don't think that!" Amanda retorted. "I always try to listen without preconceived ideas! Unlike some," she added with asperity.

"Yet you believe Philip?"

"If I wanted to hear the other side of the story I wouldn't ask you. You've already made up your mind so your attitude would be misleading."

"It's all very well for you to come here and decide in the first five minutes who's right and who's wrong! But I was there. I saw the way Haydn coped with Heather and saw Philip walking about without a care. He gave up his job so he couldn't pay for the keep."

"That's nonsense. He gave it up with great reluctance, to try and save his marriage, and much good it did him."

"I was there. He took any casual job, just enough to feed himself."

"That doesn't sound like Philip. It's no good, Rhys, I can't see him as the villain in all this."

"One day you might hear the story from Heather and Haydn, perhaps they will make you change your mind."

Amanda looked at Rhys's face and wondered if what he said were true. Remembering Philip's sadness when he spoke about the end of his marriage made it impossible to believe.

"He's the loser now," she said quietly. "He gave up a job he loved to save a marriage that failed anyway. How much more should he suffer because Heather is unable to take the job along with the man? A man's job is a part of him, take it away and he isn't the same person. Heather tried to do that and the result was misery all round."

"What are you doing talking to me?" Rhys said angrily. "You should be running after Philip and consoling him!" He turned swiftly and hurried back to his bungalow. Shocked at the suddenness of the quarrel, Amanda was shaking when she entered the kitchen.

Catrin saw at once something was wrong. "Are you all right, dear?" she asked, handing her the ever-ready cup of tea. "You look a bit shocked."

"Rhys and I had a terrible argument," she said, sinking into a chair. "About Philip."

"Oh, I see. I'm afraid Rhys will never think anything but the worst of the poor man. Haydn is his friend and he saw the mess Heather was in at that time and he can't accept there was another side."

"But you can?"

"They were both to blame and yet neither was guilty. They

were different people who couldn't fulfil the other's needs. Rhys looks upon Philip as cruel and stubborn, whereas I look upon Heather as a weak woman who couldn't cope." She patted Amanda affectionately. "Like I say about Rhys, it would take an angel to marry him and accept his wanderings. Philip thought Heather could, but he was dreadfully wrong."

Amanda wondered if the tension in them both after the accident to the car had made their quarrel more severe, or whether it was a symptom of the fact they were psychologically unsuited. She wondered when they would meet again and how they would react after such a violent disagreement.

In fact, they met in the company of Heather and Haydn.

Amanda had gone to collect some items for the school jumble sale which was to take place the following term.

"If you can take it now," Heather said, "it would be a great help. I want to start spring-cleaning and there'd be less to move."

"Spring-cleaning, she calls it," Haydn teased. "I'm asked to move the furniture and decorate the rooms, she puts up fresh summer curtains and that's her cleaning done!"

Amanda listened to their light banter and knew they were happy. Something good came out of the mess of Heather's marriage to Philip. Why was Rhys still so unforgiving?

They were having a cup of tea, with biscuits handed around by Jane, when there was a knock at the door. Haydn went to answer it and returned with Rhys.

Amanda looked at him, her heart racing at the sight of him. Why had things gone so terribly wrong? She waited anxiously to see how he would greet her. The two girls ran to him and he ignored her to talk to them. Moments dragged as she waited for him to speak to her. Heather handed him a cup of tea and everything seemed to be in slow motion. But at last he turned his head towards her and smiled. Her spirits lifted but when he spoke it was to the children.

"Are you trying to keep in teacher's good books by inviting her to tea?" he asked.

160

"I'll show you teacher's good book," Jane said seriously. She took out her school book and proudly read to him.

Amanda stood to leave. She hoped Rhys would follow but he did not. She left him still talking to Helen and Jane and it was Haydn who helped her fill her car with the boxes of jumble.

Ten

R oy was soon a highly popular citizen of Tri-nant village. He endeared himself to the elderly by working on the gardens of those less able to pay, for nothing more than a cup of tea and a slice of cake. A few of the more wealthy paid him extra in appreciation of his kindness.

When he lost his bicycle, someone found him a replacement. He couldn't explain that he had thrown it into a quarry some twenty miles away, having been involved in a accident while travelling home from a break-in! He said it had been stolen.

"The biter bit, eh, Mand?" he said cheerfully as he showed her the rather neglected Raleigh Sports he'd been given.

The bicycle needed attention and with brazen nerve Roy asked Rhys to give him and the bicycle a lift to the Harris house so he and Mr Harris could do the repairs.

Seeing a scar on Roy's arm, Rhys said, "No ill effects from your knock with the car, apart from that graze?" Rhys smiled as they put the bicycle in the back of the Landrover.

"Knock with a car? I never had no knock. Pity I didn't, I'd have been able to demand a new bike. No, pinched it was, and from the front garden under my bedroom window. Now there's a nerve some have got, eh, Rhys?"

Rhys stared at him hard, wanting him to know how certain he felt that Roy was the person he had hit that dark night a few weeks previously. Roy whistled insouciantly, apparently without a care.

Mr Harris was pleased to see him and called for his wife as Roy stepped out of Rhys's car and struggled with the bike. He began at once to sort out the tools they would need, humming cheerfully and chattering about how they would set about bringing it back to a good condition.

"We've missed you, boy," he said, as he tugged to remove the back wheel. "A bit dull it is round here without your ol' nonsense."

Gillian was working, but when he and Mr Harris had spent a few hours in the shed, stripping down the bicycle, he went to meet her.

She was working in a shop, selling men's clothing and when she stepped outside, her greeting was more ecstatic than her father's had been, throwing her arms around him, her face held up to his for his kisses. They went back to the house where a meal had been prepared in his honour and then to the pictures.

They had met from time to time, making love in the back of the car and once at night on a distant beach under a starry sky, but Gillian had despaired of them ever returning to the close, loving relationship they had enjoyed while he had been her mother's lodger.

"Won't be long before we're really together," he assured her as they finally parted. "Savings coming on a treat. But I got to go now. I was hoping to ride back on the bike but your Dad has stripped it so it looks like a Meccano set! There's more parts to that bike now than even the inventor would believe. I'll have to get the last bus and come back for it next week."

"Unless we can persuade Mam to let you stay the night," she said. "It's very late for you to be out, knowing how tempted you'd be. I think it'll be for your own good, for you to stay, don't you?"

"Very much for my own good," he grinned, then, arm in arm, they went to ask her mother.

Imperceptibly, a veneer of disapproval settled around Amanda as people wondered why she had not offered a home to her brother before he came to the village, and even now saw fit not to invite him to the cottage for more than the occasional cup of tea. In vain she explained that the cottage was not yet hers, that, as a lodger, she was not in the position to invite whom she wished to come for meals. Overhearing this and misunderstanding her reasons, Catrin reassured her.

"I enjoy Roy's company, Amanda, dear. If you want to ask him here for a Sunday dinner you can, you know. You don't have to ask each time."

But Amanda shook her head. He was her brother and she loved him but didn't trust him not to be summing up the houses he would rob. He probably wouldn't disappear after getting what he could from those who trusted him, no, he would face it out and deny any complicity. Dave was still around and the possibility was that, between the two of them, Roy and he could make sure of an alibi which, together with an attractive face and an honest expression, would clear Roy completely.

"What about asking him for Sunday for our celebration lunch, dear?" Catrin suggested and Amanda agreed; it would have seemed churlish to refuse.

"I still wonder if he was the one who broke into those houses some months ago," she admitted to Philip and Catrin one day.

It was July 1954 and they were planning a meal in celebration of the end of rationing. At last, almost nine years after war had ended, the beige and green books were being burned in the streets, or stored away as unnecessary souvenirs of a time most would never forget.

Rhys came less often to the cottage, now. The typing he had been bringing for Amanda was apparently done. Jessica Maybury was often seen around the village and Amanda presumed she was staying with Rhys, although she didn't ask. She would rather not have her suspicions confirmed. The idea of them together was a pain which increased every time their names were mentioned.

"I haven't seen Rhys for a while, is he away again?" Philip asked.

"No, but I think he's busy working on his book, and content at home. While Jessica's there he doesn't need his aunt's company as much as usual." She spoke lightly but Philip was not fooled.

"Jessica isn't living there if that's what you're thinking.

And," he added, "don't think her constant presence in Tri-nant is Rhys's doing. She spends her time asking about you."

"About me? Why should she be interested in somone she doesn't know?"

"Strange, isn't it?" There was something in Philip's voice that made Amanda stare at him, but he didn't explain.

"Does she know something about my family? Perhaps some scandal, and she's afraid of being involved if I find out?"

"Perhaps. Although with someone like Jessica, I doubt we'll ever get any straight answers."

They were in the garden behind the cottage and Catrin was busy cooking dinner, to which Philip had been invited.

Catrin had made a sponge pudding with butter, to which she had added fresh fruits and would serve with a jugful of thick cream. From the oven a tantalising smell of roasting lamb issued forth, and fresh mint chopped ready for the sauce was adding to the promise of a delicious meal. All the vegetables were from the garden, tended by Philip, and the first course was melon sprinkled with ginger and decorated with slices of orange and a few grapes. Although the real celebration would be on the Sunday, with Rhys and Roy invited, this too was a fitting tribute to the final end of austerity.

Since the day when he had spoken of his marriage to Heather and its devastating end, Philip had spent a lot of time with Amanda. With the unhappy situation between herself and Rhys unresolved, Amanda was glad of his company. She watched as he finished tidying the flower bed and collected the last handfuls of weeds, and she waved to him as he slipped through the hedge, to return as a dinner guest an hour later. She put away the tools and stood for a while in the quiet garden, thinking of the rapidly approaching day when all this would be her own.

How would she feel with both Catrin and Philip gone? They had become an important part of her life and the resulting loneliness was a fear. What if someone unfriendly moved in next door? Then living alone might not be as pleasant as she imagined.

Not for the first time, she wondered if the solution was to

invite Catrin to stay. Somehow she knew that was not what Catrin had in mind, although she couldn't see any other way 'fate' might intervene. There was still time to work something out, she decided, as she went indoors. But not the solution she dreamed of, with Rhys sharing her life.

When she went into the dining room she saw the table was set for four.

"Who else is coming?" she asked Catrin.

"Just us four, dear."

Amanda's heart sank. Rhys was invited for Sunday. Surely Catrin hadn't also invited him today, expecting him to eat and be sociable with Philip?

"Yes, dear. I did. I thought it was time they were grown up and faced each other. You never know, they might even agree on something!"

"That you're supplying an excellent meal, maybe! I can't see them seeing eye to eye on anything else!" Amanda groaned.

She dressed with care, choosing a summery green suit which flattered her bronzed skin and emphasised her blue eyes. Confidence was badly needed tonight if she were to avoid another quarrel. She determined to stay out of it and allow the men to find common ground. Surely they would, if only out of respect for Catrin?

Philip was first to arrive, wearing casual slacks and an open-necked shirt. At Catrin's insistence, Amanda sat with him while she attended to the meal. She heard Rhys before she saw him. Her nerves were jangled and the pulse-beat in her neck increased alarmingly although she tried to stay calm.

He had come through the back door and had spoken briefly to Catrin. Entering the room, he stopped on seeing Philip. The two men looked at each other, both waiting for the other's reaction. Rhys glanced at Amanda, suspicion in his eyes. She pleaded silently for him to stay, not to walk away.

"Hello, Rhys," she said after a long pause. "I'm glad you could come. Catrin has gone to such a lot of trouble." There was a warning in her voice. He mustn't leave. She gripped her chair tightly as he hesitated, then to her relief he removed his coat and sat down. The urge to run into the kitchen, away from the tension of the meeting, almost won over her determination to stay. She offered drinks and the men visibly relaxed.

Catrin called to say the meal was ready and once the four of them sat down, things improved. Catrin ignored the possibility that the men wouldn't speak and soon involved them in conversation. If she doesn't solve the problem she's at least achieved a temporary lull in the fighting, Amanda thought admiringly.

Philip mentioned that as the one-year lease on his cottage was almost up he would soon have to search for accommodation.

"Like me," Catrin said brightly.

"Catrin, you know I'll—" Amanda began.

"Don't say it," her friend interrupted. "I know you'd offer me a place with you, but it wouldn't be fair. One day you might want to sell, or invite someone else to share with you. And there's Roy to be considered. No. I want you to feel free to plan your life and accept changes as they occur."

"But what will you do?" Rhys asked.

"Too early to say, but things are working out."

"What things?" Rhys wanted to know but, as usual, Catrin wouldn't say.

When Catrin and Amanda went to prepare coffee, Catrin laughed like the conspirator she was. "D'you think it's working?" she whispered.

"At least they're talking to each other," Amanda smiled. "Why are you doing this? Does it matter if they don't agree?"

"It would be nicer for me if they did."

"Catrin?" Amanda looked at her with a suspicious frown. "What are you up to?"

"Me, dear? Nothing. Nothing at all." But she gave one of her saucy winks.

Philip left early but Rhys stayed on. He asked Amanda if she would type some more pages for him. "There are a few changes the editor recommends and I'd like them sent off without too much delay."

"Of course," she said, thankful he felt able to ask.

"Can you come and fetch them tonight?"

"If you wait while I help Catrin with the dishes."

"Amanda, dear. I told you this was a dinner party and no hostess expects her guests to help with the dishes!"

"But I live here," Amanda laughed.

"Tonight you're my guest. Now go on, the pair of you."

Lights were showing when they reached the bungalow and Amanda stepped back when Rhys put his key in the lock. What if Jessica were there? She steeled herself as the door opened but her fears were groundless. Yet she stood in the hall, unsure of how she was expected to behave.

"Are you in a hurry?" Rhys asked when he returned with some untidily scribbled pages. "We could go through what I've done so far if you've time?"

"I'm in no hurry." She took off the light coat she wore and went through to the lounge. As she began to sit, Rhys pulled her towards him.

"Was this evening arranged to introduce me to the idea of you and Philip announcing your engagement?"

She was so surprised by his question she took a moment before saying, "Of course not!" Then some devil made her add, "What if it was? It's no business of yours!"

"I'd hate you to get hurt."

"There's no reason to suppose I would. Philip has a lot to offer."

"Ask Heather about their marriage!"

"Ask Philip about their marriage!" she retorted. "He has a story too!"

"Talking about stories, did he tell you he wrote a story about her uncle, bringing out accusations of fraud and deceit? Did he tell you that the uncle killed himself? Heather was very fond of the man, he was almost like a father to her. Yet given a choice between his wife's peace of mind and a damned good story, he chose the story!"

"I'd better go."

"Yes, you better had."

As she opened the door he looked at her, his brown eyes serious. "If only things had been different."

"How different?" she demanded.

"I can't tell you that."

"It must run in the family," she said in exasperation. "You and Catrin are both fond of mysteries and half-said trifles." But she knew he was thinking of his work, that barrier to loving her, erected by himself with the help of Heather and Philip.

Walking past Philip's door a few days later, Amanda heard typing and wondered if it meant Philip had taken her advice and was starting to work again. If he was good, and the job he had previously held suggested he was, then he should be able to start again on a journalistic career.

She asked Catrin about the story he had written that Rhys had mentioned with such bitterness.

"Rhys can hardly blame Philip for doing the job he was paid for," Catrin protested. "It was a court case and every newspaper followed it. If Philip hadn't written it someone else would. It's unfair of Rhys to hold that against him, dear." She sighed and went on, "But then, Rhys and Philip have never tried to understand each other. They haven't talked through their differences, they seem to prefer prolonging them."

The clatter of Philip's typewriter filled the air every time she passed his house. She also had been busily typing, completing the work Rhys had given her. She was dismayed to see the same pages over and over again as he scribbled out and added new thoughts as they occurred to him. "He'll never finish at this rate!" she complained to Catrin.

She was on her way to the bungalow one day to leave the newly-typed pages when, after a few yards, Philip called, and caught up with her.

"I'm off to the pub, d'you fancy coming?"

"I'm putting these through Rhys's door but if you can wait, I'll be glad to."

At the gate of her destination they stopped, both seeing Jessica at the same time. She was walking towards them and to Amanda's surprise, smiled and joined them.

"Hello – er – Amanda Brighton?"

"Clifford," Amanda corrected.

Jessica turned her lovely eyes to look at Philip. "And you're the man who came with her to seek some mysterious relations, aren't you?" she asked Philip.

"That's right. And you're the lady who said she couldn't help. Had any more thoughts?"

"How could I possibly help? I'm an American."

"Your parents weren't," Philip said, watching her closely. "They were from Tri-nant, weren't they? You were born here too."

"Where did you get such a preposterous story?" Jessica laughed.

"According to my enquries, your name is—"

"Oh dear, you sound like an investigator. Now what could you be investigating about poor little me?"

"Not an investigator, just a defunct reporter with contacts. I'm told your real name is Sian Talbot."

"You have been busy, haven't you?" she drawled in a bored voice. "So what? It wasn't a name I felt happy with. It didn't suit me so I changed it. But that doesn't mean I can help find your goddamned family so forget it, will you?"

She hurried off and Amanda and Philip looked at each other, Amanda confused by the look of distress on the woman's face.

"Run after her," Philip urged. He too had seen the woman's distraught expression. "Go on, ask her again. I'll give this stuff to Rhys. Go, quickly before you lose the chance!"

Without understanding why, Amanda followed Jessica and walked beside her along the lane leading to the school.

"Who are you?" Amanda asked softly. "You do know something about me, don't you? Why won't you help me?"

She was startled when Jessica turned sharply and glared at her. "I'm your mother, damn you! I thought you'd never find me!"

Amanda was stunned. She reached out a hand to grasp the branches of the roadside hedge. "My mother?" she gasped, staring into clear blue eyes which were very like her own. Tears welled up as she thought of the thousand ways she had imagined this scene. Never in her dreams had she envisaged

170

standing facing such bitterness as she saw now in Jessica's expression.

"But – your name – my name is Clifford," she stuttered as thoughts began to overcome distress.

"I used the surname of the family who took you on, hoping it would stop you finding me. If it hadn't been for Aunt Flora leaving you the cottage you never would. Did it for spite, she did. She always hated me, and this was her revenge, bringing you here to pry and ruin everything."

"Perhaps she wanted to leave it for you but couldn't find you?"

"She knew how to find me all right. D'you know how she found you? I'll tell you. A burglar, breaking into her cottage when she was on an overnight stay. How's that for bad luck! This thief talked about you and she set Philip onto you like a terrier after a rat, and look what he came up with: a daughter I'd tried so hard to forget!"

The words didn't penetrate Amanda's brain. All she could think of was that this woman was her mother.

"Please tell me, why did you give me away?"

"I was fifteen and very ambitious. How could I face bringing you up on my own? I had a career to build. Dammit all, girl! Aunt Flora was the only family I had and she hated me. I managed on my own, why couldn't you? I wasn't able to help you. There was the stigma of an illegitimate child – I couldn't face it."

Yet she had two children, Amanda thought curiously, herself and Roy. And now she was causing lively gossip by spending nights with Rhys. Stigmas and scandals could be managed when it suited her, it seemed.

"What shall we do?" she asked. "I mean do you still want it kept secret? Is the 'stigma' still there?" Amanda was shivering with shock, her legs were in imminent danger of giving way. Surely she wouldn't be turned away? She looked at the expression on Jessica's face searching for a glimmer of hope.

"I'm going back to America. I don't want these small-minded people looking down on me for something that happened when I was still a child."

"But we'll keep in touch? You'll want to know about me now we have met? I'd like to know about you."

For the first time Amanda saw distress in her mother's face. Perhaps, she thought with relief that made her shake even more, Jessica wasn't as hard as she pretended. But Jessica said, "I made my decision twenty-four years ago and I'm not starting to regret it now. You were born in a farm shed with an old woman to help me. She bundled you up and you were given to a couple foolish enough to want you. I heard they died a year or so later and you ended up in a Children's Home. I did check to see if you were safe, but that's all I did."

"But now I've found you, don't you want to know me?"

"I've learned all I need to know. Goodbye, Amanda. Don't try and reach me." She walked away leaving Amanda white and too shaken to move. After a few yards, Jessica turned. "I suppose you'll tell Rhys?"

"Yes," Amanda said in a small voice. "And Catrin. Philip has guessed, I think."

"Yes, damn him. That's the only reason I've told you. You wouldn't have been told otherwise. But no one else. Right?"

"Oh, I'll have to tell Roy, of course."

Jessica increased her pace until she was running. If she heard Amanda's last remark, she didn't reply. She was running away from her daughter and the memories of a sadder time and Amanda didn't try to stop her. At least she had learned the most important thing, who her mother was. She had learned a most important lesson too, she wasn't wanted now any more than at her birth.

It was a long time before Amanda could walk back to the cottage. Even that was spoilt for her. Aunt Flora had left it to her out of spite, so she would be led to Jessica Maybury, or Sian Talbot, who would reveal the sordid truth about her birth. A dirty shed and the ministrations of some old woman. Secret and shameful.

Her first task must be to tell Roy. Hating the life Roy had led and the numerous times she had been embarrassed by him, the friends she had lost because of his behaviour, all these things now seemed of little importance. She had found their mother.

Forgetting Philip, she ran into the cottage and fell on the bed stunned by the revelations of the past half hour. From when she was a small child she had imagined a scene in which she and her beautiful mother would greet each other with delight. Mother would explain how she had to leave her adored child. She would understand, and they would promise never to lose each other again. The reality was far from the fantasy. Jessica was going back to America, almost as far away from her as it was possible to go.

She heard voices downstairs and guessed Philip had come looking for her. She stood up and began to wash her face. It was no use hiding. The truth was out and she had to live with it.

She brushed her hair and tried to calm herself before walking downstairs and facing Catrin and Philip. Philip glanced at her distressed face and guided her to a chair. Catrin handed her a steaming cup of tea.

"You know?" Amanda asked.

Catrin nodded. "Philip and I guessed. We couldn't tell you, dear. It had to come either from your own deductions or from Jessica herself. You've worked it out? All of it?"

"It was a complete surprise," Amanda whispered, tears hovering.

"How does Jessica feel about you?" Philip asked. "She must be thrilled to have such a lovely daughter."

"Oh yes," Amanda said bitterly. "So proud she's off to America as fast as she can go!"

It was after Philip had gone and the two women were discussing the implications that Amanda asked about Aunt Flora. "Jessica said she'd left me the cottage out of spite. Did she mean left it not to her, but between Roy and me? She implied it was left to me to bring me here where I might learn about Jessica, or Sian I suppose I ought to call her."

"I only remember Flora as an elderly woman who had once worked as a parlour maid in one of the larger houses. She never talked about her family. I have no idea what Jessica meant by spite, dear." She didn't look at Amanda as she spoke and Amanda had the feeling she was hiding something. What else had she to learn that would distress her? Was it something about her father? Was that another shock in store? Catrin reassured her on that.

"From what I have gathered from general gossip and rumour, dear, your father was a married man who moved away to live in London after his marriage all but broke up. Strange, isn't it, so many stories about unhappy families and in such a tiny village as Tri-nant?"

Later that evening as a sort of codicil to the day's happenings, Amanda spoke of her love for Rhys. "I'm very fond of him," she began, wondering how much she could tell Catrin who, after all, was Rhys's aunt. "But, knowing he's had an affair with – my mother – I can't think of him in the same way any more."

"You think they had an affair?"

"I'm sorry, Catrin. I shouldn't be talking to you about this, but there isn't anyone else."

"I don't object to hearing it, but are you sure you're right?"

"About Jessica and Rhys? There's no doubt. She's been staying at the bungalow and with her own house only a few miles away it's impossible to imagine an innocent reason."

"I wouldn't know. But Jessica's devious enough to think of one!" Catrin touched Amanda's cheek affectionately. "Why don't you talk to Rhys? Tell him all this and don't make up your mind until you have the facts."

"Please don't tell him how I feel," Amanda begged. "What's the point?"

"Because if you don't discuss this and sort it out you'll spoil my plans. I thought from the moment we met that you were right for Rhys. I didn't think I'd have to leave the cottage, you see dear. If you two married, you can hardly live in both and the bungalow is much larger.

"I'm so miserable," Amanda whispered. "And everything could have turned out so wonderfully."

Catrin stood up and hugged her. "Unless you clear the air with my nephew, you'll spoil things for Philip too. I intended to invite him to be my lodger!"

"So that was your little plan!"

"Seems I was wrong, unless you and Rhys can sort out your differences, dear."

Amanda wanted to run to Rhys and insist on talking everything through, but she was unconvinced about his non-involvement with Jessica – her mother – and so did nothing.

She knew she had to tell Roy and, the following morning before school, she knocked at the house where he lodged. There was no reply – he started his garden work impressively early these days – so she left a note asking him to call. A few days later he did. But when he came to look for her she was not at the cottage and he went to Rhys's bungalow and found her there.

Roy's thick fair hair had grown into a tightly curled mat, which with his intensely blue eyes made every woman's expression soften with admiration. Invited in, he strolled through to the lounge in his confident way and sat in a chair overlooking the garden.

"Hi, Mand," he said, as she looked up from the papers on which she was working. "What's this you want to talk about then?"

"I'd rather not talk about it here," she said, while Rhys was attending to drinks. "Can't you come to the cottage later?"

"Not really, Mand. Got a date, see. Me and Gillian is going to the pictures. I think her Mam and Dad are softening towards me, now they haven't seen a police car for a few weeks."

"I'll talk to you tomorrow then."

"Don't worry, you can talk privately here," Rhys said and went out into the garden.

"It's about Jessica Maybury." Amanda touched Roy's arm, trying to soften the blow. "She's our mother."

"Never!" He walked away from her to hide his agitation. Surely she'll realise we're not related now she's discovered her mother, he thought with sickening disappointment. His chance of sharing the cottage was fading fast.

"She refuses to acknowledge us though," Amanda went on. "She said I was born in some old barn with a woman from the village helping with my birth. I was so shocked, I didn't ask about you. But it must have been something similar."

"Now there's a thing, eh, Mand? Us related to a glamorous woman like her."

"Only a child she was. Fifteen years old. I suppose we should understand how impossible it was then, but why doesn't she accept us now? To late for any scandal to harm any of us, after all this time."

Roy looked upset, wary even, but then he smiled, as if in sudden revelation. "Talking daft she is, Mand. Made it all up."

"No, she was speaking the truth. Pretends about her age though. I suppose it would give the game away, wouldn't it, admitting to us?"

Rhys returned to replenish their drinks and with great deliberation, Roy talked about anything but the discovery of their mother's identity. He alone knew Jessica was not his mother, only Amanda's, that he and Amanda were not brother and sister. If she found out, there was no chance at all of her giving him a share of the cottage. Once she had agreed to make him a half owner, persuading her to sell wouldn't be that difficult. Strong sense of fair play, Amanda had. And playing on brotherly love was going to make everything simple.

Before Roy left he made some admiring remarks about Rhys's home. "I'll have a place furnished smart, like this place one day," he said. "Filled with souvenirs of my travels. Mind, I haven't been further than Cardiff so far," he laughed. He commented on several items and Rhys explained their origin. Roy was particularly interested in the masks.

At the door, he smiled and thanked Rhys for the pleasant hour. "I like the house Rhys, specially them wooden masks and things. A bit creepy mind, specially the one of the wide-eyed man with a monkey on his shoulder."

Rhys frowned as he closed the door behind him and turned to Amanda.

"Now when would he have seen that?" he asked. "This is supposed to be the first time he's been in my house, isn't it?"

"He had a good look around," Amanda said, dread in her heart for what he was thinking.

"He'd have needed a very thorough look. Can you see it?"
She glanced at the shelves and shook her head.

"No, you can't. Because I put that particular carving away after the burglary as it's of great value."

"You think he was the burglar?" Amanda asked sadly.

"Don't you?"

After he had explained his suspicions about the accident in which he was sure Roy was also involved, she could only agree.

Eleven

A few days later Catrin asked if Amanda had any plans for the evening. On being told no, she picked up the telephone and began dialling. Amanda didn't hear all of the conversation but heard Catrin say, "Can you come over?" As Philip was their most usual visitor and he only needed a knock on the wall to invite him in, she was curious.

"Who are you ringing?"

"Rhys. I am inviting him here and I am going out! It's time you two silly people talked to each other."

"There's nothing to say."

"Say what's in your mind. Be truthful and sort out your differences for good," Catrin said firmly. "I can't bear seeing the two people I love most in the world so unhappy when there's no need."

"Where are you going?"

"To talk to Philip."

Rhys arrived about ten minutes later.

"Where is she?" he asked, smiling. "Don't tell me she asked me to come and then forgot!"

"No, Catrin went out deliberately."

Amanda stood near the window looking out into the quiet garden. Birds were flitting about and a cat stalked threateningly across the lawn, made larger by the late evening shadows. She was remembering how happy and excited she had been at the thought of living in this cottage, that had once been owned by distant members of her family.

Now she had found the one person whom she had always thought would make her happiness complete: her mother. The end of that search had meant losing Rhys, and the end of her contentment.

"What is it?" Rhys asked, puzzled by her silence. "Has something happened?" He moved towards her but she hastily stepped away to avoid the contact that would have undone her. She couldn't tell him. She couldn't.

"It's just that I don't want to be involved in any more of your photography trips. That sort of thing isn't really for me."

"Why?" he demanded.

"It's become rather boring," she said, intentionally hurting him in her determination to keep the meeting brief. "With the best of summer still ahead of us I want to do more exciting things. I want to dress up again, wear feminine clothes to remind myself I'm a young woman. For me, wellington boots are out from now on."

"You mean I'm boring!"

She didn't answer. Something funny was happening to her throat and she was afraid her voice would let her down. How could she answer, when she was destroying her only chance of happiness? She straightened cushions, giving herself time to recover.

"You told me you wanted to revisit the cave. D'you mean you didn't enjoy our last trip? It was all a pretence?"

"Once was interesting, but I wouldn't want to spend every weekend doing such uncomfortable things."

"You moved in here with my aunt, giving the impression you liked us, that you felt we were almost a family to you. Through us you've established yourself in the village and now you've achieved that, we can go hang!"

"That isn't true. I'm very fond of – Catrin."

"But not me? Well, I won't be bothering you any more!"

She continued to stare into the garden, waiting for him to leave. Before he could do so, Catrin came in.

"Hello, Rhys, dear. Will you stay for coffee?"

"No thank you." He didn't say another word, he just walked from the room and hurried away.

"What happened?" Catrin asked, a frown of concern on her

kindly features. "Did you tell him about Jessica's announcement?"

"No, I just told him goodbye." Amanda ran to her room, leaving Catrin open-mouthed, staring after her in dismay.

For the next few days, Amanda went through the motions of her work without any real thought. She deliberately closed her mind to her feelings, numb with the knowledge that her mother had rejected her for the second time and had succeeded in taking Rhys from her.

She had concern only for little Jane, who became a kindred spirit. She discussed her situation with no one and remained islanded in her misery.

Catrin and Philip were aware of her unhappiness but made no attempt to persuade her to discuss it, knowing she had to work things out for herself. Heather unwittingly added to her rejection by saying casually, "I saw Rhys and Jessica leaving for the airport with masses of luggage. Where has he gone this time?"

"America, I presume," Amanda said, as if it didn't matter.

"Just as well," Heather said, bitterness making her expression harsh. "I have the feeling you were getting too fond of Rhys. A life with him wouldn't be much fun. You'd spend all your anniversaries alone."

Amanda didn't reply. It wasn't his absences she minded, it was the thought of him making love to the woman who was her mother.

Amanda was aware of a difference in Heather and she wondered what had happened to make the usually pleasant young woman tense and full of anger. Unbelievably, she was rarely seen with the girls. It was usually Haydn who brought them to school, but sometimes a neighbour would meet them and take them home for the afternoon and that was something Heather would never had permitted only weeks before.

The school gate looked strange without her lonely figure standing there. Amanda knew she should be pleased but instead the change made her uneasy.

Besides Heather not being with the girls all the time, there were other changes.

Whenever Amanda called at the James's house, loud music could be heard long before she reached it. For several days at a time Heather would be playing Mario Lanza singing 'Because You're Mine'. Then it would change and Alma Cogan would be belting out 'Bell Bottom Blues' for days on end. Frankie Laine was a constant favourite and Amanda sympathised with Haydn for having to listen to the same record, however good, hour after hour. She wondered how Haydn could work with such a racket. But besides the irritation there was a serious worry. Philip had told her of the obsession with music that had accompanied Heather's previous depression, when she had left Philip. Amanda was afraid there was going to be a repeat.

The end of term and the end of the school year was a very busy time and gave Amanda little time to brood on her situation. There was a summer fair in the grounds of the school, for which each class managed a stall. Also a Sports Day, a Fun Day during which the children came in fancy dress, and a jumble sale, which besides taking jumble from the parents got rid of the left-overs from the Fair. And finally, an Open Day for the parents to come and view the children's work. This entailed many extra hours, as Amanda wanted to make sure every child had a picture on the wall and a page or two of work mounted and on show. Displays were prepared for the children to make, and several evenings she worked until after ten o'clock to be sure of everything being ready on time, often with Catrin's help.

The Open Day was a great success, with parents and grand-parents and proud aunts and uncles attending, so the school buzzed with excited voices, oohs and aahs and laughter. Every class had chosen a theme for their display and Amanda had, not surprisingly, chosen 'The Countryside'. Besides pictures and models, they had their small pond on display, plus a real bird's nest, a snake's skin and an old wasps' nest which caused great interest. Many people had lived in the country all their lives and never seen them. It was only when the last of the parents

181

had gone and she was setting about the clearing up that she realised that Heather hadn't been there.

Her first thought was that she must be ill. Haydn had been among the first but there had been no sign of Heather. She wondered who had collected the girls and was told it was her brother Roy. Heather must be all right or she would have heard, but why hadn't she shown her face on this, the children's most important school-day?

Catrin could shed no light on it so, after a reviving cup of tea, she drove to the house next to the Cwm Gwyn Arms to enquire. The girls were ready for bed and their welcoming kiss smelled delightfully of toothpaste and soaped skin.

"Heather went out for the day," Haydn told her. "To do some shopping she said. Summer clothes for the girls, I expect."

Although he smiled and sounded casual, Amanda was made curious by the frown on his face. "She's all right, isn't she?" she asked. "It isn't like her to miss something at the school."

"Fine – I think she just wanted a break; her last chance without the girls tagging along. I think she said she's meeting a friend."

"Do her good," Amanda agreed, but wondered who Heather's friend might be. She was so rarely in anyone's company except Haydn and the girls.

There were records spread over a low table, their sleeves spread out in a precise pattern. Amanda looked at them and Haydn shrugged.

"She makes a fuss if I tidy them away. She loves her music."

"There are some for the children too, are there?" she asked.

"Oh yes. One or two."

He had said very little but he left her with the impression that he was a man with shoulders heavy with worry. She wished she could discuss the situation with Rhys, but that wasn't possible.

On the last day of term the children went out loaded with their work, plus the display material Amanda shared between those who wanted it. Large pictures, ungainly models, which their parents wouldn't thank her for passing on, she thought

182

with a chuckle, but which made the children so proud as they staggered to the gate with them.

She planned a lie-in and a lazy day on the Saturday but woke early, with a feeling of emptiness, to look out at a gloomy, overcast sky. She looked out of the window at clouds that glowered and matched her mood. This was the day on which she and Rhys were to have made their second trip to the cave to the colony of bats. But his previous filming had been successful and he didn't need to go for a second attempt. There was only the equipment to collect and she wouldn't be invited now, not even to help carry that. No, it was well and truly over between them. She was here, Rhys was in America and Jessica was with him.

"What are you planning to do today?" Catrin asked.

"I haven't any plans, but I feel restless. I always do after the hectic end-of-term week. Perhaps I'll go for a drive."

"Fancy a trip into Cardiff?" Catrin suggested, but Amanda shook her head.

After a light breakfast of which Amanda ate very little, Catrin said, "I'll see to the dishes, dear, if you want to get off." She frowned at the sad expression on Amanda's face. "But remember, you don't have to be alone. I'll come with you if you wish."

"Thank you, Catrin, but I wouldn't be very good company today. I'm tired. It's been a busy couple of weeks."

"Why not go and see your friend Gillian? And Roy? You haven't seen either of them since Roy went back to live at the Harris's."

Amanda collected her camera and the flask of coffee and some sandwiches Catrin insisted on her taking, and set off in the car without any goal in mind.

She drove past Rhys's bungalow without a glance, but at the cottage where Jessica had been staying she stopped the car. If only I could talk to Jessica once more, she sighed.

The place was empty of course. Jessica had been afraid of criticism and gossip and had left at once for America, where no one would learn about her less than perfect past. She had taken Rhys away too, leaving her with nothing.

Looking at the empty house, it was as if Jessica had been nothing more substantial than a dream. And Rhys, was he a dream too? Was love something unattainable for her? Something she would never win?

Guiltily, she reflected that she had taken something from Jessica in her search for her family. Jessica's peace of mind, her confident conviction no one knew about her being a mother of two. Children in their twenties at that. What distress that must be causing, and all for no purpose. What a mess.

She returned to the car swamped with a feeling of guilt. She was shamed by her mother's final rejection. But she had forced the woman to look at something she hadn't wanted to face. Jessica had a life of her own and she had forced herself in and tried to disturb it.

She suddenly wanted to see Roy. At least she had him, and she should be grateful. Roy was comfortably settled back in his own room at the Harris's. Still working around the houses of Tri-nant, driving to and fro in his impressive car, but living in an uneasy peace with Gillian's parents.

The reason for the change of attitude was an ultimatum from their daughter. Gillian had told them she was expecting a child and was going to marry Roy.

Their first reaction had been to refuse to allow it. Why compound one mistake with another, they argued, but Gillian threatened to go away and never see them again if they refused to accept Roy, so they surrendered.

When Amanda knocked on their door she was surprised and, at first, delighted to become involved in the preparations for the wedding, which was to take place on August twenty-first.

"We're goin' to have a baby, Mand. What d'you think of that, then? You'll be an auntie and I'll be a dad!"

Shock was brief and delight was her emotion when the news was given.

"Our own family, Roy! We're starting a family of our own!" she said, hugging her future sister-in-law.

"The Clifford dynasty, Mand," Roy said hugging them both. "Them two weren't best pleased at first, mind, but they're happy now. A baby is always good news, eh, Mand?"

"Yes," Amanda laughed. "Wonderful news."

"What about us coming to live with you in Firethorn Cottage?" Roy asked. "Plenty of room for us all and Catrin will be out of it from October, won't she?" He turned to look affectionately at Gillian. "Imagine, love, our first being born in a place where our ancestors lived. Romantic, eh?"

"Sorry, Roy, but I don't even know if Catrin will be leaving. As for myself, well, my plans are far from clear at the moment."

"Mand. You wouldn't let a stranger live in the place and see me and Gillian and our baby without a home, would you?" He looked at her, his smile trying to force her to copy it, using every inch of his charm. "Jokin' you are, aren't you? Yes, for sure. There's a tease you are, Mand. Didn't I tell you she's a terrible tease, Gill?"

Realising it wasn't working, he felt a sudden and rare surge of anger. She owed him this. Hadn't he played the role of brother all these years? She wasn't going to find out he was no relation. That Jessica woman would have known, but she was safe back in America. She'd have to be reminded about how close they were and that her duty was to share her good fortune with him. "Come out and have a spot of dinner with me," he offered. "Gill and Mam will be busy talking frocks for ages yet." He would have to make her see how wrong it would be to refuse them, her own kin − or so she thought!

They ate at a small café, eating fish and chips and a plateful of bread and real butter which was still a luxury even after several weeks of ration-free shopping. While they lingered over a pot of tea, Roy persuaded her to talk.

"Where you off to then, Mand? Going somewhere nice?"

"I would have been going to a cave, miles from any main road, to collect Rhys's equipment after some final filming of the bats flying out late in the evening. But he's in America and I can't go alone."

"That cave you told me about, where you and Rhys went a few weeks back?" He gave Amanda a mock serious frown.

185

"You mean his expensive gear is up there in the mountains and you aren't going to get it? Fine friend you are!"

"It's nothing to do with me."

"Have you had a falling out?"

"Well, yes."

"Then go and get it for him, do it for a friend, wouldn't you?"

"I can't go there alone, and it's his worry, not mine." She was aware of sounding childish, but it was easier than trying to explain.

"But it's Rhys's stuff and even if he isn't the love of your life, like Gillian is mine, you would like to be friends, wouldn't you? Or can't you manage to be a friend? Love or hate, nothin' in between? You aren't one of them, are you, Mand?" He smiled, punched her shoulder playfully. "Go on, go and surprise him by rescuing his stuff before it's ruined or stolen. Expensive stuff, that camera equipment. Show him you're a friend, Mand."

"I hoped to be more," she said.

"Better than nothin' though, being a friend." He watched her for a while then asked again about letting Gillian and himself share the cottage.

"No, Roy," she said firmly. "But I will help you find somewhere really nice, I promise."

"Thanks Mand. And I hope you and that Rhys get together so you and I will both be settled and happy. Go on, go and get his stuff from that cave, is it?"

It seemed the most sensible way to spend the day. Plenty of daylight left, it was July after all, and probably light until ten. Three hours to get there and an hour to walk back down to the car. She'd do it and be back before Catrin began to worry about her.

When Roy told Gillian about their conversation, he looked up at the ever-darkening sky and shuddered. "I 'opes she isn't thinking of going today. Look at them clouds. Rain for sure before tonight."

*   *   *

186

The sky hadn't broken, it was darker and lower if anything, Amanda thought. There was a strong threat of rain so she stopped in Barry and found a camping shop and bought some waterproof bags she could use to protect the items as she carried them down to the car. It would be a pity to rescue them, then ruin them by carelessness. That wouldn't endear her to Rhys, even as a friend! Getting into the car she almost threw the packet of sandwiches away but decided that even after a huge meal, she might be glad of them before she got home.

She drove without thinking, following the route she had taken with Rhys. The journey was dull as low clouds obliterated everything except the road. The distant mountains changed from grey-blue to grey-black and deep purple before disappearing altogether in the gloom. Carrying only a small shoulder bag with the pack of sandwiches and the flask, plus the waterproof covers, she began to follow the animal tracks over the soft, springy turf away from the road.

There were no spendid views today when she reached the top of the rising ground. Everything was hidden by rain clouds. She looked back and noticed that the car was almost invisible and the other side of the road, which dropped down into a valley, was already lost to her sight.

She should have been warned but her mind was so numb with misery she was not thinking in her usual clear-headed way. She walked down into the valley and up the other side and when she crossed the shallow stream she felt pleased that she had remembered the way so well.

She found the path up to the cave and stopped inside it for a drink of coffee and a rest before strapping Rhys's electronic gadgetry around her. She made sure it was all safely covered in case the threatening clouds precipitated into a downpour.

Before she had travelled more than a few yards down from the entrance, the rain began falling heavily and hissing with a vehemence that blocked out all sight and sound. She bent against the force of it and increased her pace, running where the terrain allowed. The act of bending over misled her and instead of retracing her steps, she over-ran the downward path and soon realised she had wandered too far before changing direction and heading downwards.

Looking around she was frightened. Visibility was absolutely nil. She heard running water and sighed with relief. If she could find the stream she would know where she was. But the fast running stream she found was a new one caused by the rain.

Further down she did find the right place, although she doubted it for several moments. She was horrified at how it had swollen. Again and again she checked but no, she remembered a large stone where she had rested briefly. This was the place, but how was she going to get across?

It widened as she watched. It was no longer a gentle innocent stream such as she had easily crossed before, stepping from stone to stone, but a dark angry torrent. The heavy rain, running so fast over the rocky ground, had filled the river bed and made crossing it by the stepping stones an impossibility.

With the rain pounding the rocks around her, she could not stay there, without shelter or warmth, idly waiting until it eased again to a passable wading depth. It might be July but she could soon be too weak to help herself and be dead by morning. She scrambled back up the way she had come, intending to retreat to the cave. If she could find it again!

Everything looked different. Small spurts of water leapt out to make waterfalls where there had been none, bursting out of small fissures and sending small stones hurtling out of their resting places. And all the time the rain was beating down on her, sidling down her neck and seeping through her summer-weight coat with ease. Thank goodness she had brought covers for the cameras.

The thought of not locating the place of safety in the night-like darkness made her want to shout in despair. It was four o'clock. If she couldn't find the protection of that cave she might have to spend the night hours alone with nothing to ward off the coldness and wet.

Trying to walk upright and look around her for clues, she went up what she hoped was the correct path, instinctively bending into a crouch to avoid the needle-sharp attack of the raindrops then forcing herself to straighten up again to see her way. In the gloom she searched for a gap, a niche in which she could stand out of the ceaseless torrent. Those she did find had their own individual waterfall and were useless.

Every inch of her was wet. She looked down at the summer jacket she wore, wishing she had thought to put on waterproofs. But she hadn't intended to climb mountains when she set off that day. That, she thought with growing misery, had been Roy's idea.

She touched the flask of hot coffee but decided to wait until she reached the cave. Thank goodness she'd had the sense to bring that, there were still several cupfuls left. And the sandwiches were still there, soggy no doubt, but better than being hungry.

She knew her life was in jeopardy. Just looking around her told her that her life could be forfeited unless luck stayed with her. It had happened so simply. A walk that she had done with Rhys, and which had been like a summer picnic, had become a situation fraught with danger within minutes.

How she would be criticised for being so stupid! But it hadn't been like that, she wanted to shout. She hadn't been deluded into thinking the mountains were harmless playgrounds, or beguiled into trusting they would always be the same innocent landscape they had been on that calm clear spring day. She knew the dangers, but her misery had made her careless.

With hands stiff with cold she rearranged the straps around her and, with the rain still beating down, she began to climb again. She was better on the move; standing against a rock face which offered no shelter was pointless.

The weight of the extra luggage pulled on her shoulders and they ached terribly. A sharp pain across her back made her long to leave everything behind. But that was too much effort. She had fixed most of the bags inside her coat for the slight protection it gave and thought sadly that she had probably ruined the equipment she had tried to save.

She felt like crying. The rain showed no sign of stopping

and she was stiff and tired, and very chilled. Exhaustion hung about her like wet blankets dragging her, trying to persuade her to lie down, but she moved on, her progress slower as weariness and the weight of her wet clothes weakened her.

She lost all idea of time but a glance at her watch told her she had been searching for two hours. With the coming of evening, darkness closed in and just when she was thinking she would never find it, the cave opened before her, a blacker black in the gloom. She fell inside and lay for a while without attempting to do anything more than rest.

Slowly she removed her drenched coat. There were a few dry branches which she gathered together, wishing she had the means of lighting them if only for momentary cheer from a blaze.

With them she made a bed and with her wet coat around her she sat and drank from the flask. Immediately she felt better. Looking out at the slanting rods of rain which showed no signs of easing, she tried to assess the situation.

It was bleak. No one knew where she was. Even if someone saw the car – and that was unlikely – they would have no idea where she could be found. Roy might have phoned Catrin, but whether he had mentioned their talk about the cave was doubtful. Why should he? And Rhys – Rhys was the only one who might guess and he, she reminded herself sadly, was in America with Jessica.

The storm increased in strength through the hours of darkness. It lashed against the rocks as if determined to smash them and dislodge her. She slept a little but most of the night was spent thinking of Rhys. Should she stay in Firethorn Cottage or sell it and start again somewhere? Loving him and seeing him so near would be hard to take.

The bats didn't leave their perches, perhaps instinctively knowing that no insects would be flying in this weather. She fancifully pretended the tiny creatures had stayed to keep her company.

Towards dawn she finally woke and looked out. The storm still gusted but the rain had ceased, leaving a fast-moving pattern of clouds. She was stiff and chilled, the coat she had used as a blanket was soaked and she had to force herself to put it on. It would offer some comfort once it warmed.

She stared out at the bleak scene and wondered fearfully how she would cross the stream which by now must be seriously swollen. The remaining coffee was cold but she drank it gratefully and ate the last of the sandwiches. Leaving the cave with the equipment belonging to Rhys once more draped around her, she left the flask behind – no point in carrying unnecessary items – and set off.

She was stiff and tired and hungry, but knew she had to move, get down lower where there was at least a possibility of seeing someone. She was surprised to find that her feet hurt. They had swollen and her shoes were painfully tight. Her muscles were reluctant to move and as she slithered down the path she wondered just how far she could walk.

It was sensible to head towards the car but it seemed a long way off and if she couldn't cross the stream, what then? Perhaps there was an easier way down if she went across the range rather than down? Rhys was not a mountaineer and he wouldn't necessarily have chosen the easiest route to the cave, simply the shortest.

Staggering as she made her way downwards, still undecided, she eventually caught sight of the stream now a foaming, turbulent river, wild and certainly un-navigable. She turned to walk upstream; there the stream might be smaller and should be easier to cross. Everyone knew streams and rivers widened as they reached the sea, she thought logically.

She fell as she tried to climb higher in the hope of seeing a likely place to cross, and panicked at the sudden sharp pain in her knee. This was not a place to lie injured. She choked back a sob as she faced the fact that she was in danger of losing her life.

She sat for a while and rested her knee. Loaded down with Rhys's equipment was making walking more difficult; the cameras swung unexpectedly and tilted her off balance. But she had brought them this far and couldn't leave them now. The prospect of giving them to Rhys, unharmed, was what kept her from the edge of despair as she moved further from the cave into unknown territory.

Rhya had been alarmed when he had returned home from dropping Jessica at the airport to find Amanda missing. Philip had already searched the local area and now, with a night having passed and evening approaching once more, they were both seriously alarmed.

"The cave," Rhys said. "I have a feeling she's gone to the cave. We were going there together but, well, you might say Jessica changed our plans."

Philip wasn't convinced. "Why would she go into the mountains on her own? No, I think we'd do better by talking to her brother again. She went to see him before she disappeared and he might remember something she said that would help find her."

"You go if you wish, but what d'you think you'll accomplish that can't be achieved on the telephone? He insists she was heading back here when they parted."

"You're right, Rhys. There are plenty of people looking in the most likely places, let's try the unlikely." The two men forgot their differences and, after making sure they had ropes and extra clothing and food, they set out for the mountains.

The weather was closing in and the rocks were slippery as Amanda made her way forwards, following the sound of the stream, walking alongside it at times and at others high above it with steep rocks dropping down and separating her from its hopeful presence. She trod awkwardly and, trying to save her already painful knee, she tripped and rolled down and down a fall of scree, landing breathless and tearful not far from the water. She lay there wondering whether she could find her way back to the cave. At least with evening drawing in she would have somewhere to rest and its comparative warmth was a goal.

Time was a blur; she no longer looked at her watch. She turned to retrace her steps with the feeling she had been walking for days. In fact she had covered very little ground.

*   *   *

Rhys and Philip reached the cave and Rhys gave a shout of joy as he recognised the cheerful red of the abandoned vacuum flask. "She's here," he called and hurried on. But the cave was empty and he shouted his rage to the sky.

"She has been here though," he said. "All my equipment has gone. She came up her alone to collect it." His shoulders drooped with despair. "But where is she now?"

It was tempting to split up and cover more ground but both men knew that idea was fraught with even greater danger. Instead, they headed downstream, calling as they went, both convinced that, for someone lost, that would be the wisest choice.

A short distance away, in the opposite direction, Amanda huddled under her coat and closed her eyes. A rest was what she needed, then she would walk out of the mountains with ease. Just a short rest.

Rhys and Philip had been walking and calling for half an hour, unaware they had been increasing the distance between themselves and Amanda, when Philip stopped.

"Would she have got this far, loaded with your cameras? I think we ought to go back and try the other direction."

Rhys didn't argue, he had been thinking similar thoughts himself. Still calling, they followed the turbulent stream back the way they had walked as darkness began to fall like a grey sodden blanket around them.

Amanda was dreaming. She was warm and cosy in Catrin's favourite armchair and the warmth of the fire was soothing her aching body. She wondered vaguely how she had got home. She heard Rhys calling and smiled. She was too comfortable to go and see what he wanted.

She relaxed again into sleep and in doing so slipped a little. The jerking movement woke her from her pleasant dream. Voices were calling.

She woke and struggled to stand. "Rhys?" she whispered

aloud. Then, as the voices continued she raised her voice and called back, looking around her for the source of them.

In the distance she saw two figures. At once, unbelievably, she recognised Rhys. "He's in America!" she said aloud. "How can he be here, looking for me? Rhys!" she called. "Rhys. I'm here!" She watched as he waved excitedly before hurrying towards her in a stumbling run. They met as she reached the scree slope and clung to each other. It was a long time before anyone started asking questions.

"Thank goodness you're safe," Rhys repeated over and over again.

"I thought you were in America," Amanda said.

"I took Jessica to the airport." he explained, staring at her as if unable to believe she was safe.

The second figure materialised into Philip, who stood a little way off waiting until the ecstatic reunion was over.

"How did you know where to find me?"

"Come on, back to the cave," Rhys instructed.

"What? You aren't going to make me wait while you film!"

His smile widened as he removed a rucksack from his back and handed it to her. "Dry clothes. Change in the cave, it'll be easier than the car, and the sooner the better."

While Amanda changed into the dry clothes, which turned out to be Rhys's and far too large, Philip unpacked food and coffee.

"The whole village has been anxious." he told her. "Catrin has had dozens of calls all suggesting where we might look. People have been out all night. Several men have been driving around looking for your car."

"Haydn and I formed search parties," Philip told her. "And we've been out most of the night but it wasn't until Rhys came back at five this morning that we knew where to look."

"I knew at once where you were," Rhys said.

"But how? I didn't know myself. It was only Roy suggesting it that put it into my mind."

"I don't know how. But I knew," Rhys said.

"Catrin hasn't slept for a moment," Philip said. "She'll be so relieved to know you're safe."

"We'll phone from the first box we see."

Amanda had barely given Catrin a thought. All through the long, lonely night she had thought of no one but Rhys.

Now she saw clearly for the first time that although she had no family, she was not alone and never would be. Catrin was her family; Heather, Haydn and Philip dear friends. And Rhys? She looked at him holding out the flask to refill her cup, his face lit with the smile of relief that hadn't left him since he had found her. What role would he play in her future? A friend, like Roy had suggested? Would that be enough to keep her in Tri-nant?

With the luggage shared between the two men, Amanda set off down the now clearly discernible path to the stream. The water still flowed furiously and Rhys led them downstream to where it widened, and assured them it was shallow enough for them to walk across. Amanda looked doubtfully at her shoes, already ruined. It seemed she was in for another soaking.

Rhys picked her up and said briskly, "No point in you getting soaked again."

"Give me your car keys," Philip said when they were at last on the road. "I'll drive it home for you."

Rhys held out his hand. "Thank you Philip," he said gripping the man's hand firmly. "I'll never forget what you did."

"Just keep her under lock and key till she's learned her lesson," Philip grinned. He drove off in Amanda's car and Rhys opened his car door for her. There were blankets there and he wrapped them around her lovingly.

"I was frightened that I'd lost you," he said, and something in his voice told her he cared. She had to speak out; even if it meant losing him, she had to tell him about her mother.

"Jessica is my mother," she whispered.

"I suspected as much weeks ago," he said, starting the engine. He didn't drive off immediately but looked at her, trying to read her thoughts. "She and I weren't lovers, if that's what you think. We met in America and although she gives the impression we were more than friends, that was not the case. She tried to commit suicide, and I found her. I feel responsible for her safety. I befriended her, that's all there ever was between us. She has an ego that needs constant feeding. She has to pretend that every man she meets falls desperately in love with her."

"And you didn't?"

"I don't find glamorous actresses irresistible. I'm more for practical souls who wear jumpers too large and stagger about in wellington boots."

It was so ridiculous they both laughed and Amanda knew that, against the odds, the tangled web they had created had unravelled itself and they were going to be all right.

He searched in a pocket and handed her a note. "Jessica asked me to give you this."

The note was brief and rather sad. Jessica wished her luck and promised that one day, when things had settled, she would write and try to be a friend. 'But,' the note ended, 'don't *ever* call me Mother!'

As the car warmed her she relaxed and every time she glanced at Rhys he was smiling. It was going to be all right. She settled under the warm blankets and slept.

Rhys looked at her, loving her, and wondered how he could ever ruin her life by asking her to marry him and share a life as disjointed as his. She woke as they stopped outside Firethorn Cottage and smiled up at him. He scowled back.

During her sleep, his feelings had changed from grateful relief to a deeper, unselfish love. He had to let her go. It was kinder to walk away from her. A husband should be there always, not just when his busy schedule allowed it.

He hid disappointment and regret in his anger and, as Catrin ran down to open the car door to greet her, he said sharply, "Don't do anything as idiotically stupid again! If you can't think for yourself, consider the people who have risked their own lives searching for you." He got out, opened her door, slammed it shut and drove off.

Amanda burst into tears and was helped up to bed by Catrin, who put it down to shock.

Twelve

Amanda suffered no ill effects from her night on the mountain. She was fully recovered the following day when Philip came to ask after her.

"As you see," she smiled, "I am perfectly all right. But I don't know if I would be if you and Rhys hadn't found me. I wouldn't have found the way to cross that stream, would I?"

"Of course you would, a resourceful young lady like you. You'd have followed the banks until you reached the ford."

"Thank you for all you did, Philip."

"Get on with you, it's Rhys who guessed where you were. Though what made him realise you'd be daft enough to go clambering about collecting cameras in a storm like that, I don't know. As soon as he knew you were missing he sensed where you were. He must have very strong feelings for you, wouldn't you say?"

"Just an intelligent guess, that's all."

"What possessed you, Amanda?"

She shook her head. "I really don't know. It was the end of term and with no plans and feeling a bit fed up, I just wanted to fill the day. It was Roy who put the idea into my head, suggesting that Rhys might be pleased that I'd bothered."

"You mean he sent you up there on a day like that?"

"No! I didn't think of it until after I'd left him. He just thought that I might collect the stuff as a surprise for Rhys when he got back."

"He put the idea into your mind? That's all?"

"That's all."

"Pity he didn't remember and let someone know where you might be."

"He didn't know I was missing, did he?"

"Yes," Catrin said. "Gillian phoned at about ten o'clock to tell me you'd forgotten a headscarf. I told her you weren't back and we were getting worried. She didn't mention anything about where you might be."

Philip said nothing more but there was a strange look in his eye. He would be asking a few questions as soon as he could get to see Roy Clifford.

Rhys called several times to make sure Amanda was all right but he only glanced at her as if she were a part of the furnishings, questioned Catrin about her progress, and left.

Amanda wondered what had happened to change his attitude so dramatically. There was no doubting his genuine relief at finding her safe, or the warmth of his concern as they travelled home. But the moment the car stopped outside Firethorn Cottage, there was that sudden coldness, which hadn't thawed since.

One day during a warm spell in late August, Amanda and Catrin set off for a leisurely drive around the villages of the beautiful Vale of Glamorgan. They stopped to eat at a small tavern specialising in fish and sat for a while looking out over the calm blue sea. In contrast, they then went on to Barry Island where trippers flocked in their thousands and covered the warm sand with a cheerful patchwork of family groups colonising the beach for the day. Mums and dads, children of all ages plus uncles, aunts and grandparents, all enjoying a typical seaside day out. Sandcastles were built and flattened into tables on which fresh white cloths were spread, and there was the usual assortment of food, games and paddling causing laughter and contentment.

They were just leaving when they saw Philip carrying a couple of ice-creams along the promenade, staring at them with concentration as if willing them not to melt before he reached his destination. They continued to watch with mild curiosity as he reached a group and pushed his way through, to hand one of the piled-up cones to a young woman.

"So Philip has a friend, I see. And about time too," chuckled

Catrin. "Shall we go and say hello, or wait until later so we can tease him?"

"I don't think we should do either." Amanda stared at the couple in shock. "Look who it is." The young woman was Heather James.

They hurried back to the car as if guilty of snooping. When they were moving away, Catrin said, "I wonder how long that's been going on?"

"Nothing's going on. How could it be? She and Haydn are so happy together. Heather and Philip must have to meet sometimes to discuss things. Helen and Jane are still Philip's children, even if he has agreed never to become involved."

"But all the way out here? Haydn has been telling Rhys how pleased he is that Heather has started going out again. First into Cardiff to buy the latest records and the odd item of clothing. I wonder what he'd think of this? Meeting Philip, hiding away in a place where she's unlikely to be seen by anyone from Tri-nant. Big hat and sunglasses in case she is!"

"We mustn't judge," Amanda said. "Not without knowing the facts."

"Poor Haydn. She wouldn't do it to him again, would she? Not even Heather could be that cruel."

"Rhys told me Haydn was intending to marry her, then she left him for Philip."

"Practically on the eve of their wedding, dear. They went to live in London, Philip and Heather. But she couldn't cope with the life of wife to a travelling newspaper reporter. She loved London and having plenty of money at first, but then Helen came along, and being forced to stay in was hard for her to take, with Philip away so much. There was no one she could to go to for help. Heather isn't very good at coping, I'm afraid."

"Philip was offered the job of Far East correspondent, you know," Catrin went on, "and he turned it down. Heather told him she couldn't live anywhere but London. Then she persuaded him to give up his career, threatening to leave him if he didn't . . . After messing up his life she left him anyway. She came back here and fell into Haydn's arms once more. Now it seems she's off again."

"She probably can't help it," mused Amanda. "She's help-less in some ways, isn't she? Just not good at coping with what life throws at her."

"Weak and helpless, afraid of her own shadow? Perhaps. Yet she has a remarkable skill at getting what she wants, and for landing on her own two feet. Poor Haydn," she said again.

Amanda groaned, the irony of the situation becoming appar-ent. "Just when Rhys and Philip are talking with some civility to each other, this is going to start the war all over again!"

The day had ended on a solemn note and they were both relieved when Philip didn't appear that evening.

Philip had travelled with Heather as far as Cardiff and put her on the train back to Tri-nant, then he had gone to see Roy and Gillian.

"I'm trying to sort out the facts for Amanda about you and your family," he explained. A fussy little Mrs Harris, covered with shiny jewellery and dressed as if for a summer ball, invited him inside and began to prepare a tray of tea and cakes. Sitting in the small 'best room' which was overcrowded with highly polished furniture, he talked to Roy. He gave out a little information, hoping Roy would fill in the rest.

When he realised Roy was not going to be forthcom-ing, he said with a sigh of impatience, "Roy, you know damned well you aren't Amanda's brother. Why keep up the pretence?"

"What? Of course she's my sister. Brought up separate, but that's only because of the Children's Homes' rules. Close we are, always have been. What a lot of ol' rubbish to suggest different!"

Silently, Philip handed him the details he had copied from the register. After Roy had read them, he said, "Convenient, wasn't it, to go on pretending, so she'd help you and support you in between your prison sentences? Wanted a share of the cottage, did you? Afraid she'd find out you aren't her brother before she'd been persuaded to give you half? Is that why you sent her off up into the mountains hoping she wouldn't come back?"

"What you talking about? Slander that is and I'll damned well report you for that!"

Philip could see Roy was shaken.

"Why else did you suggest it?" he demanded.

"Because she was on about how Rhys was cold and didn't seem to want to know her no more. I only said that if she did that for him he'd at least be a friend and that was better than nothin'. That's all I said, honest. I didn't dream she'd go off there and then with them clouds gathering up for a storm. Where was her sense, man? Where was her sense?"

"I believe you," Philip said. Then, "I just had to be sure."

"You're right about the other thing, mind," Roy said. "I did find out she wasn't my real sister. And I did hope for a share of the cottage. Not saying what I knew, that's all I'm guilty of, man. I'd never have sent her into danger like that. She isn't my sister but she's the next best thing."

"And you've no objection to her being told?"

Roy shook his head sadly and asked, "Tell her you've only just told me, èh? Nothing lost by that. I'd hate her to think bad of me."

When Philip got home that night he heard the usual coded knocks on the wall and went in. Amanda was holding a flimsy airmail letter in her hand.

"It's from Jessica," she told him. "She says Roy isn't my brother. Oh Philip, I've been so stupid. I should have worked it out. If she was fifteen when I was born she'd have had to be very precocious to have had Roy eighteen months earlier."

"Actresses are notoriously unreliable when they talk about their age, but in this instance she's been honest. Roy was the son of the couple who adopted you, Gareth and Frances Clifford. They died soon after you arrived and you were both put into care under the name Clifford." Philip handed her the paper on which he had written it down. "I've told Roy and he's upset," he added.

"He's still my brother. We can't forget each other after being brother and sister all our lives. I'll write and tell him nothing has changed."

"So, dear, you've found your family. Now you can relax

and forget all about who you *were* and enjoy who you *are*," Catrin said.

"I still don't know who my father was," she said.

"Does it matter? He hasn't shared your life so far. Even if we found him, he wouldn't take on the role of father now."

"I was called Clifford; d'you think—?"

"No, I don't think Gareth Clifford was your father. You aren't even half-sister to Roy, best to face it," Philip said.

"I still feel that Roy is my brother. We've shared so much over the years."

"He feels that too," Philip assured her. "He and Gillian are coming down at the weekend to talk to you."

"Instead of finding a family I've lost the only member of it I had." Amanda tried to smile at the irony.

"And what about you, Philip?" Catrin asked with a slight tilt of her white head. Her blue eyes looked piercingly into his. "Have you got any news for us?"

Philip stared from Catrin to Amanda in surprise. "News? Me? My life is as dull as the proverbial ditchwater and far less interesting." He looked ill at ease though, and after another glance at the sharp-eyed Catrin, he left.

When school began again, Amanda was no longer Jane's teacher as she had moved to a higher class, but she saw her often and quickly realised that all was not well.

Once more, Heather was over-protective to the point that Jane was never allowed out of her sight for longer than was absolutely necessary. Heather would be at the gate long after school had begun and again twenty minutes before school ended. From Jane's teacher, Amanda learned that the child spent a lot of time looking out of the window waving to the lonely figure standing just outside the gate and Amanda realised with a jerk of anger that it was five-year-old Jane reassuring her mother, and not the other way about, as most would presume.

Resolving to go and visit Heather after school in the hope that she could persuade her to talk, she told Catrin at lunchtime that she would be late.

"I thought I'd call and see Heather and talk about how Jane is getting on in her new class," she said.

"Not to find out if Heather and Philip are meeting in secret?" Catrin queried.

Amanda put down the sandwich she was eating and said, "Well, I do feel there's something wrong. Heather is back to her old possessiveness where Jane is concerned. I want to find out why, if I can." She told Catrin about Heather waiting at the gates as she had before, and Catrin frowned.

"Then you think there might be something going on between Heather and Philip?"

Amanda shrugged. "I just want to see if I can help Jane before she slips back to her previous withdrawn state. I don't want to pry, but it is part of the job as you know, solving any problems that affect the child's progress when you can."

"Be careful, dear. Concern can easily be misconstrued."

When Amanda had finished tidying the classroom after the afternoon session, she ran to the gate in time to catch Jane and Helen with their mother. Helen was talking animatedly, Jane was walking with her head hung low and Heather seemed unaware of either of them. What a sorry little group they make, Amanda thought as she caught them up.

"Hey there," she called. "Any chance of a cup of tea at your house?"

"Mam, can I put the biscuits out?" Helen said at once. Heather turned and smiled.

"Lovely. We haven't had a chat for weeks."

Amanda took both Helen and Jane's hands and talked to them as they walked to the house next to the Cwm Gwyn Arms.

The house wasn't in its usual state of orderliness. A pile of washing covered one armchair, waiting to be ironed, and toys had been left where they had fallen. A bowl of flowers drooped miserably, long dead, and the grate was filled with the ashes of a previous fire.

"Sit down, Heather," Amanda said. "Jane, Helen and I will make the tea." Going into the kitchen she found the same disorder. Unwashed china, potatoes and vegetables cut and left, with stale cabbage filling the air with its pungent and unpleasant smell. She didn't say anything to Heather, who had come to the doorway and was surveying the chaos, she just found a teapot, washed a few cups and set a tray. She handed a plate to Helen and asked her to arrange the biscuits as prettily as she could.

"No biscuits," Heather said wearily. "I forgot to go shopping today."

"Bread and jam then!" said the capable Helen.

"There's so much to do," Heather excused.

"Because you've let things slide. Jobs pile up if you don't keep on top of them, don't they?" Amanda said rather sharply.

When the children had been given a snack of toast and marmite – there having been no jam – they went to play in the garden and Amanda sat beside Heather and put an arm on her shoulder. "Now, are you going to talk about it or would you like me to go home?"

"I want to go back to Philip," Heather said.

"But what about Haydn? What's gone wrong?"

"Nothing's wrong. I just feel trapped with the wrong man. The girls should be growing up with their father. I want to move to Cardiff, with Philip."

"Why move to Cardiff?" Amanda asked. "The children are settled in school and with their friends. You too are surrounded by friends. So why leave?"

"I couldn't live here with Philip after living here with Haydn. They all think Haydn's my husband but we've never married, and Philip and I have never divorced."

"But you can't do this, Heather. You can't disrupt people's lives like this. Haydn doesn't deserve it and what about the girls? They look on Haydn as their father. Where is Haydn?" she asked.

"Staying with his mother for a couple of days while I think things out."

"Think about this carefully, Heather. About what it will do to Haydn, who's been good to you. Think how it will affect little Jane to leave everything she knows, including the man who has been such a wonderful father to her. You can't leave Haydn."

"I belong with Philip. Philip loves me."

In what Amanda took as a dismissal, Heather leaned over and started the radiogram. Touching the edge of a record with the needle, the room was quickly filled with the lively sound of Frankie Laine singing 'Sugar Bush'.

Walking down the road the sound followed her as Heather increased the volume.

The following day Amanda was surprised to see not Haydn, but Philip waiting outside school with Heather. She gathered her things and hurried out as soon as the children had gone, curious to hear an explanation.

"We thought now the children are older they should know who their father is," Heather explained hurriedly. "Haydn understands."

"Oh I see. Yes. Probably a very good thing. Nice for you all." Amanda thought she had better shut up, she was babbling mindlessly.

In the hope of being able to help, and out of concern for the family, Catrin called on Heather when the children were at school. Presumably because she had telephoned first, she found the place in its usual neat state. Heather was playing for a few different audiences it seemed. Pathetic and helpless to some, efficient and misunderstood to others.

Heather said very little and Catrin did not stay long. She admired the garden, said what a pretty little cottage their home was and left in time to meet Amanda from school. She did learn, to her regret, that Heather and Haydn no longer shared a bedroom. Things seemed to be getting worse, she reported to Amanda.

Apart from talking it over with Catrin, Amanda didn't discuss it with anyone, wanting to stay out of what was bound to become a difficult situation.

Over the following weeks Philip was frequently seen with Heather, Haydn and the girls, and if it worried Haydn he seemed not to show it, although, Amanda confided in Catrin, he didn't seem quite as relaxed as usual.

"Bound to be afraid, dear. She's left him before and I doubt he's ever felt secure. Pity they haven't had another child. That might have made them legalise it all."

The usual loud music was playing when Amanda called one evening with some photographs she wanted enlarging, and the door was open. She called, but there was no sign of the children, who were usually in the garden. She called again then went inside, intending to leave her photographs on the hall table. Haydn and Heather walked in immediately after her, unaware of her presence, and they were quarrelling.

"If you love the children you can't do this to them!" Haydn was saying.

"I haven't any choice. He's their father and they need him."

"I thought I'd provided all they needed in a father. Have I failed you? Or them?"

"No, Haydn, but Philip belongs with us."

Horrified and dreadfully embarrasssed by her unintentional eavesdropping, Amanda slipped out of the kitchen door and scuttled around the house out of sight, hoping she hadn't been spotted. Running past the Cwm Gwyn Arms she saw Philip with Helen and Jane, all on bicycles, heading towards Heather and Haydn's house. She hid around the corner of the building, feeling more like a criminal by the minute and when they had passed her, ran on. A nervous chuckle escaped her lips, as she remembered a similar situation in Rhys's bungalow.

She heard Philip call her but she ignored him and hurried on. She didn't want to speak to him. If what she had heard was confirmed, and he was taking Heather and the girls away from Haydn, then she had nothing to say to him.

Slipping through the front hedge, damaging the firethorn in her haste, she almost fell through the kitchen door.

"A burglar, but a clumsy one I think," Rhys's voice announced as he offered a hand to steady her. "What's happened? You look as if you've had a nasty fright."

"I was in Heather and Haydn's house thinking it was empty. I was only going to leave some photographs," she defended, when he began to frown in disapproval. "Well, they followed me in and from what I overheard before I ran out of the back door, Heather is leaving Haydn and going back to Philip!"

"What!" Rhys looked around as if searching for a weapon and Amanda tried to calm him.

"Rhys, it's nothing to do with you or me. It's for Heather, Haydn and Philip to sort out."

He relaxed and nodded. "But if I see Philip I'd want to attack him for what he's done to Heather and Haydn."

"And what's that then?" Philip's voice announced his presence and they both turned to the doorway where he stood, panting, looking huge and dangerous, his face a trifle red after his fast cycle ride back after depositing the girls. "Well Rhys? What d'you want to attack me for?"

"For messing up Haydn and Heather again. That's what!"

Amanda backed away from Philip's anger and tucked herself into Catrin's armchair. But Philip was unaware of her, he only saw Rhys.

"For your information, I have no intention of getting back with my 'devoted' wife. She has been using the girls to try and persuade me. Her life is in a rut and, as with several times before, she doesn't mind who she hurts to change it. She left me once before, you know. For a man who ran the local grocer's shop. She came back fast enough though, when she realised she was expected to help him run it. Then there was Haydn, and he, poor fool, promised her a life of comfort.

"Heather is selfish and devoted only to her own comfort," Philip went on, "so you can give over making excuses for her and blaming me! This is the tragedy of a silly woman who can't make up her mind. She's psychologically incapable of staying true to a commitment. This time I won't be a part of it. Right?"

He walked forward in a crouch, his arms hanging loose but looking dangerous. "You're so high and mighty, Rhys Falconbridge, always knowing what's best, always judging others, usually when you only know half the facts. I didn't ruin Haydn's life, he did that on his own, by believing he could make Heather happy. I tried once and I won't try again. I know when I'm wrong!"

"I've always believed the reason Heather left you was because you didn't want Jane," Rhys said quietly.

"It was Heather who couldn't cope with another baby. Little Helen had spent a lot of her time with people who would mind her for the afternoon or the odd evening while Heather went dancing or just listened to her records. She knew she wouldn't get away with it with two children. The girls only had a play session or had a story read to them when I or someone else was there to do it. Heather blotted everything out with music." He continued to glare at Rhys. "There, now you have it. So, what are you going to do about it? Eh? Sort me out for being a wicked husband?"

Amanda sat there, white-faced, expecting at any moment that the shouting would become a fight, but Rhys's voice was low and apologetic when he spoke and she felt the tension leave her body in a long slow breath.

"I'm going to say I'm sorry," Rhys said. "I really believed Heather's story." He looked across at Amanda still cowering in Catrin's chair. "I remember Amanda telling me that there was a danger of believing the first version you hear and refusing to listen to the other side. She was so right. I really am sorry, Philip and, well, I'm impressed by your loyalty. You didn't even try to convince me otherwise, you kept faith with Heather and took the blame."

"I did try to talk to you once or twice," Philip said dryly. "Pompous old sod that you are, you wouldn't listen."

"Am I a pompous old sod?" Rhys asked later that evening when they were discussing all that had happened with Catrin.

Amanda and Catrin answered in chorus, "Yes!"

Summer passed and autumn came rolling in with mists and extravagant colours transforming the area with a different scene each day. The time for Catrin to leave Firethorn came and went without anything being done. Amanda began to think once more about the preparations for Christmas at school.

Heather and Haydn were still together, but now Philip visited and occasionally took the girls out. The gossip this caused went round and round, changing form as frequently as the clouds, as people tried to fit what they knew into some sort of story, but the truth, that Haydn and Heather weren't married, seemed to elude them all.

One day in late November, Roy and a noticeably pregnant Gillian came to Firethorn Cottage. Amanda was enchanted to see how attentive Roy was to his bride, and not only when someone was watching, either, she noticed with pride. He was genuinely caring. And, from the way he spoke, he was looking forward to the baby with great excitement.

"That'll be enough to keep me on the straight and narrow, eh, Mand? I wouldn't want to miss a day of him growing up. More special for people like you and me, not having a home when we were small."

"Thank goodness for that!" Amanda laughed. "I'd begun to think nothing would cure you!"

"It's still hard not to take something when it's asking to be nicked," Roy confessed. "Seeing a shopping bag with the purse perched on the top, or seeing an open window with a wallet on the window sill like I saw the other day. Or when I see someone picking up a mat and taking out a front door key, something clicks into place in my brain and I start planning to use it and go and see what I can find." He looked a bit embarrassed, pushing his fingers through his thick blond hair, looking away from them. "You don't know how hard it is to ignore all that, you really don't."

The beautiful Riley was parked outside. The road was narrow and the cottage was near a corner, so there was no room for Amanda's Ford Popular when someone else parked there. Today she had moved her car further along the road in readiness for her visitors. When Roy looked ouside he saw an old man leaning on his walking stick, admiring it.

"I had one of these once," he called, seeing Roy's face at the open window. "Beautiful they are. Can't drive no more but I often think about it."

"I'll take you for a ride one day," Roy promised. "Go on, sit inside, she isn't locked." He opened the door and walked

209

down to where the man was getting into the driving seat with some difficulty, being obviously a little lame.

"Who is it?" Catrin asked and looking out, said, "Oh, it's Mel Griffiths. You know, Philip walks his dog, Ben."

As they watched, the old man stared at Roy then raised his stick to him and beat Roy across the shoulders.

"Whatever's happening?" Amanda and Catrin ran out as Roy managed to get the stick out of the old man's hand.

"What's got into you, you silly old fool?" Roy demanded.

"It was you! You're the one who broke in and took my electricity and rent money! Saw you I did and I'm going to call the police now this minute! Got your fingerprints I have, so you won't get out of it!"

In vain they tried to reason with him. He went into Philip's house and a few moments later, Philip came to tell them Mr Griffiths had identified Roy as the man who had stolen from him and insisted on calling the police. "I tried to stop him," Philip said. "Told him about Gillian and the baby but he was so furious. Strong man he was once and I think he was humiliated that he couldn't stop the burglar that night. It's rankled ever since."

"What's happening?" Gillian asked, and when she was told she collapsed.

The ambulance arrived at the same time as the police and Roy just managed to get inside the ambulance to go to hospital with his wife before the police could ask him to accompany them, in their politely-phrased demand, to the station.

The baby was born that night, a little girl they planned to call Sarah. Two hours after the birth, Roy was arrested.

It was Rhys who came to tell Amanda. At eleven o'clock that night, when she was undressed and ready for bed, having heard the glad news of the safe arrival of Gillian's daughter, she opened the door to be greeted with the other, devastating news.

"It's Roy. You've got to be brave, Amanda, Gillian will need your support. Roy's been arrested for the burglaries in Tri-nant last summer."

210

"But he wouldn't! Knowing I live and work here he just wouldn't be so stupid or unkind. It isn't true. He wouldn't break in. There has to be an explanation of him seeing that sculpture in your house."

"We've both known for some time it was he. He couldn't have known about the sculpture. He's guilty, Amanda. I'm sorry."

"And you'll give evidence?"

"Of course not!"

"Thank you."

"What will you do?"

"Nothing, I'll deal with it just as before, but this time I'll have Gillian to look after as well. Nice really, having a sort of sister-in-law. And a sort of niece."

Rhys put his arms around her. "Amanda, I'm so sorry."

"It won't make much difference. I'm used to it."

But it did. The first thing that happened when the news reached the school was that someone else offered, rather firmly, to hold the money being saved for the Christmas Pantomime outing.

During the same week, the offer she made to collect a few pence each week from the children towards the school party was also refused. It came to her with a horrifying rush that she was no longer trusted to hold other people's money. Having even a reformed criminal for a brother was affecting her life once more.

"I intend giving in my notice at the end of this term," she told Catrin.

"Please don't," Catrin urged. "It will all blow over. I suspect that one or two people with loud voices have convinced the rest that you are a criminal by being related to one. How ridiculous people are. As if having a doctor for a brother would make you naturally good at first aid! Or a brother who's a singing policeman would mean you'd go around singing and arresting people!"

Amanda laughed but it was forced and died quickly. No matter how Catrin tried to cheer her, her mind was made up. She couldn't possibly work with people who didn't trust

211

her. "I'll open a nursery school," she said. "It's something I've often thought about. Then only those who trust me would come. I'll stay in the village though, they won't make me leave."

Over the next few weeks she pored over catalogues to decide what equipment she would need to buy. Premises would be difficult but with the church hall and an ex-army hut both being possibilities, she was confident she would find something when the time arrived. She had no intention of leaving before finishing the school year. She owed the children that.

She bought several large toys, a swing, see-saw, prams and bikes, and, with Philip's help, repaired and re-painted them. The garden was more like a park playground until they were dry and packed into the shed. One swing was erected at Catrin's request, and she often sat on it to read her morning paper when winter offered up one of its mild, sunny days.

Rhys was away but he arrived home as Christmas approached. He walked into the garden to find Philip and Amanda dressed against the chill, covered in red paint and trying in vain to finish the final coat on a tricycle by reaching underneath to places Amanda had missed.

"Next time you'd better leave all the intricate painting to me," Philip was laughing. "Slides and pedal cars, yes, bicycles definately no!"

"What's going on?"

"Hello, Rhys. Philip is helping me get this ready for when I open my nursery school. What d'you think?" She spread an arm for him to admire their work.

"Nursery school?" he queried.

"I'll leave you two to talk," Philip said reaching for a cloth and the bottle of paint thinner. "I'll come back this evening and finish the rest, right?" He slipped through the hedge into his own garden, where he was building a small frame with steps and hand rails, for children to learn to climb in safety.

"I'm going to leave Mill Lane School," Amanda told Rhys when they went inside to make some tea. "I don't feel happy there any more." When she told him why he looked at her quizzically and told her she was an idiot.

"Call a meeting of the teachers and the Head, together with any of the parents you think would be on your side. The ones who started this nonsense must be known, so invite them too. I'll come and chair a meeting and we can bring it all out into the open. I don't think the parents or the teachers would like you to leave. Will you give it a try?"

She was doubtful. "It's been spoilt irreparably, in my opinion. The edge of distrust will never completely leave me."

"Nonsense. Now, I'll go at once and talk to the Head. He'll agree, I'm sure."

Roy was remanded in prison awaiting a trial and his Probation Officer's report. Amanda went every weekend to see Gillian and baby Sarah. Gillian was philosophical about it, prepared to wait for Roy to be released and convinced that he had spoken the truth and had given up crime for her and the baby's sake.

"It was such bad luck, that man recognising him," she told Amanda sadly. "Roy had told me about the robberies in Tri-nant. He told me about the man trying to stop him too, and how he could have pushed him out of the way like a matchstick but he didn't. Whatever you say about him, he has never been violent, even then, when he was faced with being recognised."

Eventually, Mel Griffiths gave evidence to that effect, and together with the fact that he had not offended since and was apparently going straight, with a job, a wife and a child, his sentence was limited to the time he had already served on remand. He came out a chastened man and hugged Gillian until she thought she would break.

"Thanks Gill. I'll never let you down again, never," he promised.

"You don't have to say it any more, Roy," Gillian smiled happily. "I believe you. So, shall we go and see Amanda this weekend? I've had the car checked over and filled with petrol all ready for you."

"I don't deserve you," he muttered into her hair.

Heather left Tri-nant, leaving Haydn behind and taking the

girls. She had found a job as housekeeper to a man in Dinas
Powys with a large house on the common where the girls could
play, and with horse-riding stables close by owned and run by
the same man. He promised lessons for the girls and offered a
car for Heather's use so she could take them to Barry Island
at weekends. She wrote to Amanda and told her that this time
she intended to stand on her own two feet and not depend on
anyone.

"Doesn't sound very independent to me," Amanda said.

"And she's made sure Haydn has her address, in case it
doesn't work out," Catrin said sadly. "I don't think he's free
of her or ever will be."

"Philip isn't either. He'll want to continue to see the girls
now they know who he is," Amanda said. "And Haydn will
want to keep in touch with them too."

"Two men attendant on her and a home in a beautiful place
like Dinas Powys, what more can she need to keep her happy?"
Catrin looked at Amanda. "And what about you, dear. Are
you going to arrange this meeting? Stay on at the school? I
do hope so."

"We'll see." Amanda was undecided.

The meeting lasted only twenty minutes. Everyone there –
and the school hall was crowded – insisted she stayed. It
was pointed out that only two people in the whole village had even mentioned a connection between Amanda and
her brother. The reason for the removal of the money collecting was kindly done, it was because the other teachers had agreed she was doing too much. It was that simple.

"What will I do with all the equipment I've collected?" she
asked Rhys. "I've collected enough toys to fill the shed".

He looked at her strangely and said, "You'll find a use for
them, I'm sure."

Nothing had been said about Catrin leaving Firethorn Cottage
and as she brought out the Christmas tree and all the decorations were put up, Amanda hoped nothing would. On the few

occasions when she thought Catrin was going to discuss it, Amanda quickly changed the subject.

It was Rhys who eventually made her talk about it, one Saturday morning, when he had called and invited himself for breakfast. He had just driven back from Cornwall, where he had been working on trials for filming advertisements for the newly approved independent television authority.

"When is my aunt leaving Firethorn Cottage?" he asked.

"There's no hurry," Amanda replied. "She can stay as long as she wants to."

"Philip's lease is extended but he has to get out in April," Rhys added. "Are you going to take him in too?"

"Hardly. I don't intend making Firethorn Cottage a boarding house!"

"You know that was her idea, don't you? That you and I should marry and live in the bungalow so she could invite Philip to be her lodger?"

"She told you that?" She forced a laugh. "She told me too. What a preposterous idea. As if you and I could settle happily together."

"Once I would have agreed with that sentiment. My attitude was coloured by my belief that Heather had been treated shabbily, by having a husband who travelled frequently and was never there when he was needed."

"And now?"

"Now I think we could, and should."

She turned to stare at him, convinced she had misheard him. "Couldn't and shouldn't! Well yes, that just about sums it up," she laughed, deliberately misunderstanding.

She turned away thankful of the excuse of cooking breakfast, concentrating on the bacon and mushrooms under the grill and the eggs crackling in the frying pan. "Would you like fried bread?" she asked casually.

"I'd like you to marry me, Amanda. I'll never be happy unless you do. Please, say yes."

Slowly and deliberately putting the food onto a warmed

plate, she reached over and put it in front of him. "Sorry, Rhys, I wasn't listening. Did you say something?"

"I want to marry you." He pushed his chair back and stood beside her. "Amanda?" he asked, when she was slow in replying.

"Oh, I see, and when were you thinking of arranging this little ceremony?"

"Amanda!"

"Yes?"

"Will you marry me?"

Still she didn't reply, but stood looking out of the window at the wind-blown garden, and the shed bulging with children's toys.

"Well, I suppose it would be better than wasting all those toys Philip and I have repaired," she said, still talking as if they were discussing next week's milk bill.

Catrin burst into the room and said with what was for her high irritation, "Amanda. Answer the man!"

"When he makes it sound more important than where we'll park the car, I'll answer him."

"I love you. I would never be happy without you. Your car is constantly blocking the road and my aunt wants the cottage," Rhys said and now he was trying hard not to laugh.

She turned and there was laughter and tears brightening her eyes as she threw herself into his arms.

MAINDEE 4/60